by R. V. Cassill

The Father and other stories
The President
Pretty Leslie
Clem Anderson
The Eagle on the Coin
Fifteen by Three (with Herbert Gold and James B. Hall)

The Father

and other stories

by R. V. Cassill

Simon and Schuster
New York

FIRST PRINTING

The following stories have been published and reprinted as noted:

"Larchmoor Is Not the World"—Published: *Furioso;* reprinted: *Best American Short Stories, 1951,* Foley, Ed.; *Stories of Sudden Truth,* Greene and Abell, Eds.; *Stories for Study,* Kempton, Ed.; *Patterns for Living,* Campbell, Van Gundy and Shrodes, Eds. *Fifteen by Three.*

"The Prize"—Published: *Perspectives;* reprinted: *O. Henry Prize Stories, 1956,* Engle, Martin, Urdang, Eds.

"This Hand, These Talons"—Published: *Western Review;* reprinted: *Perspectives, USA.*

"The Biggest Band"—Published: *Western Review;* reprinted: *Fifteen by Three; Svetova Literatura.*

"The Inland Years"—Published: *Western Review;* reprinted: *O. Henry Prize Stories, 1955,* Engle, Martin, Urdang, Eds.

"When Old Age Shall This Generation Waste"—Published: *Epoch;* reprinted: *O. Henry Prize Stories, 1957,* Engle and Urdang, Eds.; *Elle.*

"The Goldfish"—Published: *Fifteen by Three.*

"And in My Heart"—Published: *Paris Review.*

"The Father"—Published: *Esquire.*

This book is for Kay and her good children.

I love you for not knowing how to live today. . . . For thus *you* live best.

—ZARATHUSTRA

Contents

Love? Squalor?

JUST RECENTLY, by the Village grapevine, I heard about a wedding that's supposed to take place in my neighborhood during what my landlady refers to as "the cruelest month." It's a wedding I probably won't get to, though when I first heard about it I lay around my pad, deep in thought, trying to compose what I call a *stance* to take during the services. "Something incomparably light and deft," as my landlady says—an attitude and a grimace that would con*trib*ute to the occasion. Personal judgments be hanged, I'd like to be able to go there and smile. However, to keep from thinking too deeply about all this, I talked it over with my landlady, a remarkably demoralized harridan, and decided against it.

For one thing, as she pointed out, I hadn't been invited. And moreover my presence there might cause the groom an uneasy minute or two, because as I'm given to understand, Nathan has spent a lot of time refining the bride—like, her language and the things she's apt to talk about spontaneously.

As my informant, who's known Mesmé at closer range than I have in the last several months, says, "It was an apotheotic moment for Nathan when she walked into his office from the *street* and said she 'couldn't cope,' she simply 'couldn't any longer cope,' with the horror of looking through the Village for an apartment.

"Of course first of all she reminded him of all his years in England during the war—he wasn't even in London, for Gawd's sake, but *Bristol*—while he was waiting to come to the States; waiting loyally enough, but at the same time wishing he could have been *there,* in the ideal Britain, when there wasn't the war and the Empire wasn't dissolving, and if he could have spoken English then. And, fifteen years later, there *she* is, the reasonable facsimile of Unity Mitford herself, with her gargoyle voice, wiping the sweat of August off her lip and asking him couldn't he please help her find something with bawth inside that wasn't for a working girl—and part-time at that—'too deah.'

"And it was a great thing for Nathan to be able to say and believe that he *was* helping her then 'because she had suffered so much she deserved a good time' even, or especially, when he followed her into the apartment he showed her—and subsequently didn't even bother to rent to her—on Barrow Street, and in that same August sweat and heat tasted the facsimile of Mitford-flesh on the Salvation Army couch that she pronounced 'not posh but homely.' And because for any man the occasions of lechery and charity are rarely simultaneous, Nathan was already, in that first down-sinking, reassured and reassuring embrace, wound and knotted not only in the tentacles of his exile dream come true, but was grasping the opportunity to atone for gouging his myriad other tenants.

"One fly alone sullied his ointment. Before they even got back to his fern-filled office to sign the lease, she said in that voice of jaded Empire, 'Now that you've _____ me . . .' and the next day, while he was explaining in his inimitable confusion of senses that she needn't really make a payment until she was on her feet again, she said, 'I anticipated such an offer now that we've _____ each other ____ . . .' At which Nathan, like any man, felt his charity lose its bloom, and, being a practical man, he set about with carrot and stick to clean up not only her language but her memory as well, restoring, if not virginity, at least the paradigmatic *tabula* on which only the future may inscribe."

Yes. And since I knew the bride before purification and the obliteration, the *rasa,* I have the feeling that her history might break out on me like a childhood contagion, and right there at the service while I stared at the well-scrubbed and rosy groom, my lips might whisper that language once so familiar —"Mesmé, do you really ＿＿ ＿ ＿＿ when he ＿＿＿＿ you? Though you are even more fastidious than when I knew you in your emigration, do you really like for him to ＿＿ in your hair?"

Nevertheless, I'm setting down these notes in payment of a debt to Muse Clio, her of the sardonic silences, the lady of the white lies and gaudy ellipses, *mater narcissus* herself. I don't want to make any public opposition to charity, or even to its side effects, or even want to doubt that it endureth forever. For the sake of the bride's multitude of former friends I'll shore these fragments against their ruin.

A few years back, in April, I was traveling home from France on a British ship. For the voyage I shared a cabin, forward and low beneath the water line, with two Britishers on their way to Canada, and with a dark, discreet gentleman from one of their recently liberated colonies.

The Englishmen, called Dexter and Billy, had been hired to work for an American contractor on some Thulean defense project. The bigger one, Dexter, never left his bunk, as far as I saw, for the entire trip, and I remember him as permanently propped on one elbow, his huge, tattooed biceps glowing like a fish belly under the gray short sleeve of the underwear he slept in. He was handsome in what I was to have explained later was a lower-class style, and except for the cowardice that kept him permanently in bed from dock to dock, might have effectively bullied all of us cabinmates throughout the ship. As things were, he could only work his tyranny while we were in the cabin. It seemed to me that every time I was preparing to leave it he would call down from his perch, " 'i, mite, if you see the steward in the hall, ask 'im if he's got a bit of chicken or a chop, wot? Gives a man an appetite, this sea air." The air was musty and ammoniac in his corner of the cabin, and, after the second day out of LeHavre, there was usually a semicircle of chicken bones beneath him, like refuse beneath the nest of a loyal mother vulture on her eggs.

Since I was out of the cabin as much as I could be, I know the duty of attendance fell mostly on little Billy. The two of them owned a gramophone without a changer, and Dexter never tired of listening to *The King and I* and *My Fair Lady*. Not only was it incumbent on Billy to keep changing the records, in rough weather he had to hold the tinny machine in his lap to keep the needle from skidding. He rolled on his bony little hips against the roll of the sea and hugged the machine as if, in the event of shipwreck, he and it would gurgle down together, emitting, "The chillll-druhn, the chilllll-duh-runnnn," or "Why can't the English teach their children how to speak?" which Dexter, broadening his accent, would take off as "oh-ah-ee cawnt thee Inklish tich theh chi-ow-druhn a-ow tee-oo spih-eek?" Then he would comment, "True. You Yanks have got everything now. Even our bloody language; we can't speak it no more." Accusingly he would ask, "You know how much I'm going to make up there north? Bloody more in a month than I'd make in six, home in Yorkshire."

"England is done for," I said agreeably.

"Bloody well right it's done for," he said. *"I* never want to go back. 'ow about you, Billy?"

"Not me," Billy said. "You know, mite, London's filling up with niggers. You chaps know how to handle your niggers. More'n what we know any more."

Fleeing Dexter and Billy, the chicken bones, and the death of Empire one rough morning, I took my reading to the salon forward on A deck. And that, of course, is where I met Mesmé.

I didn't right away see that straight, upper-class ash-blond hair, her exquisite forehead, or even her hazel, sated eyes, for the simple reason that she was huddled—almost enveloped—in a huge, furry coat. The coat seemed to cover the green lounge chair and occupant entirely except for one protruding, shoeless foot. Her chair was near one of the front windows, and with a cold, blasting rhythm the sea banged those windows with black and white explosions of foam.

Seated fifteen feet from her, I caught her as a forlorn detail, an undigested lump in the attention I was unavoidably paying to the threatening clamor of the water. I've been on ships enough to know they're all unsinkable these days. I always say so, but on mornings of bad weather my eye and ear go on responding as if seafaring were still hazardous. And it was my anxious, uneducable eye, scared of the sea, that began, all of itself, to marvel at my swaddled companion.

She and I were practically the only occupants of the salon that morning, though a few hardy old ladies were spaced unsociably across its rear wall. I brooded and watched, and presently it occurred to me that the girl looked somehow like a caterpillar on a drifting shingle—so forlorn—but nevertheless like a caterpillar which had already had its chance as a butterfly and was reverting back to a condition safer and cosier in these mid-Atlantic circumstances. She looked, for the moment at least, safe against the morning wrath of water, and, if it hadn't been for the butterfly foot exposed, perfectly invulnerable.

Maybe the fortieth time my gaze gyroscoped in her direction I saw a raptured eye staring back at me out of the sworling coat. When it was steadfast through the fiftieth, on that hint I spake.

"I suppose you're wondering where I got this military-looking wrist watch which tells at which velocity one is walking if one wishes," I said, approaching her chair in a series of lurches and clutchings. She pulled even her foot inside the coat to make room for me to sit on the footstool anchored against her chair. "I got it from a chap in the army. Writing fellow who called himself Corporal X and was medically discharged for that and other reasons. I understand he is now profitably employed repeating the Jesus prayer without cease and flattering fat lady readers; but wherever he is—I might say *who*ever he is—he don't need this watch any more, for Gawd's sake."

The rapt eye looked at the watch—which I held right up at the opening of the coat—and blinked. Then the impeccably Aryan face was exposed while she said, "Have the bitches been around with tea yet? Do you suppose the chemist's would have some aspirin?"

I explained to her how bloody *awful* aspirin was if—as I suspected—she was seasick. I offered Dramamine, which I just happened to have a little vial of in my jacket pocket. She asked what on earth that was and while I was explaining, I could see her purposely, regally cast away the thread of my lay discourse in favor of what it sounded like.

"An intellectual?" she asked. I showed her the heavy book I was reading, but that didn't seem to pertain. "I know hundreds of intellectuals in London, but no American intellectuals, though I know dozens of Americans."

I persisted in offering her the Dramamine, and she took it, at length, rather suspiciously, as if it were some miracle poison that could change her on the spot into a conformist or Mc-Carthyite and spoil her taste for the Third Program. She set it just on the tip of her pale spiky tongue and tossed it backward like a musclebound child throwing a rock over his shoulder. Her eyes seemed to follow the pill back on its inner trajectory and fix on it when it landed—the first time I noticed her talent for absolute withdrawal when a memory or a visceral sensation claimed her.

It was weird enough to see this reaction, and momentarily she convinced me I had got the wrong vial somehow and had poisoned her. Her grip on that rug of a coat relaxed and it gaped in front.

"Is that a Campbell tartan?" I asked excitedly.

"Fortune and Beasly," she said. "It is rather *like* the Campbell tartan. I couldn't say what it is, really. I know the Duke of Argyll through H. E. Martin Pummer's daughter who was a deb three winters ago and knew his grandniece."

I said that London seemed to be a very small place where everybody knew everyone else, and she said Oh, it *was*. She peeked back at the pill again and said with conviction, "Most debs absolutely wear themselves out in their first season. They sleep with everybody, because it's the thing. I wouldn't sleep with everybody. They've lost their figgers and their complexions and look ancient. How old do you think I am?"

I told her not to be silly, that I knew very well she was twenty-eight, had a title that she preferred not to use—par-*tic*ularly while traveling third class—that her father had been killed in the North African campaign, that she had a real boy's boy of a brother, and that she had been raised, after her untimely orphaning, by a noble aunt.

"That's not *quite* right," she said. "How did you know?"

I explained to her that she had once and for all been definitively described as one of the two kinds of English girl encountered by our forces during the war, and that the other kind had been somewhat older than she at that period, had had husbands overseas, and believed that if they remained standing they would remain guiltless.

"Knee-tremblers," she said with an explosive, extroverted laugh. "You're entirely right, except, of course, I don't have a title, though Mother's great-great-great was noble in the eighteenth century and my father's great-uncle, who was in the forces, should have been knighted after Mafeking. Jealousy, you know. It's all politics there. My brother's not so boy any more. He's married a Bonstacker and opened a shop in Kent. Scabby girl, but no character, and they've produced an *enfant*. No future."

"Out of Harrow to a Kentish shop," I said, clicking my tongue with dishonest sympathy. I was braced against any I-knew-the-juke-in-London snobbery—braced a little too hard, like being braced for a pitch of the ship that didn't come.

"He would so have gone if the RAF pensions weren't so mean. It's rotten not to have a parent. Mother's gone out to Canada, you know, and *she's* all right, but Charles and I haven't et very high on the hog."

"You're going to join your mother?"

"Jesus H. Christ, no! I'm going to New York. All my friends said I wouldn't do it and here I am."

"High on the—? Jesus H.—?"

"Texas," Mesmé said. "One meets lots of Americans, though intellectuals very few."

I ventured that most of them had been cleaned out of the services at the same time as Corporal X, and she agreed, but said she knew a lot of Americans besides those in uniform— journalists, barristers, and movie people, and that none of them were intellectuals either. "I like Americans because they're so demonstrative, though. The English men—well, most of them —don't marry until fairly late, because they can't afford it or don't want to and in the meantime they develop a most in-*diff*erent attitude. They don't *try*."

"Texas tried?"

"Oh," she said. She got to her feet and stood there, very tall, her ash-blond hair bordering those crazy eyes with a straight severity. "Tex came into the bar where I worked and, as he told my best friend, before he even saw my face, the moment he saw my hips, he said to himself, 'That's my girl.' He used to call me Slim." She flashed a sick smile, hummed a few bars of "Deep in the Heart of Texas," kicked her feet—I thought she had lost her balance from the pitching of the ship—and said, "See? The English can still dance. That Dramamine of yours is no bloody good. I have to go to my cabin for some aspirin."

And with that she left me. I thought I might not see her again, except as one sees everybody again on a seven-day passage— going to meals, playing horse races, in the bar, the writing room, or on the deck if there is good weather.

But that same afternoon she descended on me in the smok- ing lounge, towing a young man whom I might as well call

Corporal Y, since he is going to be the straight man of this narrative—the crude, uncouth, unquiet American. I'd had some talk with Corporal Y, since we sat together at a large table in the dining room, and so I knew that he had spent some months in Germany as an agent for a company that supplied local products for Army PX's. Corporal Y hated Germans and was constantly pressing me to read a book called *The Scourge of the Swastika* which he said "finally" told the truth about Hitler's Germany. I said I had hated Germans for twenty years, but since I wouldn't read the book, he remained a little suspicious of my politics, and I was a bit sur*prised* to see him allow Mesmé to come to my table.

"Meet Lady Brett," he said, "for Chrissake. Hey, okay if me and Lady Brett *Ashley* proceed to forget the terrible wound I got in the goddam war by joining you for a goddam *pernod* or something?"

"He's an intellectual, too," I said to Mesmé, rising and bowing slightly as I pulled out a chair for her. "You got the wrong goddam war," I told Corporal Y. "Mesmé's nothing like the Lost Generation. She's more the detritus of Their Finest Hour."

" 'Their Finest Hour.' Will lovable, crotchety Uncle Winston bow to the Loot Waffy? Will Paddy Funyoucame get his baling-wire and orange-crate Spitfire airborne in time to meet the dread Stukas?" Y demanded of his audience. "You know what Hitler planned to do to every potent male in England if he conquered?"

Mesmé said, "Aunt Cecile used to wear a pistol around the garden. She was going to shoot me if the Germans landed. We were just playing a guessing game of the capitals of your states and we couldn't agree on the capital of South Carolina. I said *you'd* surely know. So we've come in search."

"Charleston," I said. Corporal Y guffawed loudly and offered to bet me ten goddam dollars that it was either Columbia *or* Sumter, while Mesmé, he said, was holding strongly for Columbia.

"Do you know this other guessing game?" she asked,

chewing off the tip of her left little fingernail. "The one in which it is the object to guess whose is a certain quotation? Who said, 'Kiss me, Hardy'?"

"Mrs. Hardy," Corporal Y said. He emitted an artificial yak and slapped my shoulder and Mesmé's knee.

"Lord Nelson," she said. "He had been struck at Trafalgar. He knew he was dying."

"But who was Hardy?" Y said. And in this pleasant way the three of us fell into the infinitely slow-paced comradeship which means so much on ocean voyages. In fact, by the time we'd had our third bourbon—a drink suggested by Mesmé, who 'lowed as how that was what they drank in Texas—we were all three sure we were fond of each other.

Y had begun to recite many limericks from a collection he had bought in Paris and memorized. Mesmé laughed at them so hard that our sheep-nosed waiter was lurking near the table to get the overflow of jollity. She asked, "What's that one again about the girls at Fortune and Beasly? Really I must learn that one. I've worked at Fortune and Beasly in the holiday season, you know. Tell!"

It came to me with one of those little jogs that show the pattern in what you've been hearing awhile that I hadn't, before the limericks, heard Mesmé *con*centrate on a single topic. I mean, now that it was dirty, she re*sist*ed the impulse to tell us who came into the store and what they said to her while she was on duty at Fortune and Beasly. ("Fulke-Binsmith, who used to live with Molly Proudflesh, has done certain art criticism for two or three of your better journals, *he* came in one day to buy Sally Gunn-Tewksbury a *souvenir sentimental* and saw me at the cosmetics counter and said . . .") Well, there was *none* of that now. She was listening to gospel.

I mean I already saw what would be confirmed later, that she was reverently listening for the single theme that could make both her memory and attention cohere enough to convince her that she *was* a survivor amid the English ruins. This story is going to have a numinous moment and a moment of illumination that I trust will make clear why Mesmé would lay off nail biting and stop reversing her eyes when the talk was sex. But for the time being, since what I knew of her was known because of certain unprovable intuitions I got that afternoon, it's got to be a kind of *pas de deux* for a while. On certain points you'll just have to take my word that I knew them until I get around to explaining why I was sure.

Through that afternoon and in the evening when the three of us got together after dinner, I kept watching and listening. When Mesmé egged Corporal Y on to tell about the time he played doctor with his little cousin in full view of the IC trains, I thought she had a goal in mind. She was like a tomboy daring her guileless buddy to leap off a bridge so she'll have nerve or at least justification to do the same. And as soon as he had ended with a self-amazed, Philistine chortle, she said, "I believe we haven't such a game in England, but I am reminded that when I was visiting the Earl of D———'s daughters, the eldest sat on my head while her sisters stuck straws up my arse. It was three to one. Most unfair. Though I suppose I didn't really mind. If it's one's natural bent. . . . One takes to that sort of thing like a duck to water and from an early age."

"How early?" I had to know.

"Nine. Well, not really, though an aggressive boy my age attempted to have at me. I suppose nothing really happened. Eleven. We'd been evacuated to my aunt's. George and I were put to sleep in the summer house because we were the children, though George could hardly be called a child. He was about to be called up. George was a sort of cousin, though the Bevilles—"

"No genealogy," I said. "Leave me with pity and terror." As a matter of fact, she had struck for the heart and nailed me. I saw the child in flight, the old evil confusions of the blitz. "Bad George." I could have shot him with Aunt Cecile's pistol.

"He had to go in service," Mesmé justified sulkily. "And it was pleasant. We didn't do anything really, anyway. I put my hand under the sheet as directed."

"My Cousin Imogene—" Corporal Y began. But by this time Mesmé was talking only to me. In implying a moral judgment, I had stirred up a bristling response.

"I did nothing definitive until I was twenty and had gone to London," she said. "I startled the physician who examined me in my first pregnancy by being *intacto*. 'Intacto,' he said. I hadn't really done anything and it was most unfair that I should have got caught. Marriage was absolutely out of the question because he was colored. Not terribly. Merely a lovely, lovely shade of pale chocolate. Yum. At any rate, his father was a prince and it was out of the question his marrying *me*."

"Well, this here ticktacktoe—how could you get in trouble without . . . ?" Corporal Y asked.

He tried to kick me under the table, but since Mesmé had her foot up my pants cuff, he kicked her instead. I'm not sure he realized that, but she interpreted his move correctly and, turning to him, blushing and defiant, said, "I suppose we were petting. What you Americans call necking."

"*I* call that *necking*? Wheeew. Taken this reader up too high. Need oxygen. Not *necking*. No, no, no, we neck them all," Y said. He began to twitch in his seat and turned, now and then, to make commanding gestures at the waiter, who ignored him. In a moment, assisted by a roll of the ship, he lunged up from his chair, and in a half crouch went lurching toward the bar to serve himself. He called back, "Hold it, hold it. I want to hear about this. I don't wanna miss a word. I mean, I need *instruc*tion."

"Was I that funny?" Mesmé asked.

"Very funny."

Both of us bent our attention to some matchbooks that just happened to be lying on the table among some soggy paper napkins, and I, at least, began to read mine. I mean, I didn't want her to think I was goading her to go on with any tales that might be painful to her. We were only strangers on the same boat. We weren't the goddam Canterbury Pilgrims.

I glanced up to see Y fighting and elbowing his way through the pile-up of after-dinner drinkers around the bar. I glanced at Mesmé's face and saw her skin glowing bright rose. "Take me somewhere and ____ me," she said.

I fitted the cover of my matchbook carefully under the striking strip and dropped the thing an inch and a half to the table top. I reread it carefully. It could have had the Ten Commandments on it. "Get a high school education at home," it said. I thought of Dexter, who never left our cabin—then of Billy and the King of Siam—all of the detriti of the humpty-dumpty empires.

"There isn't any place to go," I said. " 'There's no upstairs to go to,' " I said.

But there always is. I mean, if you've really got through the wars with all your faculties intact except those that might save you from peeking over the rosebush edge of the pit and discovering the female damned writhing below you, then you're capable of wandering around the windy and half-lit decks of a goddam ship until you discover the cranny where the deck chairs are stacked, tarpaulined and roped down. You're capable of anything, even coupling while you lean against the stacked rungs of the deck chairs, both of you as much inside that monstrous coat as possible. I said, "Kiss me, Hardy."

And I gathered even then that it wasn't any friction or contact of our goddamned epi*thel*iums that counted as much as the moral fact of having done. It was to be a fact that won her certain privileges of frankness and even *lèse-majesté* with American me. She was paying in advance for an intellectual confessor to hear the brag of herself, the pitiful brag that was all she had to set against the terrors of emigration. She wasn't bringing very much with her, she would confide later. Oh, she had been traveling light since Cousin George was called up—lighter than ever now.

We didn't have to stay on deck very long for the moral accomplishment. Less than an hour, certainly. It was cold and we
would have got moody, and there was no point in *that*.

Apparently we were even looking to rejoin Corporal Y when
we climbed back down and went into the bar. He wasn't
around. Whatever he made of what he'd heard, he wasn't
around much for the rest of the voyage, though we saw him
once a day, here or there, with a homeward-bound girl from
Barnard. He and I would have a little talk—about Mesmé, of
course—before we reached New York, and I'll come to that
later.

The bar had filled with people while we were gone. The
only point of relative isolation we could find was a long couch
by the window that looked onto the rear deck. We flopped
onto it like athletes returned from the games. Mesmé's cheeks
—only her cheeks now—were shining like spots of health paint.

"Now you've had a Limey," she said gravely.

"What were you telling me when we were interrupted?" I
said. "Pale, yummy chocolate prince, whose hand was ever at
his lips, bidding adieu . . . ?"

Now that she had earned the right, she didn't tell me everything. Only as much as there was time for and she could remember. And now that we have finished the squalid part of
the story and are ready for the love part, I will remove myself,
insofar as possible, and tell it as I heard it. I heard it in a voice
which, though it may never have breathed over Eden, has certainly breathed through our commercial dreams of what a
lady *ought* to sound like; and even I, who probably heard more
than anyone else has ever had time for, kept to the end doing
double takes when she said things like "I'm very fastidious, but
I let him ——— in my hair" or "Donald and Esther ate each
other's excrement. I shouldn't do so in any circumstances." I
would think for a minute she'd said, "I'm very fastijjous,
therefore only Yardley's Old Yeoman Downyflakes ever touch
my dainty things," or, "Donald and Esther use tea bags; I de-

mawnd Lipton's prime leaf, properly brewed." Now what I'm
not trying to say is that the elegance and the apposite trench-
ancy of her phrasing redeemed the grossness of her goddam
subject. I mean, redemption doesn't grow on any goddam trees,
and you have to muster a lot of faculties to extract it. Just
think, for the time being, that I heard a curious tension of op-
posites between manner and material of what she had to de-
clare.

Our girl had gone down to London, then, after that first
operation, which to the confounding of all expectations had to
remove not only the royal chocolate polyp in the womb but nature's Aryan-pink demishield. Had gone down to seek her
way because RAF pensions are mean and the money once set
aside for her schooling had been badly diminished to pay for
something the Health Plan didn't cover. Had gone (I mean to
follow the straight road of how she told things, not yet involved with the deviousness of mere chronology, since I suspected all the while I listened to her that Time was the gray
lecher she sweated under on those innumerable cots, beds,
swards, tables, benches, and blankets where she, taken to water,
had no more questioned her element than old Drake himself.
I more than lightly toyed with the idea that it was really she
who had tried to break this goddam wrist watch I got from
Corporal X, and you know what *that* means)—had gone to the
second abortion that both the frustration and the demoraliza-
tion of the first had rendered as inevitable as the abortion of
peace in our time. I mean the climax—the culminative disaster
which or whose consequences she was running from now on
her way to America—was the natural point for her to begin.

This second time she " 'lowed as how" it had been the
Texan done it, he who had called her Slim after he found her
in the bar where she was working to support Jerry. (Jerry?
Later . . .) She was carrying a picture of Tex in her purse the
morning she told me about *him,* not an ordinary snapshot, but
a clipping from the *Express* that showed him with a slanting
cartridge belt, low-slung holster tied above his knee with a

bootlace, and wearing on his head what might have been either a cowboy hat or an Aussie bonnet. Since restrictions against killing niggers had tightened up in his home state, he had been off in Kenya scoring against the Mau Mau. The caption said he claimed ninety-two.

At the time she knew him he still seemed to have some hush-hush connections with either the CIA (for whom he had probably run guns into Cuba and Vietnam) or British Intelligence. He seemed to have plenty of money from somewhere and used to drop out of her sight for days on end with no explanations to her, and this at a time when they had become so firmly engaged he was able to persuade her that dutch cap and french letter were as abhorrent as bob-wire to a freeborn puncher from Texas. "Bastard even went up with me to call on Aunty and the Vicar," Mesmé said. "He charmed them, of course. So frank and open. Honestly, you Americans all tend toward candor and liberty. We do find you so."

Happy-go-lucky Tex didn't turn a hair when she gave him the big glad news. He just *disappeared,* as if the Commies were rampaging again and his fast gun was needed in the jungles or on the beaches. She was two and a half months along when Scotland Yard called to ask if she knew him and could account for his presence in London on a certain day in July. She could indeed, since she had marked all his "visits" in her diary, cross-referenced to her menstrual cycle. In exchange for her information she was finally told by Yardsmen that Tex was in jail. Whether or not she would be called as a witness depended on the Foreign Office. But, whether or not, he would undoubtedly have to serve time for passing bad checks, defrauding a landlord, and violating currency regulations.

Could she see him at his place of incarceration? Inadvisable, since that might upset his wife, she was told.

From the purse that had yielded Tex's picture, Mesmé produced another clipping, notably less worn than the first. This one was from the *Mirror.* Smiling staunchly into the camera was a wee, pretty Indonesian woman embracing two cold-eyed,

double-holstered, booted and lank boys of about three and
five years. Beneath this family grouping the caption read, "I
Married a Cad."

"And to think, so might I have done," Mesmé said. "He was
a Libra and I was a Taurus. I should have known better from
the beginning."

Plainly she could not go again with her trouble to her
mother, who had once arranged "the best Harley Street attendance" for the defloration-curettage that had saved a royal line
from mongrelization. "And I hadn't thruppence to my name,"
she said. "I couldn't very well get a loan from Jerry, as he was
terribly angry with me at just this point for what he called my
treachery—though what I owed him after keeping him a year
while he read every day in the British Museum, I can't say—and
besides he hadn't thruppence either, poor dear, for Mavis Burke-
Lancaster had just put him on the street as well. I had to sell
my cello. Nasty instrument anyhow. I had never cared to
play in public. The big, bulgy thing seemed somehow like personal ostentation. I might have had the creature, as Vive Roye-
Cutter had and no one was the wiser until her Gran came on
her in Charing Cross Road looking as if she'd swallowed a
football. Poor thing, it died and Gerald buried it on the Embankment. None of that for me, especially as I was frightfully
off Tex for what he'd done. He *had* played the part of a cad,
don't you think? Quite deliberately?"

I said it looked that way, but I wondered if she had made the
mistake of confiding in Tex her misadventure with the dark
prince. She answered reflectively, "I might have done. I had no
secrets from him and why should I, since I had every reason
to believe we would marry?"

Sweet Thames, flow gently 'til I end my song. With the
twenty-five pounds she got for the cello, she went to a midwife
living in the country beyond Hampton Court. "I wasn't keen
on it, but the time had come for decision." The midwife was
most kind and sympathetic "considering the sort of person

with whom she ordinarily came in contact" and a great deal of her excellence appeared to Mesmé in her not "preaching" as the Harley Street physician had done. "Defend me from those who know what's right and wrong," Mesmé said. "I once knew an older man who said he'd be justified in turning me over to the police. I've never in my life used that word *justified*."

The midwife gave her pain killers and told her to go home and wait. Home, at that time, was a gaunt, cold, and enormous flat she shared with six other girls and a medley of masculine names—"journalists, artists, writers, producers, all really quite sedate except for Donald and Esther, though quite without a penny. A school friend of Aunt Cecile's called one time and reported home that I was living in a brothel. Not a bit fair to say, of course."

In this menage Mesmé had a room of her own, "not grand, but adequate now that Jerry had left and had taken his books and Tex never stayed overnight even before his incarceration. He hated a single bed, and I must say that I got tired of it too in the thirteen months Jerry stayed."

Alone in her room Mesmé waited until the pains "quite like labor pains as I've been told of them" came. Then, in a borrowed dish pan, and for the second time, in pain and travail she gave back to nature what nature had so blithely entrusted to her. "I didn't know what to do with it," she said. "The kitchen was at the far end of the apartment, and I'd had to wait so long I heard Rosemary and Roberta come home and some men talking. I covered it with a newspaper and went through, explaining that I'd been sick. All very well, but it clogged the sink, and I stood there poking, poking, you know, wondering if I should faint. The girls were frightfully worried about me, though I don't think they knew—thought I'd gone a bit off, I dare say. They were most gracious about bringing me biscuits while I was confined to my room later. There's a special sort of hard, dry, I think quite tasteless, little biscuit called Grugg's Delight that I'd become keen on during the war. Rosemary brought me I can't think how many tins of them in this trying period."

I said I could certainly see why she wanted to go to America, and she said that while she'd been eager to see New York and the West for some time, it had actually been Tex who had fixed her determination. "He had such stories to tell. Life over there seems so much more exhilarating. Perhaps it's your open spaces." I could only concede that maybe they *were* the key to our basic American natures.

From a climax, even if it's only to a goddam story you hear in a bar on a boat wallowing westward through a gray snowstorm, there's nowhere much to look except back. And you know what follows is going to be more upbeat just because it really, once upon a time, pre*ced*ed instead of following. What followed—running backward in Mesmé's tale—was poor Jerry kicked out, if you'll remember, of his cozy berth with Mesmé by the appearance on the scene of the overwhelmingly frank and candid Texan. Right now, on this day that we braved the Atlantic chill, old Jerry was established on some *guru* in the Midi, living high on the *guru*'s hog, eating wheat germ and blackstrap molasses. The *guru* was giving Jerry some final pointers on how to shape up the mystical book he'd been working on for so many years, and had put him in touch with an international set of Zen fags who thought his book might "go" if it was pushed right. In London, where everyone knew everyone, there were those who blamed Mesmé for making Jerry homeless. "But after all, it was summer," she said. "Jerry loved to cycle and he had a sleeping bag that the Persian had given us. There's always somewhere to sleep in the country, and from there it's only an hour and a half ride in to the museum."

I said she must have been getting more or less deformed sleeping two in a single bed for all that time. She brightened at my interest, said, Oh yes, there was that aspect, but actually she had always rather looked forward to coming home late from work and finding him there, sacked in and warmer than a hot-water bottle. They read a great deal together during the nights. All his friends were publishing in *Horizon* and the *New Statesman* and they read these new things as well as Nietzsche, Dostoevsky, Madame Blavatsky, Lawrence, Kierkegaard, Henry Miller, and Yeats' and William Blake's prophetic works. "I shouldn't like to say we merely read," Mesmé emphasized. "Indeed, Jerry was very good for me, very tender. We did seem to get rather bored with orgasms after all the trouble we'd been to getting adjusted, but at second hand I got it from Alex Du-Verde that they'd lunched and while comparing notes on me, Jerry said that my _____ always reminded him, rather, of the sporting club at Monte Carlo. Edwardian in its amplitude and elegance. Poor Alex simply hectored the wits out of Jerry trying to get the secret of how he made me come, when for all those months with *him* I hadn't. He said Jerry didn't understand it either, and I assured him I did not, unless it was that Jerry was less aggressive. Alex used to read me all the pertinent medical literature and send me out for nights with someone else. And with them I always did, and when I reported so, he was *fur*ious. I told him the watched pot never boils, and that made him no happier. Do you suppose I refused just *so* he would be wretched about it? He used to bully me so with that dirty old Freud and an American volume that I understand is found in every middle-class home; naturally I should seek some method of vengeance."

I said that seemed natural to me.

"I suppose Alex was fond of me, in his own way, though," she said dreamily. "When I saw him two weeks ago he said, 'Mes, you should know me now that I have money.' You see, I was supporting him, too, and he felt badly at the recollection. He was a sort of literary critic and I understand that he's doing very well these days. Cyril Connolly has mentioned him. He had to have at me one more time before embarkation to see if he couldn't bring it off, but it was no go."

I said it was nice they had parted friends anyhow, and she said they didn't really, for once again Alex had been unable to resist quoting Freud, probably only because he knew the great man's grandson, and she was certain (as I was, too) that Freud could not explain her.

"Only John Keats could," I said. "Your hair is long, your eye is wild."

She blinked her goddam gratitude at me for being intellectual enough to offer such grist for free association. She said, "I was once one's mistress, though never child, but I shan't say a word about him, for to talk about them is to talk against them, somehow, and he was most pitiful. *His* father had been shot down, too, over Tripoli. He taught in a boy's day school and it made him quite frantic. Of course Alex was always dabbling, you know, but that was rather different. He had such a lively curiosity. No doubt that's what gave me an attraction for him."

"Your privates, we."

"One may feel oneself basically a simple wretch who merely wants to get married and raise numerous children. And yet things happen."

Before Alex had moved in to peep and botanize there had been a doctor and a dentist who, between them, had put her in excellent health, remedying certain defects which she supposed were the result of wartime austerity, and supplying her with dentifrice and vaginal jelly enough to last a normal lifetime. Before them (or coincidental with them, since they were professional men who required neither food nor lodging from her and thus left her with a certain freedom of movement) there was the fashion designer.

"He liked my figger since no one else in the shop could wear his furs quite as I could. I appeared before the Queen Mother in a sable stole that rather drowned Priss and Con. Our Meg was there. Did you know she was practically a midget, poor thing? Comes only to one's armpit."

The designer's wife was also fond of Mesmé, but made neither advances nor protests in spite of knowing all, and to this menage a fourth member was added, a Greek nephew. "Rather like a golden, glowing fruit," Mesmé described him. "One seldom sees a tighter skin on a man—or boy, as the case may be better put. He had absolutely no mind at all. He smiled continuously, in the blandest way."

Before—I mean, if we didn't have to use that word and could just let it stand that my symbolic time piece hadn't been running all this while, I suppose I could convey better both the way I heard all this from Mesmé and the way it must have happened. I mean, anybody who's read *The Magic Mountain* knows how time is on a boat (just like in a TB sanitarium, tricky and ductile) and might very well find their intelligence insulted if I pretended we just sat on that long couch in the bar, like sitting at a multiple feature movie running backward, while I heard all her tales in sequence. I mean, even if Dexter and Billy almost never left *my* cabin, Mesmé shared hers with only an old lady, who was just mad about horse racing, bingo, and the dining-room steward.

I could go on plenty about how going furtively through the passages of our ship and into her cabin was like going through a time construction, through transitional or durational periods until I found where linear dimensions became spatial and something between us could *hap*pen. But all that's been done *before*. And yet I don't want to just throw out all the befores, because there was *a* time that all Mesmé's *temps retrouvés* were heading back for in just the same way—or rather in just the *oppo*-site way—that the ship was going on a compass track toward New York.

So, *before* serving time in the world of fashion, before the remedial work on her physical person and the broader outlook on sex given her by the professional men, before her subsidies of literary criticism and mystic thought, she had gone to France once with a "nasty little dilettante," presumably on their way to a Casals festival. They got only as far as Paris and the Hotel des Étrangers. "Nor did I get to see the Louvre," Mesmé told me. "Underneath all his pretenses, Edmund was mean to the core. He didn't even like French cookery and we ate most often in the bistros near Pigalle that specialized in hamburgers for American servicemen."

She paid Edmund off for his meanness by deserting him one night in the Flore in favor of a Swede touring Europe in an ancient Buick with two Afghan hounds. That adventure ended in Geneva when "I realized my flight was mere escapism. It's not my nature to fly reality, and that is exactly what I had done. You understand?"

With drugs?

She shook her lovely head. "I never needed those."

But before escape, in the idyllic period of her first London months, she had slept lightheartedly around "almost like a deb, but there are certain men in London whose specialty is to sleep with everyone and I was careful to avoid such. I know many stories came back to me at second hand from someone's saying, 'After all, everyone else sleeps with me. Why not Mesmé?' "

I said it was a good thing to regard oneself as an orchid and not as one of the common daisies of the field. She said, "Exactly!"

"Nevertheless," she said with a slanting, giddy grin, "one has a certain sense of control when one is able to sleep with as many as three friends in a day without one's emotions being shredded. I never thought of getting married in those days and generally I came with glorious ease."

She sat bold upright in her berth one night and hugged her torso as if in a gesture of love quite beyond anything she had felt in my arms. Her ash-blond skin was goose-pimpled. Her splay fingertips sunk in smoothly ridged dimples of flesh, and she dragged her muscles so hard that her ribs looked like the phony gill lines scored on some kind of antediluvian reptile.

"Hurry up, please, it's time," I said. Mrs. Brindleman, her cabin mate, usually came down from Bingo at ten-thirty, and we tried to allow her at least a half hour variable to be on what Mesmé called the safe side, understanding so little of either safety or its value.

"I don't mind its being *time*," she said awfully. "It's a nasty paradox. I could come with so many others I don't love. Why can't I come with you? Can you figger it?"

I didn't say anything. I don't have a faculty for taking on because someone loves me.

"It's most unfair. It's always been unfair. The night they chose to tell me about my father was when George spilled everything to Aunty. They shouldn't have done."

I said they certainly shouldn't.

"The wretched beast had put me up to it, too. I could hardly have got much fun from tossing *him* off. And yet, such fun as it was—they didn't have to punish it *so*. What are you thinking, darling?"

"Get dressed," I said. "Hurry."

"Don't you think it's unfair?"

I thought it would be further unfair if Mrs. Brindleman caught us as we were. She was not a lady who would understand why we had to undress and go through all these motions just so Mesmé could tell me how she felt when her father was killed.

When we were safely dressed and out of there, she dragged hard at my arm, as if blaming me for bringing her out just when she was on the edge of finding what was *wrong*. I think she would have gone back then and there and Mrs. Brindleman be damned, to try once more to get the secret.

"You know more about me than anyone in terms of brute detail," she said. "Can't you explain it to me without allusion to Freud?" Old Beardy was not going to have her as long as that roving hand could reach beneath the sheets of her new-found land for what had been taken away that night in the summer house. But I wasn't going to let on to her what I knew. I mean, when you're on public transportation you don't crouch in the corridors to clutch your belly and howl. I wasn't going to discredit my countrymen and Tex's by any disparaging predictions, either.

"About your daddy," I said. "It was the krauts that killed him, you know."

"Yes." She sounded like she was glad to have that straight again.

"*You* didn't do it."

"They shot him under the ear. He had parachuted safely, you know. It wasn't the worst time in the war for them, either. They might have taken him prisoner. They shouldn't have done. . . ."

Well, as Corporal Y never tired of repeating, it's taken a long time to get the *real* dope on the scourge of the swastika. That same night after I'd got tanked up enough to stop saying the Jesus prayer (which I pronounce with a high, whistling sibilant) and had taken Mesmé back properly to her cabin where she would sleep above Mrs. Brindleman, I ran into coarse, crude Y and we had our talk.

"You know something about that girl of yours?" Y said.

"She's not my girl. She's being met at the dock. There's a man who's been after her for years. He's flown over to Hollywood and will be back in New York."

Corporal Y gave me one of those gross, shocked but insensitive looks with which he is so prodigal. "Oh," he said. "Anyway, you know something? That girl is sad."

"It only hurts when she laughs."

"I mean, her story is *moving*."

"She tell you all the gore, too? About the drain stopping up?"

He nodded. "She tells everybody. She's compulsive, and I mean that's what's so goddam sad. I should think you'd be full of lousy tics and twitches if you cared anything about her at all."

I held out my hand to show him. My knuckles were snapping all by themselves with a noise like celery being snapped. I hoisted a drink to my lips by using my necktie as a sling to elevate my right hand, but my lower lip kept jerking so fast that I spilled part of it anyway.

"That's better," Y said approvingly. "You know Mesmé wouldn't be such a de*praved* orphan if it wasn't for what happened to England and her during the goddam war. Did you ever think of what her life might have been like if she'd kept on in school and practiced her cello and her father was maybe an air marshal now? You know he was a brigadier when the krauts murdered him. I mean, did you ever *think* about that?"

I said I hadn't given it as much study as it probably deserved, but once I got safely back on dry land I would sit down to think about it lots.

"If you think about it you'll see that why she's a nympho is her goddam aunt caught her practically in bed with the cousin and gave her a hell of a guilt feeling by telling her right on the spot that her old man is dead. So she keeps trying to repeat that night—that one lousy night—trying to make it come out different, so that after she's been had someone will, like, whisper in her ear that her daddy's safe. I mean, he parachuted down and according to the rules of the Geneva convention they got him in a PW camp with his gallant buddies planning how they're gonna fool the slow-witted Bavarian guards and escape, see?"

I said even if I could see it I didn't know what it was I saw.

"Don't know *what?* What part of it? Whether I'm right or not? Listen, my ex-wife taught psychology at Western *Reserve.* I did plenty of reading trying to keep up with that girl. Mesmé's fixated on that one moment out of all time, when, for every English girl, it is still beddy-bye time on September sixth, 1939, or whatever day the war hadn't started, and Daddy's up there in his unsinkable Beaufighter and the smuggled copies of *Lady Chatterley's Lover* have made the simultaneous orgasm practically a national goddam insti*tu*tion. And whatever it may have been for the lower orders, for people of Mesmé's class, England was still merry. Why shouldn't she want that back again?"

"I don't know," I said. "I just don't think she wants it any more. And I'm sleepy, and we have probably passed the Nantucket Light. I've got to go to bed."

Well, we know what intellectuals go to bed for. It's to think. That's what we get drunk for, too, and as I came into my cabin that night, bouncing off the walls, I could see I was really ready for the old skull practice.

It was awfully late, but as I entered I heard *The King and I* going full blast, and there was little Billy with the machine in his lap and Dexter in his top berth practically covered with plates, cups, and saucers. They said that since this was our last night on board they had decided to celebrate and probably wouldn't sleep a wink. Dexter belched and said, "Laddie, m'scouts tell me you've been knocking off 'er lidyship. Har, har."

I reeled into my bunk and said word certainly got around, didn't it?

"The stewards keep their eyes peeled, they do. Laddie, let me give you a bit of advice. English girls wot's traveling third class, they ain't often no better'n tarts, whatever they talk like. There ain't no bleedin' morality left in our time. So don't let her hook you, lad. Tike your bit of pleasure and go your way."

I said that certainly *was* sensible advice and I rolled into my berth and covered my head. Even though I had so much I could have thought about, I decided it had better wait until it didn't have to compete with "the chill-duh-run, the chill-duh-run." For his celebration, Billy was playing it louder than ever.

It was Sunday morning when we came into the harbor, and *you* know what New York looks like on a cold, crisp *Sun*day morning. It looks like something abandoned on a dead planet —all that stone and no movement. It was so still. When Mesmé and I walked out on deck to have a look, we had just about passed Canal Street; then they shut off the screws and we coasted slower and slower into the Hudson current. It really was ghastly quiet then. There weren't even any gulls that morning.

"It's very un*like* London," Mesmé said uncertainly. She had made herself up gaudily to face her new home—bright-green eyeshadow, black penciling in the corners of her eyes, and a real paste of lipstick for her unchaste mouth. "In London they shouldn't be allowed to build so recklessly. I must say it looks a bit forbidding."

"Just tell yourself there are many warm, kind, friendly people dwelling in those cliffs," I said, already anticipating Nathan, I suppose. I mean, with all my pent-up thoughts and with my increased sensibility that could detect (hell! could hear, like the slam-bang from the village smithy) the ticking of my symbolic wrist watch, I knew the numinous moment was practically on me, so why shouldn't I speak from second sight?

I said, "Somewhere in that forest of glamorous stone, perhaps snoozing at this very moment, while visions from Masoch and Sade dance through the glades of his dreams, is the man you've been unconsciously looking for ever since that night in the summer house."

"One has to trust to fate," she said, with an ever so tiny smirk.

"And one dare not learn from experience," I said loyally. "I hope with all my heart I'll see you again often. But we'll never know as much about each other as we know just now."

She put her gloved hand fondly on my bare wrist.

"I don't have any more faith in Freud than you have," I said, hearing the crazy bang of that old timepiece under her fingertips. "But he can sometimes help us make up fables about ourselves. For kicks, I mean. I myself pass much time in Village bars and at home in Freudian speculation. It would be most valuable to me, *when* I think about you, if I knew the answer to one elusive question. Now if Tex and I—each in our characteristic American way—represent some facet of the ideal man you're seeking, may I infer that you want, not your father, but the man who killed your father?"

Projected against the rosy and buff towers of our island, motionless as goddam stalagmites, there was nothing less than a vision of beautiful orphans running to present themselves with servile curtsies to some two-gun, hypocritical intellectual. Their clear voices sang, "Daddy's dead and you are now king of the wood."

So much for retaining the faculty of seeing visions. They just generally upset you and make you say silly things like "Mesmé, take the next boat back" to a girl who's just arrived.

And you take a girl who knows what she wants, and she shakes off such advice like a duck shaking water off its back. For instance, Mesmé kept staring at the Sunday-morning shark's teeth of the Manhattan skyline, and pretty soon I knew she was rolling over in her mind my encouraging comment about the man who might be there waiting for her. The not literally impossible he who was morally prepared to match and mate the circumstantial devastation of her life.

Her eyes rolled back to follow the dream. Her lips rounded in a gloating smile. "I'm just a poor wretch who wants to get married and have lots of children," she said.

I said, "Kiss me, Hardy," and she reminded me that she already *had,* quite enough.

Larchmoor Is Not the World

IN THE winter the glassed arcade between Thornton and Gillespie Halls was filled with potted flowers so it smelled and looked like a greenhouse. Last night's storm, blowing in across the athletic fields of the Northwest campus, had left a shape of frozen snow like a white boomerang in the corner of each pane behind the rows of geraniums and ferns.

The first time Dr. Cameron walked through the arcade on this particular day, he stopped to point with his pipestem at the ranked greenery so slightly and perilously separated from the outside cold. "There," he rumbled to Mr. Wilks of History, "is your symbol for this young women's seminary. There is your Larchmoor girl cut off by a pane of glass from the blast of your elements. A visible defiance of the nature of things, made possible by a corrupt technology."

Mr. Wilks grimaced and chuckled, weighed this illustration of their common attitude toward the college in which they taught, finally amended, "The glass is wrong. Glass they could see through. See the world in which they don't live, even though. . . ." His thought trailed off in a giggle. At Larchmoor, Mr. Wilks seemed to spend most of his energy looking behind him to see if he had been overheard.

"True," Dr. Cameron said. As they loitered through the arcade the music and the rumble of the student lounge rose to them from the floor below. It rose, mixed inextricably with the smell of baked goods from the dining hall and the moist smell of steam from laboring radiators. Now and then a cry, barbaric, probably happy but otherwise meaningless, punctuated the noise. "The analogy breaks down, true. Listen to them down there. One gets to be like an animal trainer. Sensitive to their noises. If I had no calendar I could tell by their tone that Christmas vacation started this afternoon."

"Then there's an identifying noise that distinguishes Christmas vacation from the beginning of—say—spring vacation?"

"Hmm. Yes, that's right. In seven years my ear has become acutely attuned to it. You'll pick it up eventually. Unhappily, in learning their mass sound you'll become unable to distinguish one of them from the others. Compensation at work. They will seem to you one single enormous female juvenile named Shirley or whatever the name would happen to be of the child movie star ascendant in the year of their birth." Dr. Cameron's baby-pink face grew almost radiant. "Tomorrow," he said, "the sons of bitches will all be gone home and we'll have three weeks of peace. Shantih."

The second time he went through the arcade that day he met Sandra White, dressed for her journey with high heels now and a fur coat, looking like the ads in the fashion magazines with the good sharp empty Nordic shape of her head an appurtenance to the excellent clothes—looking five years older than she had looked that morning in his American Literature class. Her manner, too, had been changed with her clothes, so that she spoke to him as a young matron patronizing an old and crotchety, really lovable duck who had "made his lah-eef out of literature."

"Dr. Cameron. Thank *you* for the list of books," she said. "I don't think I'll give any presents this Christmas except books and I. . . ." Yet because this was so obviously a statement coined to please him, both became momentarily embarrassed. It was the girl who first recovered and went on, "I think I'll get Daddy the Dos Passos' *USA*."

"Hmmm." He chewed his pipestem and stared at the glass roof of the arcade, then smiled.

"Well," she said in defense, "Daddy is really searching . . .

for . . . *that* kind of Americanism. He's not just a businessman. He's really—"

"Yes," he said. "I understand you to say you wanted this list of books for yourself, not just for presents."

"Oh. I'm going to ask for the Yeats for myself," she said. Her tone, demanding that this would please him, produced from the efficient catalog of his memory the image of her eyes becoming feminine-dramatic in that class hour a week before when he had quoted, "An aged man is but a paltry thing . . . unless soul clap its hands and sing and louder sing for every tatter in its mortal dress." Well, the quotation had been an indulgence for him and not intended for the class at all. It had been a parade before their innocent minds of a conscious expression of his own dilemma. He had spoken the lines to his class with the motives that lead a man to confess to his dog the sentiments for which he has no human confidant. But this little female, Sandra, whatever those words may have meant to her, had caught something of their importance to him and trapped him now into paying for the indulgence with a compliment to her taste.

"Fine," he said, "that's fine."

With a still doubtful look she said, "Merry Christmas," and let him go on to his office.

Here was the sanctuary which he had been seven years in building. A desk barred off one corner of the room. When students came in he sat behind it like a magistrate at the bar. Three walls, excepting door and window spaces, were lined to the ceiling with books. "I bought them," he once told Wilks, "but only for insulation and display. It's fatuous to assume that anybody can own books. I think that President Herman is pleased to find them there when he brings down parents and the prospective customers to exhibit me as a mechanism of the English department."

His swivel chair took most of the space behind the desk. It made of the corner an efficient nest, for he could swing to any of the cabinets and drawers in which he filed themes. Also within reach were the two material items he needed for his intellectual life. One was a bolt tied on a length of wrapping cord that he sometimes swung as a pendulum. The other was a motto that he had lettered painstakingly on colored paper. Originally it had come from an examination paper handed in to him during his first year at Larchmoor. "Shelley's main purpose was to write a lot of poems," it said. "This it came easy for him to do." Sometimes, when he was alone, he would place the inscription before him on his desk and sit laughing crazily at it until all the stains of teaching at Larchmoor were washed away. Then purified, without moving except to throw his shoulders back, he would watch that fraction of the campus where the pendulum of seasons appeared before his window.

This afternoon, the sunlight was a strange and clamorous orange that moved on the black tree trunks and the snow. Here nature dramatized the quality of a Beckmann painting—black cedars over water, it might have been, or such a landscape as the horns in Sibelius presented with not so much art as longing, such a landscape as might contain a golden mute princess called out by Death, that central myth that all the Romantics had exploited.

The embroidered, death-bidden, golden will-o'-the-wisp (and Sandra White now drifted on his mind's screen in a role that would have surprised her. Not as an intellect that shared his understanding of poetry but, wrapped in a rich cocoon of fur, wool, and silk that protected her delicacies from the blowing cold, as the image itself which the poets had conceived and desired—the figure on the Grecian urn, the witchlady on the mead, or that which Malraux's Dutchman saw on the Shanghai sidewalks, proud and strutting beyond the reach of the proletariat's desire) which like Shelley's Beatrice must be the fairest, youngest, purest of flesh to satisfy the snowy mouth of the Death the Romantics had imagined.

The peacefulness of snow is pure commercial folklore, he speculated, and in art the cold North always somehow emerges as the symbol of hungry frenzy—like the gelid and perfect tyranny which Plato described as the worst disaster of all that society can manage. The disorder of cold which had wrought the counter disorder of Northern art—the wind-whipped fires in the snowfield—with its load of desire protesting too much.

If Dr. Cameron had moved closer to his window, he would necessarily have seen more than this private landscape of a few trees, snow, and sun in which his mind pursued the lost girl. He would have seen more than twenty Larchmoor girls standing in the slush in front of the Kampus Kabin while they waited for taxis. They bounced, giggled, sang ("a woman, a woman, a woman without a man, teedlededum, bumph"), chewed gum, shifted packages or suitcases from hand to hand, stamped their fur-topped boots in the muck of the road. He knew they were there, not five degrees outside the arc of vision which the window gave him. "But I have the right not to look."

With the arrival of each Christmas vacation since he had come to Larchmoor, he had discovered himself confronted with a particular crisis of fatigue and depression. The beginning of yet another school year and the first exacting months hollowed him emotionally, and the pleasures of intellect had lost their recreational power. While the girls went off to whatever indulgences the society provided for its most expensive and pampered stock, he went to his bachelor rooms to read and smoke incessantly, and considered how he might get a job elsewhere until always, with the passing of the actual and figurative solstice, the change of renewal occurred. What was compounded of hatred and contempt for Larchmoor led him first to review the other places he had taught—the two big universities where the younger assistants whinnied like mares around the head of the department, and the religious college where he had been forbidden to smoke on campus and required to attend chapel daily—then led through a couple of drinking bouts with some one of his friends, like Mr. Wilks. There had always been younger men like Mr. Wilks coming and going as Larchmoor instructors. Just out of graduate school, they regarded Larchmoor as a stepping stone to bigger schools, but while they

stayed—one or two each year succeeding those who had gone
—they formed a fit audience though few for such occasions as
the Christmas drunks. Those times gave him the chance to
elaborate with perverse brilliance on the attractions Larchmoor
had for him.

They would be sitting in the easy chairs of his rooms with a
litter of crackers and cheese on a card table between them, the
black windows frosting over, and in the late hours the monologue would pause only when one or another went unsteadily
to the bathroom. "Do you remember reading about that Jap
general on Iwo Jima . . . said, 'I will die here' . . . the com-
ponent of all the forces of his life . . . so that even the melo-
drama was right for the bandy-legged little bastard. Fitting.
The answer is a kind of balance—not balance—but that second
in the pendulum's swing when all the forces are composed so
there must be an instant of harmony that the eye isn't quick
enough to catch when one reasons that there must be no motion. Still . . . The effort of the mind to perpetuate that second
by selection out of all the comic and vicious flux in us and
around us is the same as the slave's impulse to throw off his
ropes. . . . Larchmoor locks up kids that should be out and
doing things. Their bad luck is good for me. There are different ages, and for me freedom doesn't exist in the world. It's
an asylum growth. . . . I've got my office for asylum like a rat's
nest in the corner of a busy house. I don't huddle there because
I'm interested in the house. Nobody but a damn fool would be
concerned with Larchmoor as Larchmoor. . . . It gives me
a stable place to sit and watch the 'pismires' "—here he smiled
—" 'and the stars.' And don't you know, Wilks, that a man
has to actually utter his ideas? Your gloomy newspapers tell
you that. It's such an undeniable premise of the search for freedom. Here I can say whatever I please to my classes. Elsewhere, in these days, I might be quickly apprehended as a Com-
munist or an atheist, but when I say something to my girls they
put it in their notebooks and there's an end to it. Oh, I have my
disguises here. On another level I can talk to the vermin Her-

man"—Larchmoor's president—"the same way. As far as that goes. When he asked me what I thought of the new dormitory with the air-conditioned bedsprings, I made some trivial remark about painting 'our outward walls so costly gay.' And he thought it was my stamp of approval, yes he did. . . . And then we mustn't fool ourselves. Where else could I go? I'm not a scholar in the sense that I've ever felt a mission to get my name in *PMLA,* or write a book on Chaucer's cook's marmal. I'm a reader, that's all I amount to. 'Whatever games are played with us, we must play no games with ourselves, but deal in our privacy with the last honesty and truth.' Larchmoor not only lets but forces me to be honest with myself. The games it plays with me are not much bother. To them I'm just an old gaffer that talks like Bartlett's quotations. I have a place here. They pay me as a fixture. . . . The girls are pretty. Like old David's, my bones need the warmth provided by a moderate proximity of young female flesh. My disguises . . . I look too old to notice them. I am too old to letch for any of them, but by God they're pleasant furniture. . . . At Larchmoor I come close to balancing. If it were any better I'd get involved with it. No doubt I've searched subconsciously for Larchmoor all my life. I'm preoccupied with how I die. Like the Jap general. That isn't morbid at my age. More natural. I want to die in this moral Iwo Jima . . . and be buried under the hockey field."

He had put on his overcoat to go home when he passed through the glassed arcade for the third time that day. This time a clatter of heels on the tile floor rang behind him. There was a hand on his arm and Shirley Bridges' face suddenly thrust so close to his own that he jumped back. At first, the circles of white around her eyes and the chalky stripes on either side of her mouth struck him as an antic fashion culled from the pages of *Vogue* and destined to become a part of the fluctuating uniform of Larchmoor. But even as he began to smile, her hand clawed down his sleeve until she had hold of his bare wrist and he understood that her face was marked with some girlish emotion. Her hand on his wrist was wet and cold. He felt pain in the back of his skull and then a release of anger. "What's the trouble, Miss Bridges?" He lifted her fingers one at a time from their hysterical grasp. "Are you ill?"

To his exasperation she said, "No. My grade. You—"

"I understand," he said. He cleared his throat the better to snarl. "In spite of your studious industry, I, I, I have so seriously misprized you that I reported you to the Dean, who maliciously put you on academic probation. Now you're going to be forbidden the delights of the jukebox and the downtown dance hall for the rest of the semester." The tonic of anger had blurred away any distinctions he might have tried to make between her and The Larchmoor Girl in a more temperate season. "Every coercion will be applied to force you to the unreasonable humiliation of reading your books. I am committed to the belief that you will live through it. Now, if you will excuse me, may I bid you a Merry Christmas?"

"Please," she said. In the blue expanse of her eyes the pupil diminished nastily like an insect pulling its wings to its body.

He felt the burning of his face. She'd better not put her hands on me again, he thought. "Don't take all this so intensely. There really isn't any reason you can't make up your work. Weren't you the one last fall who was, well—so sublimely confident of her ability? You sometimes make interesting comments in class. I think you just need to decide to do some work."

"No," she said. "Talk to me." Her mouth hung loose like a bright ribbon, and her tongue arched against her lower teeth.

"You're *not* well."

She nodded. "Talk to me in your office. Please."

One hall on their way led past the president's office and reception rooms. She would not go this way. Without quite knowing why, he let her guide him down a roundabout stairway.

While he lit his pipe and rocked squeaking in his swivel chair, he looked at the girl's hands. The lacquered nails were broader than they were long and the fingers were tapered like a child's from the palm. How do they manage to look like *women?* he asked himself. What corruption and tampering with mortality in the flesh is it that lets them or makes them look generally the same from fifteen to thirty-five, brushed and painted and girdled to a formula that here across his desk was breaking down into its sodden components? He noted that two beads of spittle had stuck in the corners of Shirley's mouth.

What would be the effect, he wondered, if he should announce at once that he had reconsidered her case and had already decided to give her an A for the semester?

"You restore my faith," he said. "In seven years of teaching here I have never seen a Larchmoor girl who spent the day before a vacation even thinking about the college, let alone the grades she might get in one class in Biblical Literature."

"They're going to kick me out," she said.

"Oh nonsense. No final grades go in for six weeks yet."

"They are," she insisted. "They sent for Daddy. He's in President Herman's office now. I know they sent for him to take me out of school."

"Because of your grades? Not because of your grades, surely."

"Oh. I thought if I could get my grades straightened out that would help."

"You mean you've got in some kind of trouble. If your grades were good you might get by with it?"

The note of sarcasm was heavy enough to warn her of a trap. She said, "No. I don't think there would be any trouble if my grades were all right. I could work everything else out, I know."

"If you're in difficulty you ought to have gone to your housemother, not to me."

"Honest, it's the grades and my classes and things."

Dr. Cameron shook his head. His white mustache dipped at the ends as he made a face. "I'm guilty of many things, but I have never given any grades I didn't think were deserved; so there isn't much use to talk about that. Nevertheless I might tell you something that will reassure you. Among other things Larchmoor is a commercial institution. I have even heard President Herman speak of it as a business. You pay a considerable tuition here which would have to be refunded if you were dropped before the end of the semester. I have no doubt that the administration will find some way to avoid that unpleasant necessity." This will end the interview, he thought. She can understand that better than anything. Coin is the sea that bore them hither and will bear them hence. It is the direct communication, the basis of knowledge on which whatever they might get from the library or classroom would only be fluff. "Does that explain exactly why they aren't going to kick you out?"

"It isn't that way, is it?"

He grinned like a devil. "Undoubtedly." Less because she demanded it than because of the habit of explanation he went on, "There's much more to it than that. I have simply given you a short cut to understanding why you won't be expelled. From your side of the fence everything seems to be an absolute. Every rule, every pronouncement, perhaps. I'm old enough to know there are no absolutes. Everyone here who has anything to do with your case lives in a tangle of confusions and opinions not so different from your own. Out of these will come some compromise that won't be too hard on you. That's the truth. That's the way the world goes. Compromise, compromise. President Herman's decrees and judgments may seem absolute and final to a freshman. They're not, really. He's not God Almighty."

"They're all God Almighty," the girl said. "My father is God Almighty too." He was not sure whether she meant this as a joke or as an attempt at philosophy, but whichever it was it seemed to amuse her. "That's why it's so goofy. They say I destroyed their faith. Didn't you hear about that, Dr. Cameron? It happened in your Biblical Lit class so I guess you knew about it. It's so funny because I think there is God Almighty. Lots of them. You're another one, because remember at the first of the year you told us to use our minds and question things, and then

I was the only one that argued, and you're going to give me an F."

"You haven't handed in any work," he said irrelevantly. He turned the swivel chair sharply sideways so the old bearings screamed. So the other little ones had sat in class all semester being careful to hear nothing, read nothing before their open eyes except what confirmed those memories of Sunday school they liked to call "their faith." All right. He had known that and had remarked on it caustically. But here was the other twist —that they were leagued, each little monster with her shining braids, to smell out differences within the herd which had not been apparent to him. He labored his memory for images of the class from which this one girl would appear standing like a martyr among the Philistian mob. She said that she had "argued." He could remember nothing of the sort. Each day she had seemed as impersonal as a ninepin in a row of her classmates. Her eyes had been as blue as theirs, her hair more blond than some; the courtesy of her bored attention had been the same, though she had not taken notes so assiduously as a few. Somehow, on a level of intuition that he could only guess at, they had found the intolerable difference in her. He remembered the wetness of her hand on his wrist and wondered if it had been fear they smelled.

"I thought you got along all right with the girls," he said.

"I will try. I will get along if they'll let me stay. I think I was just beginning to make some friends." She drew in her upper arms against her breasts and shivered.

"That sort of thing has to happen. I don't suppose it's possible to *make* friends."

The idea, with her own interpretation, had not helped. "I know I could," she said.

"Don't you have any—well, people, girls you run around with here?"

"Oh yes. My roommate. And there's lots of others. I know how to make them like me if I could stay."

If there had been someone impartial with them—Mr. Wilks

perhaps—to whom he could have rationalized the abyss he glimpsed, letting orderly words mount like a steel bridge over it, he might still have kept himself from involvement. "One must not seek the contagion of the herd," he would have said. "God knows what conformities they may exact from her once she has kissed the rod. Whatever it may cost to maintain even the fear, if it's only the fear that distinguishes one . . ." If he could have found the words on which he depended.

" 'Larchmoor, calm and serene on thy hill,' " he muttered. "Now Miss Bridges, Shirley, maybe we ought to look at this another way. Suppose they . . . suppose you leave Larchmoor now. There are bigger schools you might go to where you'd have a better chance to be yourself."

"Bigger?" she said. "Oh no."

"You mustn't forget that there is time for anything you want to do."

"Not if I go home," she said.

"But you're wrong. There will be fifty years ahead of you," he said, realizing that she could not believe this. "Larchmoor is not the world. Every possibility is open at your age."

"Would you go to the president and tell him I'm a good student? Could you give me any kind of a good grade if I'd work all through vacation?" She rose and came around the desk and stood just in front of him, just beyond arm's length from him. She stood very straight facing him and neither swaying nor looking at him.

"Please," he said. "Sit down. I'm afraid I don't understand at all. I can't understand why it's so important for you to stay here. You have so many years ahead of you. There is plenty of time. Go home for a while."

She sighed like a child, heavily. "I guess I ought to tell you why they sent for Daddy. It was because when the railroad agents came out to sell tickets home I was the only girl in school who wasn't going. I would have stayed here if they would have let me. Then I got scared and rented a hotel room downtown."

He was afraid to ask any further questions. Once again his necessary refuge was not in forty years of the poor scholar's study but only in the pipe which he could chew and smoke and scrape ostentatiously, as he did now. His eyebrows arched as though to admonish her to say no more.

"I can't go home. I'm afraid of Daddy. That was the reason."

"Now, now. You could surely explain to him. . . . Grades aren't that important."

"He fought me last summer with his fists. I'm not quite as strong as he is. He knocked me down and was choking me when Mother came and made him stop." The words were rushing from her throat like a foul torrent heaved up by the convulsions of her body as she writhed from side to side. "Don't know what he'll do to me now. Now. Now."

The revelation of pain, however confused, was not to be doubted.

(So Shelley's Beatrice would have said, "Reach me that handkerchief—my brain is hurt.")

Then as though she was rid of it, she quieted. "I hit him first and cut his face with my ring." She held up her right hand, showing the ring, and for the first time that afternoon laughed shortly.

Resentment mixed with his bewilderment and horror. All around about them, he thought, on the walls and towers of Larchmoor, on the stubblefields and highways for unimaginable miles lies the snow. It's as if she's trying to drag me with her into elements that neither of us, teacher or student, should ever have to face. She's trying to elect me not just her father, but as she said, God Almighty.

"Why?" he asked. His voice seemed to boom.

"I don't know why he did it," she said with crazy slyness, her face weird.

(Oh, icehearted counselor . . .
If I could find a word that might make known
The crime of my destroyer. . . .)

"Are you sure you're well? Have you told anybody else about this?"

She shook her head. "They sent me downtown to see the psychiatrist when they found out I wasn't going home. I told him. He said he'd help me. I think he's the one that told them to send for Daddy to come and get me. I'm in trouble, so they're afraid I'll dirty up their college. But I would be good and everybody would get to like me if I could stay."

The president's secretary knocked on his door and put her head in. "Oh, good," she said, seeing them both, and then bobbing her head as though to confirm a suspicion that they were both quite real. "Can I speak to you privately, Dr. Cameron?" She pulled the door tight behind him and whispered, "Wheeeew, what a relief. The whole campus has been upside down looking for Shirley Bridges. Her father wants her upstairs. We couldn't find her in her room and they thought she might have done away with herself."

"Who thought that?" he demanded angrily.

"I don't know. We were all worried."

"But why should anyone think such a thing?"

"We've been having a lot of trouble with her. Her father says she gets in trouble wherever she goes. He just can't seem to do anything with her. He's going to take her home. I guess it's a good thing he came when he did. We had to send her to the psychiatrist last week."

"Oh, that's nonsense. Anyone can go to a psychiatrist."

"Well," she said. "Well, don't pick on me. Will you send her right up to the president's office?"

Instead he went himself. The noise in the halls was faint and infrequent now. Buses and taxis had carried most of the students to the depot. He passed one of the maids locking her mops into a closet and slowed his angry, absorbed march to say Merry Christmas to her.

A little man whose mouth protruded as though he were deciding whether or not to whistle sat in the president's reception room. He looked as sleek and innocent as a little dachshund perched on the edge of an overstuffed lounge. Dr. Cameron nodded stiffly to him. So this is the fistfighter, he thought. The champ.

"Go right in," the secretary said.

The hand in which President Herman held his glasses dangled over a chairback. He gestured with the glasses to indicate that Dr. Cameron should sit down.

"I'm glad you've come, Arthur," he said. "I understand from Miss Lee that Shirley Bridges has been in your office all afternoon. We've been very much concerned with Shirley today."

"As well we might be."

"Yes. Oh, yes."

"She's in a very tight spot. You might call it a kind of snare that tightens the more she struggles."

"She's not well. Upset mentally. There are always the few who can't adjust to Larchmoor. Her father is very much concerned with her, poor fellow." He sighed. His eyes rolled up under their thick lids.

"The girl has a rather different interpretation of him."

"You mean about her father's beating her? That's an unsavory story for her to tell, isn't it?" He looked challengingly across his desk like a lawyer requiring a yes-or-no answer. He's no fool, Cameron thought. This is going to be difficult. The president continued, "Shirley is quite an actress. Her talent should find its outlet on the stage. She's told that story to several people around here. Did she just tell you today? She seems to have fled to you as a last resort. If I'm not mistaken, she told the same story to the housemother before she'd been here two weeks. With different embellishments, I suppose. She'd broken this or that rule and seemed to think the story would be a kind of excuse. Don't you think a less unpleasant story might have served her better?"

"And what if it is true?"

"Do you believe it?"

"Suppose I did not. Why did Miss Lee say to me 'they thought she might have done away with herself'? Whether you believe the story or not, you seem to recognize a terrible situation there."

"I'm sure that I have no idea what Miss Lee may have meant." There was a clock on President Herman's desk with ornate bronze scrolls representing the tails of mermaids. With a lead pencil's point he traced out first one then the other of these scrolls. "I have, just as an assumption, gone so far as to assume that Shirley's story with all its—its morbid implications —might have some foundation. I have a psychiatrist's report in which such possibilities are examined. Inconclusively, anyway. I don't put much stock in psychiatry. It's best not to. But if they had any basis, I would say they were the best of reasons why Shirley—and her father—ought to scamper away from Larchmoor, wouldn't you, Arthur?"

"I would not. She needs something to hang on to. Let her stay, Dr. Herman."

"Mr. Bridges has decided, I think, that he'll take her home. That was all settled before you came up, Arthur."

"Are you going to let him? Whatever else is true, that girl's afraid of him."

"Is she? Maybe she's been up to something that ought to make her afraid of him." He sighed deeply for Larchmoor's sake. "That kind of thing has happened here before. Another good reason she shouldn't be here. Arthur, do you imagine that I am going to tell a parent—a *parent*—that Larchmoor forbids him to take his daughter home?" He chuckled at the impossibility.

("Think of the offender's gold, his dreaded hate,
And the strange horror of the accuser's tale
Baffling belief and overpowering speech.")

"Larchmoor isn't a hospital, Arthur. If Shirley is having mental troubles and her father isn't, ah, just the one to see that she's taken care of properly, some of the family will surely handle it."

"They will? How do we know? 'O that the vain remorse which must chastise crimes done had but as loud a voice to warn—' "

President Herman tapped his pencil impatiently on the desk top. "That's all very well," he said.

"It means, in the language of the Rotary Club, 'Don't expect George to do it.' "

"You think I might understand the language of the Rotary Club?"

"In the situation that's what it means. It's from a play. *The Cenci.* By Shelley. He was an English poet." He had seen the warning glitter in President Herman's eyes but he could not stop his sarcasm.

Yet President Herman maintained the reserve which had helped him greatly in administering a school so old and prosperous as Larchmoor for so many years.

"Arthur, do you realize the scandal we narrowly missed? Seems she had rented a hotel room downtown and told her roommate she was going to stay there and 'get soused.' Can you imagine?"

"So her roommate told you that? My God, my God. Doesn't Larchmoor ever produce anything but little stoolies? I don't understand that girl, but I believe she needs help. And as soon as there is some suspicion that she might, every student and old maid housemother and the administration itself set on her. Did you ever see a flock of chickens go after one with a broken leg?"

Now President Herman's face had grown faintly red. "I must say, Arthur, that I'm considerably interested in hearing your opinion of Larchmoor. You've always seemed rather reticent and noncommittal. All these years. I'm glad to know what you think of us."

The two old men glared at each other. "I apologize," Dr. Cameron said. "That was an unfortunate outburst. Let me begin again and appeal to you in the name of the Christian principles which guide Larchmoor."

"I resent your sneering when you say 'Christian principles.' "

Both of them stood up. "If I sneered," said Dr. Cameron, "the intonation was superfluous. I told that girl . . ." Compromise, compromise were the words he had in mind. He could see no reason now for saying them.

Blinded by his feeling—the whole compounded hate for Larchmoor, which must gloss over everything—he stumbled against a little mahogany coffee table as he turned to leave. This little and inconsequential piece of reality that had tripped him up was, finally, his undoing. President Herman might have forgiven him or forgotten the hot things he had said. But when he felt the table strike his shins, he stood for just one second watching it, then he kicked it with all his might. It flew against the wall, its glass top tinkling, and lay on its side.

He threw his hands above his head in a terrible gesture. "You dull, criminal, unperceiving bastards," he shouted and rushed from the room.

If Mr. Bridges had still been outside in the waiting room, he would have struck the man, and seen how good he was with his fists at anything besides beating up his daughter. The little dachshund man had gone. No one was there but Miss Lee, the secretary. She was watching him with terror, and it did him good to see her cringe.

Without beginning to think what he would say to Shirley, only aware that it was now he who must and would protect her, he went to his office with all the speed his old legs could manage.

She was not there. He hunted, ridiculously, in the offices next his own and in the nearby classrooms, almost dark now. He had a tremendous fear for the girl. His head began to ache as he trotted from room to room.

There is a long hall in the buildings at Larchmoor, beneath the glassed arcade and extending through the principal structures as an evidence that Larchmoor girls not only don't have to go out in the weather as they pass from bedroom to dining room to classroom, but that they need not even veer from a lux-

uriously straight path. After the classrooms, Dr. Cameron went
to the end of this hall. There, far off, down a long perspective of
windows and doors, he saw Shirley and her father. They were
talking, and as he watched, the dachshund man took her coat
from the rack outside the student lounge and held it for her
while she put her arms into it and flipped her hair up over the
collar. They went out the front door together.

He got his coat and overshoes. He took from his desk the
gloves which he had been almost ready to put on two hours
ago. He walked down the hall toward the door from which
Shirley and her father had left, but slowly, reluctantly. Was it
all a lie that she had told him? If he were going to come back
at the end of vacation, would he have heard that one of the
busy-bodies on the Larchmoor payroll had unearthed the plot?
"She just tried to fix it so she could stay in the hotel with her
boy friend. Got caught at it." No, no, it couldn't be just that.
Whatever it was, though, however muddled and sordid, the
walls of Larchmoor—that were bigger, much bigger than
Larchmoor; as big as money and complacency—were going to
enclose it gently in indestructible steam heat. He was the only
one who had been projected, tossed, into the cold, where an old
scholar had to worry about rent.

The lights along Larchmoor's main walk had a festive air.
Each one had been wreathed in red and green for holiday. At
the bases of the lampposts and in the trees overhead, driven
back only a little, lurked the blue shadows of the absolute snow.
It was not Shirley who had lured him out of his warm corner
into this, not any real Shirley that he had been protecting or that
had determined he would die in the real cold, he thought, de-
fending himself against self-ridicule, self-obloquy. The realer
Beatrice, the gold-embroidered princess, the beautiful lady
without mercy and without hope had brought him out of the
door.

The Prize

THE FIRST prize in the contest sponsored by the Goodyear Tire Company early in the Depression was, I remember, an overwhelmingly large one. It was probably $25,000; at any rate it was a sum on that scale, one large enough to inspire a variety of religious experience among contestants, and the scattering of lesser prizes had been conceived with similar grandeur. Looking back from a removal of two decades and from some comprehension of the economic and political turns of those years I am impelled to visualize the Goodyear Co. struggling with titanic anxiety to shake free of the chaos that threatened organizations as well as individuals, and willy-nilly I have to admire the scale of their effort. They knew how big a battle we were in.

And I remember with a twinge that at the time of the contest I didn't even know there was a Depression. I knew we had moved out of the city to live near Chesterfield—where my father was to work in his cousin's grain elevator—for reasons that were not very happy or decent. But it seemed to me when I weighed everything that we had been expelled because of something ugly or shameful that my family had done or because of some shameful inadequacy in us into which it was best not to inquire too far. When I learned, from eavesdropping on adult conversation, that my father had lost $380 in a bank failure, I was ashamed of him for not having had more on deposit. We lost our car then, too, and I was pretty sure that this need not have happened if he had had more of the installments paid on it.

There was very little talk between my parents which named the name of Depression. Since they were both faithful Republicans who supported Hoover to the end, it might well have seemed traitorous to them to use such a term—I figured then it was like *not* holding your breath when something very important depended on your holding it.

A big green van took our furniture to the house near Chesterfield, and the family followed in the car borrowed from my father's cousin. We arrived on a rainy evening just before dark, and there was the van backed up to the house with the moving men carrying our familiar things into its dark interior. Our rocking chairs, the fernery, and the radio were going in where they didn't belong. The thought struck me that we were moving into a house that no one lived in. That was so strange. And whatever mystery was being enacted, I didn't want it to happen. I wanted to hold my breath long enough to keep it from happening.

Through the rainy fall of our first year in Chesterfield, while I was trying to get used to the tiny school, to the overpowering skills of the farm boys who were my new classmates, and to the big old house we now lived in, I concentrated fiercely and stupidly on the problem of our expulsion from the city and began to see it as an omen of a world committed totally to sorrow. I learned to read the most trivial disappointments as signs that the race itself was doomed.

Walking home after school between the cornfields that bordered the road I would hear the brittle noise of rain on the cornleaves and the surliness inside me would cry back to it, "Yes, that's the way things are, all right." In the dripping of the rain from the porch roof outside my window I saw a melting of even my memories of the time when things had been fun, and whatever I found disheartening or miserable I cherished.

Separating myself more than formerly from my brothers, who were two and three years older than I, I cultivated an almost erotic pursuit of tokens of decay. In this I was aided by one of the rooms on the second floor that had served all the former tenants in lieu of an attic.

Books, old magazines, a sewing machine, dress forms, and

trunks of many funny sorts were piled in this room. Probably there was some sort of stipulation in the rental agreement that we were to have only "the rest" of the house, for my brothers and I had been forbidden to play in there. But if I was quiet I could slip into it from my own room without my mother's hearing me where she worked in the downstairs kitchen.

In the room a smell of paper decomposing welcomed me and alerted my senses to a kind of dream that was detailed by the thousand articles of use and the souvenirs I stirred out of the trunks. I found an old cane with a metal bust of Lincoln for its head, the metal bearing an inscription linking it to the Republican convention of 1884. One of the trunks was half full of arrowheads and stone knives, some of them bearing paper tags that indicated they had been found in the river bluffs east of town. There was a stack of tintypes in another trunk which included pictures of the depot and the dedication of the Methodist Church. (If I wanted to I could look up and see this church through the window, sitting shabbily at the edge of a cornfield, now arched over with the elms that appeared in the tintype as twigs stuck in the loam around it. As far as one could see in such views the half-luminous white of ripe corn floored the river valley. I'd heard my father say in one of his moments of optimism that this was the richest soil on earth except for the Nile valley, and I worked on this idea too, converting it so I could gloat on these riches strung senselessly under the rains and consoling my bitterness by noting how universal the waste of things was.)

A green trunk in that room yielded a box of nickled instruments which I now realize were the old-fashioned paraphernalia of a woman's douche, and which had for me then, ignorant as I was of their function, some quality of terminated ferocity, like the arrowheads piled in the trunk bottom—no longer an arsenal, but something oddly more than a mass of junk.

When my mother found out that I had been playing in the forbidden room and asked what right I had to be there, I told her I had been reading the old magazines and books—which was not untrue. I didn't tell her that I had jimmied the locks on most of the trunks or that I had read batches of the old letters I found in them. Anyway, she discovered more trespasses by finding some of the arrowheads in the treasure box that I kept in one of my drawers and by noting small bits of vandalism. I had broken the head of Lincoln from the cane and for no good reason (except to mock at earthly vanity) had rubbed its nose off on the sharp edge of a lock.

She came after me with some determination then. She really insisted on an explanation of why I liked that room well enough to play there so much. "With that dirty old stuff," she said.

"Like with the arrowheads," I told her solemnly, "it would help me remember there used to be Indians right around here in the olden times."

"Ah," she said, mildly impressed and placated. "I see. With them you could sort of pretend that the Indians were still alive and more real. I see. Then I suppose you could understand your history better and the way things are by using that Republican cane."

She looked at me sharply. "Why did you break the cane then?"

"I don't know."

"You shouldn't have done that to Lincoln. He was such a great man," she said with a faraway look that seemed to suggest he should have been my father. "It was awfully wrong to break him up like that, but I'm glad if otherwise you learned anything."

My pretended agreement with her was a great fraud because her optimistic interpretation was so exactly wrong in its tendency. It had not been any sense of life in these trinkets that excited me. As they went through my hands I had exulted in them because they were evidence that so many who had been alive were dead and gone.

·   ·   ·

Far as she was from appreciating the content of my play in the closed room, my mother must have worried about it and found it inadequate, as she found so many things in our life at Chesterfield inadequate.

She had a bundle of grievances, and I think sometimes that what carried us through that winter and marked all of us forever with a special stamp was her refusal to admit the slipping downward that obviously accompanied our move to the little town. She had to take it, but she wouldn't have it. She was going to lure me out of the old storeroom into some healthy activity whatever the cost, and for a while there was talk of getting me a subscription to the *Youth's Companion,* even if that meant showing favoritism to me, since nothing comparable could be afforded "just then" for the older boys.

With the same frustrated force she approached the problem of utilities. There was no electricity in Chesterfield then and no bathroom in our house. From our arrival on she set the resources of her anguish to work on getting us a Delco light plant and plumbing, though with all her emotional heave in this direction and her heckling of my father she never worked out a practical plan by which we might expect to have them. She merely made us all hate fetching water from the pump more than we might have otherwise and made us all feel we would go stone blind from reading by a kerosene lamp.

What she couldn't hold on to with a full grasp she meant to cling to, as long as necessary, with her fingernails, and the obvious pity of this was that she could get her nails into nothing solid except us.

It was her passion's refusal to admit that things had changed which swept us into the Goodyear contest with such velocity and finally made it intolerable not to win.

Winter had come by the time the contest was announced. The evening we heard of it my brother George and I were in the kitchen helping my mother with the dishes while my father and older brother listened to the radio in the dining room.

"Hear that?" my mother cried out all at once. I thought she'd at least heard a car stopping at our front gate. But she motioned us to be still, and we got most of the announcement, not quite all. She marched into the dining room and demanded that my father explain the details she had missed.

"I wasn't entirely listening," he said guiltily, sleepily. "Just enjoying what they had to say."

"Enjoying? I don't see what there is to *enjoy* when he's talking about a contest. You ought to be listening attentively, or I don't know what's the point of listening at all."

"I know," he agreed. "I'll tell you what. It sounded like someone was going to get a patch of money, all right. I did hear them say there was a first prize of twenty-five thousand dollars. Moreover there's a whole kaboodle of little prizes."

"Little?" my mother wailed indignantly. "Why—why—*little!* I heard myself that there were thousand-dollar prizes."

"I meant even smaller ones. Little dee-rigibles and things."

"A thousand dollars." My mother mourned his unconcern for this. "That's not so much it would wear our brains out figuring what to do with it. I wish you'd listen at the end of the program and be sure to get the details down on a piece of paper. No. You call me in if there's any more going to be said about it."

He took off his glasses and polished them slowly. "You sit down here and listen, Mother. The boys and I can finish the dishes. You're quicker at these things than I am."

"All I asked was for you to call me. Can't you even do that?" my mother demanded. "I know you're tired from your work and I wouldn't ask any more of you today."

Since he was in our big rocker and sitting as relaxed as a man can get and since it obviously wouldn't be much trouble for him to listen to the announcement, he naturally took her comment as sarcasm. So, when she'd gone back to her work, he tuned in another program.

"You hear that, Mama?" George said, wiping away like a good fellow at the dishes. "He's turned it off."

"Well," she said, "he's tired and cranky. He worked awfully hard today. You know it's hard work at the elevator."

Then my father appeared at the kitchen door. In those days he was still wearing some of his old business suits to work, and they always had grain dust in their fibers no matter how well he brushed them when he came home. The whitish dust in his clothes gave him an air of being faded like a picture from which some of the ink has been rubbed. He made a curious gesture, half in anger, half in appeasement, like a doubter crossing himself.

"You know what these darn contests are, Sally," he pleaded. "They don't mean anyone any good. They're only done to advertise the product."

"We'll talk about it later," my mother said. This was recognized by all as a threat.

"Did you personally ever know anyone who had won his postage back in a contest like that?"

"We'll not discuss it until the boys are asleep," she warned him. I think he began making up his mind to submit right then. I saw him swallow and then nod reassurance to himself that it might not be as bad as he feared it could be.

From that first evening on, for weeks, our family had the contest like a vocation or a disease. Of course it was easy enough for my mother to find out the details of competition once she had made up our minds, and by the end of the week she and each of us boys were working on our individual lists of words that could be made from the letters comprised in the name GOODYEAR TIRE AND RUBBER COMPANY. That was the task of the contest.

You can see that the first words come easily: dog, god, ray, rite, and so on. It is when these are all put down that the game becomes tantalizing and demoralizing. Then the tongue tries nonsense syllables and combinations in the hope that some lightly hidden word will fall out to be added to the list. And that makes quite a noise in the house.

Once at supper I began mumbling to myself, and my father, driven beyond exasperation, slammed down his water glass and howled, "Groggy wayorv, boogly, boogly, woogly, arf." Then he glared around the table with the tears of the rejected squeezing angrily out of the corners of his eyes.

"Not at the table," my mother cautioned me. She turned to my father. "I don't know why you're so set against what the boys are ambitious enough to try to do. I should think you might better want to help them."

"I won't. Great Jesus, I won't," he said helplessly. "What in His name would I be helping them to do? Lose their minds and jabber like apes?"

"They've been working with our dictionary, and I don't know that *that's* bad for their education," my mother said. "The contest gives them something to look forward to." She satisfied herself with such explanations, and for my part I was thinking self-righteously that my father, in his outburst, had used *f* and *v,* which, of course, were not permissible under the laws of the game.

According to my mother's first, rather easygoing plan, each of us was to work exclusively on his own list and even keep it partly secret from the others so there would be a sort of intra-family contest as well as the larger one. We worked from the dictionary by turns. It seemed to me sometimes when I was blundering unsystematically through it, dreaming by lamplight, that each of us might win a prize that suited his own intelligence and deserts. My mother would probably get one of the thousand-dollar prizes. Dave and George might or might not get something. Maybe one of them would get a fifty-dollar prize, since they were older than I. For myself, I thought and felt that I should win one of the chrome-plated models of the dirigible *Akron,* the lowest prize offered. I think probably a hundred of these models were being given away. I remember telling my mother that I didn't think I was good enough to win more than a model, but that this suited me because I would rather have it than money anyhow. Altogether I managed to make this model into an image of what I was worth and of what the world would pay me for being what I was.

"You have to work hard if that's the prize you want," my mother warned. "Don't forget there'll be people from all over the country trying to win, just like you are."

When the deadline for submitting entries was approaching, my mother decided that we needed a larger dictionary to work from and that we should borrow one from the school. The question of who should borrow it became major. One of us boys should ask our teacher, she thought, but we all balked at this as being too embarrassing. The other boys got away with this argument, but I was caught—perhaps because I had done more excited talking about the contest than they.

"There's nothing wicked about borrowing a dictionary," my mother bullied me. "We're not doing something dishonest. We're working as hard as we know how to earn something, and if more people would do that I expect our country would be better off. Just explain to your teacher . . ."

This is odd, but maybe if I had believed that we were in the contest for the sake of competition I wouldn't have minded explaining to my teacher why I wanted the dictionary. Caught as I was in the dream of certainly winning a thousand dollars and a dirigible, I couldn't face it. It seemed to me like putting on airs to go to my teacher and admit the glory my family was headed for.

So my mother finally borrowed it. I remember her coming in through the snowy yard, a little after I had come home from school, with the big dictionary wrapped in a shawl to protect it from the mist in the air. Her face before she saw me was set with a harsh intensity, as of someone who has refused humiliation by sheer refusal to recognize it. Seeing me, she smiled and said, "Look. I borrowed it from your teacher after you'd left. She was good about lending it. Now you see that she would have lent it to you if you'd only asked her. Don't you see?"

"But what's she going to think of us?" After all, it was I who had to go to school the next day and possibly face my teacher's amusement, envy, or scorn.

"I didn't tell her what we were using it for," my mother said with a sly grimace that she meant to be comforting. "I fibbed to her, so don't you worry."

When I thought this over I announced that I didn't want to do the contest any more. My mother flung her arms around me and pressed my face very hard against her side. "Of course you do," she said. "We've worked so doggone hard this far that I'm convinced we're going to win. Maybe not the grand prize, but something. There's no reason why you can't win that dirigible if you want it. Don't you see that yet?" She frightened me with her determination, and even that was a lesser thing than the sheer giant onrush of the contest, beginning to reveal its true scope.

In the last week before the deadline—and this must have been in late January, at about the time of the thaws, when the three of us boys would have liked to be playing outside—my mother bore down on us all. Some one of us had to be at the dictionary all the time. There wasn't any more talk of the contest's being educational or fun. It was work and we had to work hard enough to win. We combined our lists now, at least to the extent that our inefficient systems permitted. We had begun without much system at all, and, except for my mother's, our penmanship was terrible. So whether a word discovered in the dictionary at this late date or on someone else's list could legitimately be added to ours was a matter none of us could be quite sure of. Certainly each of us had duplications in his list, and none of us ever had quite the same total as any of the others, though we tried to balance them for a while. Very late my mother tried to get us to alphabetize our lists, but this only got us in more tangles.

On the last afternoon Dave went to the post office immediately after school with his list and George's—that was a nervous precaution, since they had to be postmarked that day and some act of God might demolish the post office or block the road to it if we waited until too late.

On the other two lists, at my mother's insistence, we were adding all kinds of the nonsense combinations which earlier had been only a means of helping us find pure words. Some of these, she said, we might have missed in the dictionary, and it was the responsibility of the judges to decide if they were eligible or not. "*Reay*," she said. "That could be a girl's name. Put it down, anyway. *Burrec*. That sounds like a kind of donkey, I guess. *Yarg*. I don't see why that shouldn't be a word if there's a word *yard*. One doesn't sound like it meant any more than the other one, does it?"

She had the clock sitting on the table where we worked—the post office closed at six—and I knew that now nothing but time running out would stop her. My father came into this intensity and stood behind us, watching us without saying anything. Pretty soon my mother spoke over her shoulder to him. "If you're not going to help, go somewhere else. Go start the fire in the kitchen. I'll get supper as soon as we're finished."

"I won't," he said. And then, after a long deliberation, "God damn the Goodyear Tire and Rubber Corporation."

"Company," I said.

"I suppose you mean God damn me," my mother said.

"I don't," he said. "I mean—"

"Shoo. Go on. I can't think while you're staring at me."

He went into the bedroom and after some banging of dresser drawers returned to throw an envelope and two ten-dollar bills on the list of words she was working on. "There," he said in a tone that was dignified only by its slightness. "There's some money and my insurance policy. I'm leaving."

"Ha," my mother said.

"You've turned the boys against me and driven them half crazy with this contest. I warned you not to do it."

"Then leave," my mother said. "*Dooger*."

After he was gone she kept muttering more and more absurd

combinations of syllables. Her face flamed, and I could see a vein in her temple bulge with her effort, but she was not writing down any more of her inventions.

She looked up at George long enough to say, "Follow him and see where he goes." Then she glanced hard at the clock and told me to get my coat and rubbers and be ready to run for the post office. "We can't be late," she said. "You can run part of the way or go Scout's pace. You know how to do that."

With an attempt to cheer me, she said, "You and I have more words than the others now."

But, giving a last look at the physical ugliness of my list, I said I wished there were time to copy at least this afternoon's work.

"Maybe if they can't quite make out some of them that will be a good thing," she said craftily. Her imagination apparently had strained to cover every accident of incompetence, weakness, taste, or unfairness on the part of the unknown judges, and it seemed to me that she had intended that each of our lists be somehow corrupt to fit the imagined corruptness of the major human types.

As I was going out with the big manila envelopes containing our two lists, George arrived back to report that my father had started west across the cornfield, had cut back within about a quarter of a mile, climbed the fence into the road, and was right now hiding inside a culvert about two hundred yards from the house.

"Ha," my mother said. Her voice crackled with unhappy triumph. "I supposed he wouldn't go far. He'll get hungry after a little while and come in. Now *run,*" she commanded me. "Be sure you make it to the post office."

The culvert where my father was hiding was an obstacle in the road now. I could hardly bring myself to walk over him like that, but I knew I had to hurry. The road was wet. Now at sundown it was beginning to freeze, and I could feel the delicate ice crunch under every step with a beautiful sound and sensation of touch. The rosy light over the cornfield, reflected in a thousand puddles islanded in the loam, seemed to me too strongly and unhappily beautiful for me to stand, and it occurred to me that I might die right then, being so divided by feelings I had never encountered before, wakening to my first realization that living was something that one must choose against hardship to do.

At the culvert I left the road, knelt in the water of the ditch bottom and looked in at my father. He was sitting right in the middle of the concrete tube. In the dim light I could only see his silhouette and the glitter of reflected light in his eyes. I am sure he saw me, but neither of us spoke.

Then I ran for the post office. I think I ran all the way, because I got there in plenty of time to put the envelopes in the letter box. Walking home afterward I felt how my knees were wet from where I had knelt in the ditch.

Of course none of us won anything from the Goodyear Co. In about a month the winners of prizes over a thousand dollars were announced. First prize went to someone who had over three times as many words in his list as there had been in the largest of ours.

"Three times," my mother said. "That's a lie. That can't be. They must have used foreign words like French and German, Spanish and all. And they *said* that was against the rules."

My father commented, "Maybe one of you will win a littler prize. They're going to announce more next week." After the bad day of the mailing of the lists he had relaxed, had been permitted to relax, and by this time was even displaying a mild hope that something might come from all that bother.

But then the last of the cash prizes was announced and there was nothing left to wait for except the names of the winners of the model dirigibles.

"If the others didn't get any money I'm not going to win the dirigible," I said to my father, answering one of his soft optimisms aggressively.

"You don't know," he said. "I wouldn't wonder that your

list would be just right for a smaller prize. You know, it might be like having the right tool for the right job."

"Yes, the right tool," my mother said. "We should have had a typewriter. I can understand that now that it's too late. Even if they didn't specify that you had to use a typewriter."

"You told me that my words they couldn't read might be a good thing," I said.

"Well, on that . . ." Her lips worked carefully while she made up her mind how to answer me. "Yes, that may be so. Don't give up hope."

From this last posture she established against defeat and from my own premonitory sense of loss I began to develop the notion that they were all *demanding* that I win, and I added the strain of what I considered their expectations to my own. Partly for them, partly for myself I strained all the tricks of emotional force—on the order of holding my breath, crossing my fingers, figuratively—to affect what the announcer was going to say when he came to read the last list of winners. I accepted, in a subterranean agreement, that I owed it to the family to win, for if I won that would help make up for my father's hiding in the culvert, my mother's fibbing to the teacher, and our general humiliation in prostrating ourselves before a big company that had so far ignored us.

Each name on that list of winners should have been mine, and none was. I wanted to howl when the reading was over, and yet I felt that, having lost, I didn't even have the right to do that. For the first time it came to me with undeniable force that beyond our mere failure to win we had lost something that had been put at stake.

After the trial of listening my father sighed tranquilly and said it appeared to him that these last prizes had been awarded on a geographical basis. "Did you notice how there was hardly ever more than two from any state except New York? You heard how this gentleman up in Red Oak got one. Well sir, that's enough for this part of the world, they likely figured. You can't tell me these contests aren't rigged some way. Naturally you didn't have much of a chance when they did things like that," he told me.

He put out his hand to rumple my hair or pat my cheek, but I flung myself beyond his reach, behaving spitefully to cover my sense of worthlessness.

"There, there, feller," he said. "There, there, now."

"I worked hard," I screeched. "I had as good a list as anybody's."

"Sure you did. I'd lay money you had a better one than some of those as got the money."

I said, "I'm going to kill someone for this."

His head jerked as though I had burned him. Then his eyes searched beyond me for my mother, and he seemed to be crawling humbly and with awkward slowness to some complicity with her. I saw this happen, but I chose then not to understand it. I thought I understood how every man's hand was against me. From then on.

"Everything comes to he who waits," my father said. "You'll see that, because that's the way things are. You remember when we came here we had such a hard job getting along without electricity and didn't think we'd ever have any?"

He paused for me to answer and I wouldn't.

"Now they're putting a line in," he said in a hearty tone, as though I might care about *that*. "They're going to bring the wire down from Parsons to Chesterfield and we'll have it out here, too. Then we can get us an electric radio and a lot of things, maybe. They were unloading poles on the other side of Chesterfield today."

"Somebody else got my dirigible," I whined.

"It would only be a little tin thing. You couldn't have any play out of it. Your mother and I thought that when the roads dry up we'd get you boys a bicycle. Wouldn't you rather have that?"

I set up an awful racket, protesting that I didn't want a bicycle or anything else but the dirigible. To which my father replied that I only wanted what I couldn't have and if that was the way of it he couldn't help me. I believed this dictum, if nothing else he said. I heard it wailing through my dreams that night like a sentence of wrath to come. Maybe on purpose I dreamed toward morning that all my family was dead. My father was dead in the culvert where he had hidden, and I was kicking up wet grass from the ditch to cover him in.

At school time I pretended to be sick so I could stay home. As a matter of fact, I sulked with such ugliness that my mother suggested on her own part that I should go play in the store-room, where I had not been for some months. I considered her recommendation and even walked upstairs to glance in at my former retreat. The dead room would not receive me, and the chilly smell of it really nauseated me. Losing the contest had even cut me off from that.

Everything was so senseless I might as well go do it like the rest until I was dead. I would just be too smart to hope for anything again, that was all.

But they tricked me back from that state too. I came from school one evening about a month later to find my model of the dirigible *Akron* on the dining room table. There was a mass of wrapping paper broken back from around it and some excelsior that smelled like newly sawed lumber.

It was a very shiny model, though somewhat smaller and harsher-looking than I had imagined it would be. It said GOODYEAR TIRE AND RUBBER CO. on the side.

"What's it for?" I yelled to my mother as she came in from the kitchen to see how I was going to receive it. "Did one of us win after all?"

She smiled her best. "Sure," she said. "Isn't it a pretty thing, now? I guess this proves that if you do your level best and really want something you'll get it, doesn't it?"

I might have accepted the moral of her comment without argument, for moral significance seemed to me at that point lighter than air, but the practical account worried me. "How come they didn't read our name on the radio if we won?"

"We didn't *exactly* win," my mother said. "Your father and I thought that you'd worked so hard that you *were* a winner and deserved a prize. We wrote to that man in Red Oak and bought it from him."

"Oh," I said. Why did they do that to me on top of all the rest? I couldn't stand it, and I said, "Thanks a lot."

Just before suppertime my brother Dave caught me outside in the yard and said, "All right, you big jackass, you got your dee-ridge-able. Aren't you proud of it?"

"You leave me alone."

"I'm going to leave you alone. They had to pay fifteen bucks for it and now maybe we can't have a bicycle this summer."

"I never asked them to do it."

"Oh, no," he said. "Oh, no, you didn't. Just whining like a pup that you didn't get anything in this contest. Did any of the rest of us get anything?"

"I didn't want them to buy it. I didn't know they'd be such big fools."

"I don't know," he said despairingly. "I guess they were because *you're* such a big fool. Listen, if you don't make them think that you're real glad to get it I'll kill you."

It was not—or not exactly—his threat that weighed on me. When he left me I had nothing to face except—as on the evening of my father's flight—the width of sundown and spring air, empty but nonetheless resonant with things learned and half-learned, again multiplying by its beauty and silence the real threat of death if I turned away from my family and their organized ways of stinging me. I could see then that I would have to keep pretending the dirigible was fine, and I have never learned what else I could have said.

This Hand, These Talons

THERE WAS a thick mist through town and the roads were icy when they came back from hunting. They put the shotguns in the hall closet and took off their boots on the carpet by the door. Martha ran across the kitchen in her stocking feet, holding the pheasants up high in front of her and holding her hand under their necks to catch any blood that might begin to flow in the warmer air of the house. The pheasants had not bled very much when Willy pulled off their heads, holding their necks under his foot in the snow. The afternoon had been cold enough so there was not time for much blood to flow before it started to congeal.

"Willy," she called back to him, "you go and look at the clock. Could be that we're late."

As he went obediently, it seemed to him all at once, and in a mixture of sensations, very luxurious to walk in stocking feet across the warm hardwood of the floors, through two gray rooms whose windows bloomed with the dead light of the fog. The smoothness underfoot was like the rice-straw mats in a Japanese home, a luxury of touch that was one of the good things he remembered from his time overseas. And now it was just a little more than a year since the evening he and Kitz and the Australian F.O. took off their boots and went into the house in Sasebo to meet Mr. Hagawa, Hagawa who grinned and hissed like Fu Manchu himself and said, "Weh-oh-come frins," and later put them wise to a clean, exclusive geisha house.

The clock with the bronze griffins around its face had stopped; nevertheless he called, "Eleven-thirty."

"Oh, come on now." Martha said, a touch impatiently. "It must have been running backwards then. It was running when we went out. I was sure. Never mind, anyway. My watch must be in the bathroom."

He half skated, half walked, like a child discovering some novel pleasure in the matter of fact of adult utilitarianism, across to the coffee table, where the design of a Ronson concentrated most of the light there was in the room and showed it off against the dark wood. The cigarette tasted like the first one in the morning, harsh and fine. He unbuttoned his jacket, and as he sat on the davenport the shells in his pocket rattled around his thighs. The weight of his hunting clothes, the weight of his body, disappeared in the gentleness with which the furniture received him.

It was very good to come back from hunting to a house as comfortable as his father-in-law's. Such a return was the real reason for hunting, he thought, for a lot of people like himself.

The fog even, cold and distorting the shapes of the houses across the street like some malignance of decay that killed angles and straight lines, was a part of the general luxury as long as the windows kept it out where it belonged.

In his and Martha's apartment they had a reproduction of Breughel's picture of the hunters, and the good, satisfying thing about that, too, was that the hunters were almost home. Out of the spooky woods that weren't actually in the picture they had come back to the edge of their own town.

"Willy?"

"All right," he said. He went to the kitchen where his wife, already changed out of her snowsuit, was filling a kettle with water and had turned on the knobs of the electric stove.

"Willy," she said, "we do have time if we hurry. If you'll help me clean the pheasants we'll have time to get them roasted before Daddy and Mother get here. Or would you rather have them fried?"

"Either way."

"Daddy likes them roasted, then."

She stood poised briefly, with a thoughtful frown on her face, staring at him, and he thought she would probably ask him presently if he knew where she had put the roaster on Sunday. But she said, "Wasn't it a thrill? You're a good shot, Willy. I didn't know you were so good." Her smile trembled with perplexity. She put her hand in his armpit, and he could feel her fingernails punch his side.

He swung away from her, "So let's have a drink, then," he said. He reached for the bottle on the high shelf, the shelf above those where Mrs. Norton's Spode sat covered with felt.

"Isn't there any of ours left?" his wife asked, and he drew back. "Well, go ahead," she told him. "Only, my gosh, I thought there should be almost a full bottle of ours left."

"I won't take any if you don't think I should," he said.

"Don't pout like a baby. It's only that Daddy will be upset if he finds too much of his whiskey gone."

"So to hell with it."

"No," she said, "go on and pour yourself a little."

He collided with her when he went to the refrigerator for ice. With a purposeful and direct movement she seemed to come around him as he approached, and when he put out his hand, hers was already there, opening the door. "Scusee. Let me see what we have for salad," she said. "O.K. You may have to drive to the little store. I'll see."

The old man kept good whiskey, sure enough. A little more now, he thought, for the sake of coming home from hunting. It was too late now for him to say any longer for the sake of getting home from the war. That slogan had lost its humor months ago, even if the feeling had not gone. He filled the tumbler around the ice a good half full. Martha had time to watch that.

"Too much?"

She pursed her lips, her fine, plump lips. "Don't pour any for me," she said.

"Then have some of mine."

"I don't want any. I really don't," she said.

"Oh, screw. It's only whiskey."

He sat down by the cupboard, waiting for the water to be hot enough to start scalding and cleaning the birds. He tasted the very good whiskey that her Daddy portioned out so very carefully.

"It's simply that they were good enough to let us have the house for a week," she said. "That's all. I think we should respect their things."

"Sure, I know," he said. The mouthful of whiskey solaced him, and he told himself that he did respect the Nortons' things. He'd kept the old man's shotgun cleaned, used coasters when he took his drinks into the front room. He respected the Nortons' bedroom where he and Martha had been sleeping. It was as though they were somehow not absent from their room, and he had respected them and their white-legged child who lay there beside him. It had seemed prohibitively wrong to touch her in that bed except for goodnight kisses, and in the absolute quiet of twelve, one, and two o'clock he had lain there wondering why nothing belonged to him any more.

On Mrs. Norton's dressing table in that bedroom was a little collection of her souvenirs. The collection included three things pertaining to himself and Martha. There was a silver-painted doll's chair, like a little throne just two inches high. There was a photo of himself wearing dress uniform and all his ribbons. He had sent it to them from Japan last year. And there was a model, gilded like the doll's chair and mounted on a stick, of the P-51 he had flown during the war.

The street light shining through the window showed him the silhouette of the plane sitting fixed like a dead shadow or a trophy amid the junk that Mrs. Norton had collected, and he had lain stiff in the bed on those nights thinking, *She's welcome to it.*

The two pheasants he had killed this afternoon were lying in a dishpan under the sink. The bodies merged in a disordered rust-colored shape—the color of new rust—in the dishpan, and their feet stuck out. The feet were black. The points of the nails were bent in on one foot as if it were clutching hard at something.

"Yeah," he said, "it was good out there hunting today." He looked at the back of his wife's head. "For some reason you're prettier in a cornfield. With the stubble. Gloomy sky. For a background, you know." She turned from the sink and gave him the teeth in a single, efficient motion before she resumed her work. (Who was it used to say that—McElroy? Kitz? Give us the teeth, boy, the Old Man really loves you, he just don't know any better way to show it.) Those suitable, matching teeth, just what the dressmaker or the jeweler or whoever it was ordered for little Martha, the prettiest little girl they ever fixed up in Bloomsdale and sent down to be the prettiest little Pi Phi at State. Quite a credit to her, those teeth, even counting all the rest. But he really wasn't worrying about her looks so much any more or letting them bother him the way they had. During the tough week before he had gone to Student Health and begun his treatment her good looks had been a torment of accusation to him, like a ring he might have hacked from a dead man's hand, or the gold Jap molar that Kitz had carried.

He was over that part of it. He knew that Martha was all right. The trouble was not with her.

"It did me good to kill those birds," he said. "They're big enough so it means something, not like the quail. Then the place we were had a lot to do with it. Gee, it is funny the way I remember it right now. It hasn't been but an hour or so, and I guess naturally I'd remember it all right for longer than that. But it's like it was still happening, it wasn't over yet. Like you have dreams. Do you have dreams, honey, where you think all day afterward that you're still having them?" He stopped at this because he knew it annoyed and scared her to hear him talking about his dreams or the way they affected him. It reminded her of the bad week. But this was another matter, after all—he was getting well now—and he went on stubbornly.

"The main thing is the way the birds look when they're hit. You don't think they are heavy at all until they are hit and when you can watch them hang there a minute before they start to fall." He put his hand up with the fingers slightly spread, watching it, trying to make it imitate in falling to his side the plunge of the dead bird. It would not work the same way.

But without his hand obscuring the image, he could see it quite clearly against a gray like the sky that the impressed nerves of his eyes retained. That moment of suspension was the main thing. The bird all at once scattering feathers, losing what had been an almost visible course strung like a wire through the air. (Hell, but how could he explain it to her? Martha ought to turn and help him a bit. He thought there had been a time when at the crisis she pulled his ideas out of him, like the evening in '43 when the Cadets had beaten the University Freshmen at baseball and afterward in Martha's car, parked in front of the Pi Phi house, there had been a kind of glory from it to explain, something he had got from helping win the game, something solid and certain in him on that spring evening that would make whatever he was going to do soon much easier; when he had told her that he was going to act bravely through the rest of the war, she had helped him. She had not laughed or got coy when that sounded like cheap flag waving. He had put his thumb up against the side of her throat and felt the even, heavy beating of her pulse while he said it and while she had looked at him in that wonderful way that made him able to talk. . . .) That moment he had watched the bird was like the moment the Zeke had started going to pieces. The immense *slap slap* of the wing guns that made him want to yell or come, the fast silver plane that had no weight at all, suddenly getting very heavy there ahead with pieces flying out of the wing and the cockpit cowling, seeming to hang without moving while the junk came out of it, getting heavier until it seemed that he was going to run into it before it started to fall. It had looked that way then. The film from his camera had shown it just that way. It had looked like that this afternoon.

Falling after that second of suspension while the wing feathers broke and seemed to blow upward while the body dropped, the first bird had struck behind a row of corn stubble. By the time he got to it, it had propped itself upright. The neck he reached to grasp was pulled back like a snake's head, the eye a black spot on the blue feathers like a snake's eye, not frightened at all but full of hate for him. Just as he had ahold of it, everything left in the bird's body struck at him—the broken wings, talons, body itself fighting his hold until he swung it around a couple of times.

"You know," he said, wondering, "killing is a serious thing. You understand that when you do it."

With the bird hanging limp in his hand he had turned to see Martha coming across the stubble behind him. She was out of breath from running and her lips were apart. Against the slate sky her white face and almost-white hair looked like a photograph—and a particular photograph, he realized, the one he had tacked to the beer cooler at the head of his cot while they were on Okinawa, identified as the one that Kitz made the joke and the gesture about everytime he looked at it. Kitz made him mad with that at first, but later it was pleasing in a natural enough way to have someone else confirm the meaning of those expectantly narrowed eyes and the parting of the lips. There had been times later when it was reassuring to have Kitz see this thing in the photograph. There were times when he would lie there on the cot, reading the damn poor letters that Martha sent, telling about the Pi Phi dances and what her Daddy thought of Roosevelt and the war, listening to the radio play jazz in the next tent, hearing the jungle insects thump against the screen—times when he would stare at the white and gray picture and see only something smooth, toothy, and cold. Kitz, finding him like that, would sit on the cot and say, "What an expensive-looking beast," while he looked at the picture and wiped his chin. They would have a drink on that, and afterward in his imagination the picture would become a living thing again.

"Killing can be a good or bad thing. Like these birds . . ." he said eagerly and once more attempted to imitate their significant death with the dropping of his hand.

"The water's hot," Martha said. "Roll up your sleeves."

He turned red and gulped the rest of the whiskey swiftly. He said, "I bitched that, didn't I?"

"Why—what?" Then she understood and came to put her arms around him. "I heard every word you said. It was a lot of fun. I think it did you a world of good. I think you're sleeping better these nights than you have since last year. You feel lots better than when we came, don't you? You'll be ready to go back to school next week, I'll bet."

"Sure." He began to make a fuss over scalding and plucking the birds.

"We'll have to hurry," Martha said. "Mother and Daddy will be cold after their long drive. They said they'd be here tonight by dinnertime. It would be nice if we could have dinner all ready for them when they get here, wouldn't it?"

"You bet," he said. We have to make a good showing for Daddy and Mother, he thought.

"Say, here," Martha's father said jovially, at the same time with an assertive, manly deprecation, "what kind of a book is this?"

To Willy the question seemed a continuing of the friendly measurement to which they had been subjecting him since they got home. He wished he did not need to answer. This was not the time when he could talk to Mr. Norton, because he felt, after the hunting and then the whiskey, more tired and exposed, more likely to give himself away to them than he had even on the last visit. He wished he could push himself simply a little farther back onto the expensive softness of the davenport and pass strangely out of the room where he sat having to talk while the women finished getting dinner.

At the door itself, on the minute of their arrival, he had felt their eyes checking him at once as though their main interest was to find the flaw in his tall enough, athletic enough body or in his face, the flaw that had justified a university doctor's having told him to rest a week in the middle of the semester. Then, as though to hide or camouflage her curiosity, Mrs. Norton had tugged at him with her plump arms stretched over his shoulders, trying to kiss him, make everything quite ordinary enough, while he pulled away from her in shamed awkwardness.

They were after him in their kindhearted way like horsetraders who have bought some handsome horseflesh, led it innocently and proudly enough home to their stables, and then with the beginning of wonder and suspicion that they have been cheated, sense some flaw in the blood which spoils their bargain, which will make the beast worthless and in time will make them laughingstocks of the community for having been taken in by it. They had been measuring him like an animal, he thought, or going on with the idea, maybe like parents who suspect their kid has swallowed a pin or stuck a bean up his nose and are trying the means of kindness to get him to confess this so they can take common sense and practical action to remove it.

" 'Only one death to a customer, you understand,' " Mr. Norton read from the book. "I'll be damned. Is that supposed to be a joke or something? Why is it printed lengthwise like that?" He turned the face of the page toward Willy and held the book out at arm's length. "I notice the printing is queer in this book. I never saw anything like it. You have to read this book for one of your courses?"

"No. A friend of ours lent it to me."

"You like to read this kind of stuff?" He could see Mr. Norton stiffen like a pointer that has caught a red-hot scent.

"I don't know," he said. "I don't really understand it. It's a kind of poetry, I guess." And Mr. Norton relaxed with a sort of visible reassurance, still puzzled though.

"Some of those 'friends' you had when you and Martha lived in that rathole apartment house? This is the kind of book I'd expect them to read." His thin-lipped mouth fell into a smile. "God, I had a time with Momma after we'd been there to visit you. She thought she'd got the bedbugs. Myself, I wouldn't have minded that. Kids just get married, housing the way it is, won't hurt you to rough it a little. Those people, though, bedbugs and lice. Four-Fs and Jews running all over the place. You still see them since you moved?"

Willy said, "Yes, once in a while. Weiss's wife loaned me that book."

"Weiss's wife, huh? I think you introduced us to this fellow Weiss." Mr. Norton took a cigarette from his case and put it in the short black hard-rubber holder he always used at home. He seemed to be examining the implications of the fact that Weiss had a wife whom he had not seen and who, of course, might be seductive in some Levantine way. "Do you think Martha likes these people?" he asked abruptly. Then he shook his head in a hard, uncompromising gesture. "As a matter of fact, I'm sure she doesn't. Not from anything she has said to us. Martha is not the kind to complain. You know that. No, but she let little things slip out. That was part of what was behind it when we got so—ah, you know, Willy—when we got on your tail about moving to a better apartment last summer."

Mr. Norton slumped a little bit in his chair and let a tall unwavering streamer of smoke rise from his cigarette while he thought again. He said gently, "I was seven kinds of a small-town fool the way I handled that, Willy. I don't blame you for getting sore and saying the things you had to say about it. But Momma was upset about Martha living in such a place, and women are . . . You said a lot of true things then, Willy. Momma and I were talking on the way home and I told her what I thought. I said, 'Look here what we did. We jumped into the kids' affair and got Willy to make a financial move he couldn't see his way clear to taking right then and then by God I had the gall to make him sign a note for the money it would take to get this other apartment for a year.' I thought no wonder with that hanging over you when you've still got two years to go that you've been"— Mr. Norton looked as hard as he could for the kindest, most reassuring word here—*"worried sick*. So—" he fumbled in his inner coat pocket and from several papers selected one. His hard honest face turned pink in self-consciousness. "I'm going to tear that note up. Christmas present from Momma and me."

Willy said sharply, as the paper was already coming apart between Mr. Norton's fingers, "Don't do that."

"Christmas present," Mr. Norton said. Martha came into the room and sat on the arm of her father's chair while he explained the gift to her. Willy watched her beautiful silk-clad leg swinging back and forth.

Sure, he thought, that apartment house where we lived and where the Weisses live was no place for her. They had come to it in the kind of thoughtless desperation which the news that there was any apartment at all vacant in the university town seemed to stir up in otherwise sensible people. It was pure accident that he and Martha got into that building.

Right after he came home from Japan and they were married they'd got a trailer. Handsome little trailer acquired by the university for housing just such as he and Martha; but the things which had happened between him and Martha in its regimented space were not exactly what either of them had been hoping for while he was overseas. They both felt cramped in the trailer and thought they had to have an apartment soon if they weren't going to get so irritated that they would be forced to quarrel with each other.

Willy had been more afraid of a quarrel with Martha than of anything else. He had not by any means forgotten the years when he wanted her so much and couldn't have her, and a quarrel was impossible after all that waiting.

So they had held their noses and moved into the buggy apartment house. They thought they could fix their place up some. They could paint the walls and build in bookcases and have space to use the really nice wedding presents they had got from

Martha's family and friends. Some crumby-looking people lived in the house with them. Graduate students and art majors. There was no law they had to associate with them, though, just because they lived in the same building.

How they got mixed up with the Weisses and their parties and friends he did not yet know, but by now he had come full circle to the point of wondering why all these people should like him. He really didn't know what they talked about. He hadn't read the books they shouted and quarreled about while everyone got drunk. After Martha would go home to the apartment down the hall he would sit crosslegged on the floor among them, like a big innocent puppy, while the hot angry dispute went on around him. Sometimes, when they talked about the war or the desperate things they would do in case of another one, they appealed to him—the halfway hero in their midst, the fighter pilot—as a judge, thrusting their sick, bearded, myopic, pimpled faces close to his own. Or they demanded at other times that he side with them in their interpretation of Marx, Freud, or James, and he went home and tried to read the books they yelled about.

Even after he and Martha moved, they kept asking him back to the parties, and this fall he went to most of them—once a week or so—and Martha had never gone or objected to his going—"If you have fun."

It was not fun, and he knew these people were not any happier than he was, but the late drunken hours of their parties had more attraction for him than just the noise or the whiskey.

He would be sitting there maybe, among the 4-Fs and Jews, the graduate students, bedbugs and cockroaches, looking at the sea-green Kemtone (the sea far below him as it had been beyond his wingtips in the Oriental dawn) on the wall, hearing a fanatic insistence in the voice which was saying ". . . this thing of Jeffers where the soldier has his mother put her hand in the rotten hole in his side . . ." The voice sounded like the speaker was being killed himself and wanted very much to live, like the wish to live was sickening him.

In those climactic flashes he got from them the feeling he had this afternoon when the pheasant struck its broken bones against his wrist. He did not really understand the books they loaned him; he wanted desperately to do so.

He had the book in his hands now, though in front of Mr. Norton he didn't wish to read it. He was leafing through it slowly and carefully toward the passage which had so amused and outraged his father-in-law. It had sounded familiar, and he thought he remembered seeing it somewhere among the scattered fragments of slogan and typographical fancies that made up what the publishers called a novel.

Martha's mother beside him was holding her hands up in a pudgy triangle, describing to Martha a faille dress she had seen in Nieman-Marcus. "We had such a good time in Dallas, Daddy and I. They can say what they want to about California, but I think Texas is the coming place. Why, it was the best part of the trip, and the people there are so friendly. I wish we could move there for our 'old days' when Daddy sells the store . . . or when you and Willy take it over." She turned smiling to Willy, not wishing to leave him out of the conversation which she had kept up since dinner. "You were in Dallas or thereabouts when you were in training, weren't you? Didn't you find the people nice, Willy?"

"I liked them," he said.

"Such an exciting place," Mrs. Norton said. "So many nice eating places, and the stores—my!—and theaters and nice houses, not mansions but just nice. Such sunny-looking people. My, I've never seen so many pretty young girls walking along the streets. They all seemed so well dressed."

"Were there pretty girls in Dallas when you were a cadet?" Martha asked. She looked at him cutely, flirting, lowering her lashes over her blue eyes; she arched her back slowly and ran the fingers of both hands through her hair, watching him watch her.

He nodded, thinking crazily, God, she's asking for it, and she didn't dare ask until they came home to be her reinforcements; worked it out, and thinking, I owe it to her, I owe it to them.

"Then we can't move down there," Martha said to her mother. Her voice was husky and suggestive. "I'd never be able to bring Willy down on a visit."

Mr. Norton, on the other side of the room, in his own chair and under his lamp again, rattled his newspaper and cleared his throat.

"I don't think you have to worry about Willy looking at any 'other' pretty girls," her mother said and patted Martha's knee, smiling. "Willy, you wait until you see Martha's new negligee that we got her. It's—well, not for an unmarried girl, but it's pretty."

"Don't make Willy blush, Mother," Martha said. The red line of her lips was fixed in a stubborn smile. Her eyes were uncertain.

"I'll try to stand it," Willy said, and the sarcasm in his voice shamed and surprised him.

"You can, all right," Martha said.

He thought, She's already talked to her mother about me. While they were washing dishes they were talking about me, and Mrs. Norton is trying to encourage me because she still thinks I can be all right if I want to. He shrugged and said, "I'm tired," as though he meant "Leave me alone."

Something in the tension of their speech, something that had not been present before the Nortons arrived home, was heavy enough to break the conversation for a little while.

In the silence Mr. Norton snapped the paper he was reading. "Here's a story will amuse you, Willy. As a veteran. 'Sentenced for Refusing to Register. Judge Albert Minor today sentenced Orlin Johnson of Kahokia to two years imprisonment for refusing to register for the draft. Johnson pleaded not guilty, declaring that he had seen a vision'—get it, seen a vision —'which made him unable to comply with draft requirements. Johnson, the father of three children, described a series of sleepless nights preceding his decision not to register. On one occasion, he declared, he had seen a vision in which he was swimming in a sea of vomit, and after seeing this he felt himself unable to enter the armed services. Other defendants pleaded guilty and were given suspended sentences.' "

When the word "vomit" was read by her husband, Mrs. Norton waved her hand and said "Oh Charlie" in protest against her husband's teasing her by reading this dirty word.

"What do you think of that?" Mr. Norton said to Willy, folding the paper together and resting it on his knee.

In his back, just above the hips, Willy felt a surge of muscle and a tightening so intense that he thought for a minute he was going to lose his water. "They ought to beat his head between two stones," he said.

"Ha," Mr. Norton chuckled.

"The judge," Willy said.

The family group of four sat there in a sudden immobility, like the fabled people caught in the attitudes of pleasant sociability in a familiar room by an instantaneous fall of lava. As though the secret which threatened Willy's mind should have been brought to light—as they had wanted, of course—with a mad inversion of the proprieties through which they wished to see it.

First Mr. Norton said, "I've talked to plenty of veterans . . ." Then it took him several minutes of alternate rage and calming before he said, "Everybody to his own opinion. I couldn't stay in business a minute in Bloomsdale if I talked like that."

Willy shook his head miserably, "I don't have an opinion. It's the . . ." They waited for him to finish. He could see Martha getting terribly ashamed for him. He saw Mrs. Norton moving her lips as though she were trying to help him with the word, but he did not know what it was.

He heard Martha say, "Daddy!" and he felt as though he could strike her for interrupting, because he had to say this thing as soon as he could. Then miraculously it seemed that she had guessed close to what he meant, because she began gaily talking about the afternoon. "In back of Lotterman's grove," she said, "and Willy killed one before I knew what was happening. Before he knew what was happening, I guess." She laughed and her parents laughed a little, politely, still watching him.

"It's the . . ." He sat there strangling over the obscene word *death* which he wanted to say to them, so just once they would understand what his world and his war were about.

"What, Willy?" Mrs. Norton asked, softly as she would coax a child.

"Oh, Willy," Martha said sadly, disappointed in him that he would not let her smooth his way.

He walked to the stairway and then felt his way up by hanging on the banister. He did not hear them talking behind him, or Mrs. Norton's sympathetic exclamation, but he knew they would have things to say to each other in which he could take no part.

Then he was in the Nortons' bedroom, standing in the center of it like a prisoner who could not answer the accusation of its witnessing furniture. He looked at the picture of himself and the model plane on the dressing table, and now he was frightened stiff by the Nortons' having kept them there so long after the war was over and it was time to replace them. He picked up the toy chair—like a diminutive throne—that had belonged to Martha.

In a little while he reached for the model plane and was surprised to see it break from its mount, thinking he had touched it lightly. But then he picked it up and squeezed it. The wood crumpled in his hand. One by one the splinters slid off his palm. He set his thumb on the toy chair and smashed that too.

Only that wasn't mine to break, he thought in an immediate reflex of emotion. They kept that and the plane too because they loved us. He looked at the scraps on the table top and thought stupidly, They can glue them back together if they want to and keep them forever. Only to hell with it, because they would never forget that the things had to be mended.

He carried the fragments to his suitcase and, opening it, hid them under some dirty underclothes in the side of the bag where he kept things for the laundry. From the side in which his clean clothes remained he took his Japanese pistol and stuck it in the waistband of his trousers.

Martha stopped him at the back door as he was going out. "What's the matter, Willy? Don't be unhappy tonight, hon. Oh, what a silly mess, damn it."

He stepped past her into the cold night, and she followed him. "Go on back," he said coaxingly. "Shoo. I'm all right. I just want to walk by myself awhile." He saw the wind moving the beautiful tips of her hair against her cheek. "I don't feel so very well. I guess those fine birds we got didn't agree with me as well as they did with your folks. The air will fix me."

"Are you sure?" she said. "Let me come along."

He took three steps down the walk and paused as though he were going to explain something further to her.

"Please," she said.

"Naa," he said. "You're not wrapped up. Run back now. Quick." She looked as beautiful in the porch light as he ever remembered seeing her—in the photo on the beer cooler, on the campus before the war, anywhere, anytime. "You're nice," he said. "I wish . . ."

She shivered and left him with one more admonition not to stay out too long. He walked toward the edge of town, in the direction of the viaduct. When he reached it, he stepped over the guard cables of the approach and slid down the dirt embankment. He edged around the embankment until he felt his way into a clump of weeds that seemed to shelter him from the nagging cold of the air. He took out the pistol and set the muzzle against his neck. Because he was a nice boy, he felt a pang of conscience about causing the Nortons all this trouble and all they were going to have afterward, but in a way they had brought it on themselves.

The Biggest Band

THE CORN State Southern Band was a forlorn hope from the beginning, and, like other forlorn hopes, it moved within an aura of enthusiastic propaganda. Perhaps because it had hardly any distinction except size, we had it drummed into our minds that it was "the biggest band in the world." At full strength it numbered about twenty-four hundred souls, and, if we were not literally the most numerous assembly of horn-blowers and drummers ever massed in a single field, no one who ever heard us at close range bothered to contest this primary claim. All during the winter I was thirteen, I drank this propaganda of size—and of our destiny—reorganizing it all into the form of personal wishes that I would go with the other members to the Chicago World's Fair.

A dreamer named Lothar Swift had organized the band by combining the available personnel from high school, municipal, club, college, church, and lodge bands from the southern part of our state. The principle of organization was simple. Swift included everyone who had a suitable instrument—there were no kazoos or household implements used, as some of our detractors said later—and who was willing to attend rehearsals of the band's divisions, as they were called. (These divisions rehearsed separately in various county seat towns across the state. The band never rehearsed as a whole before it played in Chicago.)

Later, Swift enlarged the band even further by selling instruments to a great many people who had never played before, and by including them too. He was a partner in an instrument store in the state capital, and by dangling the bait of the band's proposed excursion he greatly expanded their sales in spite of Depression conditions.

Still, since I had shown no musical aptitude whatever up to that year, I might not have been swept into his deal if he had not known my mother from the days when she taught his younger sisters at Germany school. Though he was a big frog in a big puddle that year, he had grown up on a clay farm just as my parents had.

When he came to Davisburg to sell horns and enlist band members he called at our house for old times' sake. Before he left he had sold us the trombone. He had given us a fine reduction on price, since the bell of the horn was dented, and had promised my mother, "If the band goes—and we're going —this lad of yours will go to Chicago with us. Why, by next summer he'll be playing 'Flight of the Bumblebee.' The trombone isn't a hard instrument." He threw in with the horn an instruction book, which my mother and Uncle Lou were to use in teaching me. They both knew a little music, though neither of them knew any more about the trombone than I did. My mother suggested that once I'd advanced a little I could probably practice with the Davisburg High School band as a stepping stone to the CSS band. Swift generously countered with an invitation for me to come to a division rehearsal "just as soon as he feels ready."

By May, I had learned a few numbers. Miss Sheldahl, who directed the high school band, let me sit in regularly on their rehearsals, though she would not permit me to appear with them in public. And I had been a few times to division rehearsals in our county seat.

But though my mother and I felt that I was fulfilling my part of the bargain all right, Lothar Swift's promise that I would go to Chicago with the band seemed far less reliable. There were rumors going around that he was having plenty of trouble raising money to move his horde so far, let alone to shelter them once he got them to the city.

Presently a form letter came for me. It said that band members had been put on either an *A* list or a *B* list, according to merit. While it was still the band's intention to pay travel and lodging expenses for all its members, it appeared necessary to ask that all *B* members sell two excursion tickets to "band supporters" who might wish to go along to Chicago. The tickets cost $47.50 apiece. Naturally, of course, I was on the *B* list.

I particularly resented the fact that while I had to sell these tickets in order to go, Lard Williams, who was only a couple of years older than I, had been exempted from this condition and put on the *A* list. I would admit that he could play the trumpet a lot better than I could play my trombone, but I still suspected strongly that this discrimination between us had resulted from some kind of malevolence. I thought I might be getting my deserts for the wrong reason.

There had been a brief, bitter time when I thought it might have been Lard who fingered me to Lothar Swift's stooges for playing through a seven-measure rest during a division rehearsal. It had happened in the "Semper Fidelis Overture" when the ninety or more clarinets of this division were supposed to be having things all to themselves. After I'd blasted right along with them through the rest, Swift had rapped for silence, climbed onto his chair at the far end of the gymnasium in which we were practicing, and shouted in my general direction, "One of you trombones—some of you trombones—has lost your place." I sat there with my head down, making business with the spit valve of my horn, thinking he couldn't locate me in that crowd—even after I'd glanced at the nearby stands and discovered that it *was* the "Semper Fidelis" thing the others had been playing, while I'd been tootling along on the "Mission of the Rose Waltz."

"We can't have that happen in Chicago," Swift bellowed. "The big city critics would be on us like wolves. Now, watch it. Once again . . ."

Riding back to Davisburg later in my parents' car, Lard had whispered to me, so my mother wouldn't hear, "Why don't you just sit there and *pretend* to blow? Hee, hee, hee." So I understood that he knew who had flubbed.

He needled me about it for days afterward, while I tried to defend myself on the grounds that I had been too far from Swift to see his baton or his signal for the rest. But Lard answered me with giggles—like someone who has acted treacherously and wants to make out that there was justification for his act.

So after the letter from the band came, I made some plans for ambushing Lard and fixing his lip so he wouldn't get it into a trumpet mouthpiece for a while. I might have done it, too, if my mother hadn't come through with a timely explanation that she'd seen Lothar's "spies" snooping around in various quarters of the band, "cocking their heads and just listening for any little thing a person might happen to do wrong." I had to admit that one of those monitors might have got me on the *B* list instead of Lard.

Whoever was at fault, I was no longer willing to consider staying home while the band went. Through the winter I'd used the approach of the trip as the vehicle for too many wishes to conceive of giving it up. There were plenty of things I had to see in Chicago—photoelectric cells that opened doors, Bob Ripley's *Believe It or Not,* the Skyride and the Skyride Pylons, and the dirigible *Akron,* which was scheduled to visit the city in the same week as the Band. I meant to see them, come hell or high water. I was going to ride all night on that excursion train and stay in a big city hotel (both for the first time in my life), if I had to rob a filling station to do it.

Most of all, for just this period in the spring, I meant to see Sally Rand. Our Scout leader, who was also the high school coach, had confirmed the necessity of my seeing her. I'd been saving photos of her secretly since about Christmas, but I hadn't mentioned my feeling about her to anyone until one May afternoon at the Scout cabin when the troop came in all pooped from a hike.

Coach Douglas was sprawled out in a downy growth of ferns

and Dutchman's-breeches, while I sat against a nearby tree feeling my pulse and wondering if I'd injured my heart from too much exercise in this heat.

"I hear you're going to the Fair next month," he called.

"I hope to." My pulse was over ninety, and I didn't know if that was a danger sign or not.

"Wish I could make it," Coach Douglas said. "I'd really like to see that Sally Rand romp again."

Again! Here was someone who'd seen her with his own eyes. I jumped up and began walking around him in circles, trompling May apples, thyme, and wild fern. "What's she look like?" I asked offhandedly.

"Pretty." Coach Douglas bit through the stem of a flower and spat the fragment toward the blue sky.

"What's she do with the fans?"

"Moves them around."

"Bare?"

"Bare."

Good God. A person could live in Davisburg a hundred years, it seemed to me then, without having the opportunity of seeing a naked woman.

I practiced on my trombone for hours that night. I played all the C sharps that I'd been leaving out because the seventh position was hard for me to reach, and I smoothed out the high passages in "Barcarolle." I was driven by some sort of irrational, superstitious hope that if I suddenly improved enough I might get a letter the next day telling me that it had been a mistake to put me on that *B* list. All the time I knew that it was too late to expect that.

The next day I propositioned my father to buy the two excursion tickets I had to sell. I told him straight out what a crumby life my mother had and how often she'd come close to crying when I talked to her about all the things I expected to see at the Fair. And anyway it would have been pretty funny if they didn't want to come see me playing in the Midwest Concert, given by the biggest band in the world.

"You think I can turn up ninety-five dollars for us to go on?" he said with more solemn concern than my approach deserved. We weren't as awfully poor as we'd been two years ago, but he was just getting back on his feet then from a rough stretch. "Come on, Buddy. I'd have to sell the car. Do you want me to do that? I want you to think about that."

"Couldn't you borrow the money from Uncle Lou?"

"Uncle Lou's helped us too often when we really needed it. No use talking any more. Why don't you go hit up the Packers? That hard old jaybird is the only one in town that I know of who might have that kind of money to throw around."

Wishes gather weight through one's childhood until, mysteriously, they become necessities. I *thought* it was necessary for me to get to Chicago and see Sally Rand. That belief nerved me up to go to the Packers and try to sell them the tickets. It is easy to think now how frivolous was what seemed necessary then. And yet, of course it must have been on the hot afternoon when I went to their house that I began to learn why—really—it was necessary that I make the trip with the Band.

My first call had been pleasant and a lot easier than I had expected, but the trouble was that only Mrs. Packer had been at home. Mr. Packer was a railroad official who spent most of his time at the state capital or in Omaha, seldom coming closer to Davisburg than his big farmhouse just beyond the edge of town. I'd have to look for his car in the drive, his wife told me, if I wanted to catch him, because she really never knew just when his duties would let him come home. And she wasn't going to be the one to decide whether or not they'd buy my tickets.

She'd been so awfully nice to me, though, that I was all keyed up for success. She was a dumpy woman in her sixties, with a fresh-looking pink and white skin and very nice brown eyes. She'd ohed and ahed when I told her about the splendors of science and the glamorous entertainment she was going to see in Chicago. I could tell she wasn't just pretending her interest to be polite. She wanted to go, and I figured that was the point that really counted.

When I came back to clinch my sale I knew that Mr. Packer was home because I'd seen his big black car under the elms of their yard when I went uptown for the mail in the morning, and it was still there. I went up on the shady, wide porch and knocked at their screen door. Their collie came around the corner of the porch, prancing and panting from the heat. He nuzzled bossily at the legs of my overalls.

"Good dog. Good old dog," I said to him in the most salesmanlike way I could manage. I knocked again and the collie whined to be patted.

"Not so loud, boy." It was Mr. Packer who had come to answer the door. I had rather hoped it would be Mrs. Packer, so she could lead me to him and help explain the deal we were working out. "You'll wake Mrs. Packer," he said. "Come on around to the swing and keep your voice down."

It seemed to me that he was hardly more than aware of me as we went to the section of the porch that faced the highway and took seats in the swing. His blue eyes searched among the elms and catalpas of the lawn as though he were looking for some sly, important guest and merely tolerating me until that one arrived. In the midst of my attempt to get my sales talk started he said, "Is that your bike down by the gate? I suppose now that school is out you kids are playing, like kids will. Bikes and all." He yawned in my face and scratched the fishbelly-white fat on his arms.

"No, sir," I said. "I spend nearly all my time practicing music. I'm a member of the biggest band in the world."

If this announcement touched him he failed to show it. It occurred to me that he was looking across the highway at the purebred shorthorns in his feed lot and gloating on what they were worth, even at Depression prices. I thought that if he had any sense of justice he ought to consider how much I needed a little bit of that wealth.

"Lothar Swift, the well-known conductor and music teacher, organized it," I said. "We call it the Corn State Southern Band, and it has musicians in it from clear across the state. I play the trombone."

He looked me over then as though I were offering myself for sale. His pale lips showed that he was a little bit amused.

"Can you reach seventh position on that horn? Not quite, I'll bet."

That encouraged me, because at least it showed he knew something about musical instruments. "I can usually reach it," I bragged. Then I struck for the heart of the matter with more language from Swift's circular letters. "You may have heard that the biggest band in the world is going to the World's Fair in Chicago to play its Midwest Concert and make other appearances. Do you know that this band has twenty-four hundred musicians?"

"My God," he said absently. "That's a lot, isn't it?"

"Along with this vast assembly of musicians, music lovers of the state can buy excursion tickets to go along with it to the Fair."

"It must sound like hell," he said.

"Your wife wants to go," I told him. "She asked me to come back and talk to you about buying the tickets."

Now for the first time since we had sat in the swing he looked square into my face. There was something so savage and cold in his eyes—a gaze in which I was not a little boy but an equally responsible human—that I considered running for my bike then and there.

I went on recklessly, "I was here a few days ago and she practically promised to buy *one* ticket at least. She said she'd find out if you would go with her."

He kept staring steadily at me while he pulled the collie's head against his knee and began scratching its ears. "She told you that she meant to go to the Fair? That she'd go by herself if I wouldn't go? You're lying, boy." He was so calm in his accusation that it seemed he had spent all his life being lied to and had learned finally that all you can do about lies is to sit steady among the trees on your own farm, maybe waiting for the liars to get tired of their business.

I was scared to say anything more to him just then. We sat rocking in the swing for half an hour without a word. I saw Lard Williams and Percy Black ride past on their bikes, headed for the swimming hole in Mitten Creek, and I resented Lard all over again for his freedom from all this trouble I was having.

Mr. Packer said, "I don't think she could have said that to you, boy. Mrs. Packer isn't going anywhere. She's rotten with cancer."

I don't think I quite understood what this meant. Again he had spoken with total calm, and I took the word "rotten" as merely an impolite way of speaking about his wife rather than as a description that might be accurate. "I was sure when I talked to her that she wanted to go," I insisted, perhaps intending to persuade him not to let his meanness interfere with her pleasure.

Of course that appeal meant nothing to him. I had only one line that was not yet exhausted. "Maybe the band can't go at all unless people like me sell enough tickets. And the Midwest Concert will be something no one ever heard before. Since Mrs. Packer was so interested in it, maybe you could buy a couple of tickets and not use them. To help."

"Why should I?" he asked. His big, cracker-white hands trembled in the dog's mane. He stopped rocking the swing. The hot afternoon seemed unbearably still. I listened for the cooing of pigeons or the sound of a car and heard only Mr. Packer's slow, hissing breath.

"Why?" he asked.

"All right, then," I said. I trotted down across the big lawn to pick up my bike. I supposed that this was the end of my chances to go.

. . .

My mother arranged for me to go by beating down Lothar Swift, beating him with the flail of righteous anger. I came home one evening soon after my failure with the Packers to find her glaring and muttering to herself. "I don't care how high up in the music business Lothar Swift has gone," she burst out, "nor how many horns he's sold with all his slippery promises. He needn't think he can get away with this with me. Don't you think I remember the time he came mousing around to Germany school in the afternoon, pretending to look for his sisters, though he knew they'd gone with the other pupils, him whimpering and simpering around with his Miss Thurman this and Miss Thurman that, and it all so plain on his face what he'd come for that I finally had to take pity on him for being so dumb and say, 'Yes, if you want me to go to Hopewell box supper with you, can't you just say so?' "

While her fury lasted she called him at his store in the state capital. I stood beside our telephone, watching her face get harder and angrier than I could recall having seen it, ever. "You—told—us—last—fall. What? Why, when we bought that horn you promised he'd go if— What? Well, I suspect he can do about as well as lots of the others that you've put on that old *A* list. What? Lothar, I—don't—care. You—told—us—last—fall . . ."

In this way she beat him out of my fare to Chicago, sent me there as a musical liability, and as one who had not sold his quota either. But it cost her something to make such an arrangement. Her conscience hurt her. Later that evening she was preoccupied and nervous. She made a big effort to explain to me the kind of person Lothar Swift was. She said he was a fundamentally decent man, though he tried to squeeze too much out of life and this made him careless with the truth. "I don't want to take the bread out of his mouth," she said. "But he promised us. You and Daddy both heard him promise you'd go." Then more of her concern with the band began to come out. "Lothar's ambitious. I've never had a lot of faith he could do all he's undertaken. Your daddy and I have heard that he's borrowed a lot of money and signed a lot of notes he can't hope to pay off unless he has a lot of luck in Chicago. I just don't know how I'd feel now if he had to default his notes and they put him in jail or something."

I was afraid even now that she might weaken under so much worry—that she might pick up the phone again and cancel my trip after all. I clenched my eyes tight shut and thought of Sally Rand. I saw her only as she was in the photographs, with her fans immovably fixed where they shouldn't have been. Somehow I knew I had to see behind them, and if deception was the price, I was willing to pay it.

"But don't you think this excursion is a great opportunity for young people?" I asked her in my oiliest voice. "I mean, to learn music and to see a great American city that they'd never see otherwise?"

That took her in. "Yes. Sure it is. We've got to try things at least, don't we, Buddy?" She hugged me hard against her side. "Lothar's a clever man and maybe he can swing this project better than people think. He's bitten it off. Let's hope he can chew it."

I hoped he would have the courage to go on writing note after note to banks and backers, as careless of what came after Chicago as I was.

He had the courage. By some miracle of paper financing, artful dodging with the railroads, hotels, Fair committees, and terribly inflated promises to the gullible who went as part of the excursion, he took us.

On a rainy, muggy night in June, four hundred of us, constituting the "east-central" division of the band, boarded a special train at the county seat. We knew that some of the western divisions, with whom we had never yet rehearsed and whom we were not even to see for many hours yet, had loaded at dawn— while ahead of us, to the east, other hundreds were boarding a train that would get them to the LaSalle Street Station before us.

My father had bought me a new Brownie "to get some pictures of that Zeppelin," and my mother had packed my clothes with the abstract, enraptured sorrow that you might expect of a Kamikaze's parent dispatching her only son to the Emperor's service.

At the last minute before boarding, quite carried away by the purifying excitement of the moment, I announced to my mother, "I *won't* go to see Sally Rand." I meant it. I had not understood before how holy a thing it was that all this mob was embarking for.

"Well, I should hope not," she said. "Don't forget to get a new bottle of oil for your horn." She had not even seriously considered the possibility that I might court such a depravity. And that, I thought as I swung up, was probably just as well.

"We'll knock them dead," I screeched as the train began to move.

Once the train was really rolling—the one dependable evidence that Lothar Swift would make his promises good, I had felt—I yielded myself to the excitement of departure with a completely simple loyalty. There was a rumor running through our train that Swift had put our movement and the problems of housing us in Chicago under the direction of an Army captain who had moved troops in Flanders during the war. I overheard some smart-alec college boy giggle over this, "Swift might just do better if he'd let the captain conduct the band, too." I thought it would serve such a guy right if he were pushed into the Mississippi River for his ingratitude.

I had never seen that river before this trip, and I kept pinching myself awake until we had crossed it. Lard Williams was as impressed by it as I was. "Did you ever see anything as black as that water?" he shouted in my ear. Then he whipped his trumpet from the case and blew a few notes of "When It's Darkness on the Delta." "Do you realize that river is bigger than the Amazon?" he crowed. "It's the biggest damn river on the planet. I don't suppose you realize it, Buddy, but you ought to be plenty grateful to your parents and Lothar Swift for making this trip possible."

All these things were exactly what I had been thinking, but it spoiled them a little to hear him saying them. I grunted disagreeably and went to sleep.

I was wakened a good deal later by the passage of the sandwich butcher through the car. Careful not to wake up Lard, I bought some coffee and a jelly sandwich and leaned out the window to get the wind on my face while I ate.

We had left the rain behind us. The stars were out, but the roll of the prairie around us was as black as the river had been. I watched us zip through the night with a balancing of joys—glad that the land was so black while our train was so flashing, glad that it was silent so that the chatter of our wheels could print itself on it, like the first footstep you take in new snow.

Lard was snoring beside me. I enjoyed a lot of superior thoughts at his expense. Maybe he's with us for no better purpose than to go see some immoral Chicago woman waggle her stomach, I thought, but I'm going for something else. It seemed to me that in the hour of my success I had promised not only my mother that I would shun Sally Rand—the promise was to all those who had wanted to go where we were going and couldn't. People like Mrs. Packer. I felt terribly sorry for her, all over again, and wanted to tell her that even if her husband misunderstood her and said unpleasant things about her physical condition, I, at least, knew better than he what she had wanted. And in a way, I suppose, I felt that I was going to get it for her. Finally, I felt I knew why I'd absolutely had to make this trip. In that sweet night I imagined all my selfishness to be a kind of altruism.

We woke in a green morning before the train had passed through Joliet. A tired conductor came through and said, "You kids better keep your feet out of the windows. You'll be walking on your stumps."

I looked across the aisle at the French-horn player who sat beside his instrument case. His chin was black with beard stubble, and his skin showed that he'd been seeing some hard work in the fields. This is not a bunch of kids, I thought, telling off the conductor. You know who's in this band? *Everybody.*

Those who watched us pour into the city through the LaSalle Street Station would surely have agreed. There were old German farmers with short cornet cases, housewives with clarinets and tubas, girls with bagpipes, the whole Legion Auxiliary fife and drum corps from Osmatoc, the marching band from a Methodist college, a sect of Amish with beards and black bonnets, high school bands in a flashing variety of uniforms, and among them all the misencouraged young like me who belonged only to the totality. Counting the excursionists, there were more than four thousand people in this horde that Lothar Swift had raised up to follow him east.

All of us rallied for the first time in one of the ballrooms at the Marathon Hotel. It was a wild gathering full of noise, anarchy, and administrative ineptitude that delayed our assignment to hotel rooms for many hours. I remember an old lady—she was one of the excursionists, she said, who had paid her own good money for the trip—who whimpered ceaselessly after the first few hours, "I'm tired. I'm hungry. I want to go back." In midafternoon I heard a fat tuba player offer to whip Lothar Swift for "getting us into all this mess."

But evidently, the logjam was already broken, for a very few minutes later, the last of us bandsmen were being whisked up to our rooms briefly before we loaded to move in buses to our first concert. I had only time enough in the room to look out at the blue lake, so intimate and so strange that it was like something that might have grown inside my eye, suddenly striping its color across my field of vision—and to exult that I hadn't come all this way to face it in petty company.

There was trouble on the first day in getting us to our designated area in the middle of the Fairgrounds. Finally, a platoon of special police had to hold back the normally strolling crowds until we could all pass through into the snow-fenced enclosure that had been prepared for us.

In the push to the enclosure, I lost the other trombone players I'd been tagging and found myself in the midst of more bassoon players than you'd think lived in our state. I had to sit down there with them when the band started to play. It seemed to make them uneasy to have me in their midst.

So when the first number was over, I got up with my horn under my arm and went in search of the trombones. Presently, as I was wandering, an old man with a flugelhorn grabbed me and hissed, "Don't you know how bad that looks, romping around that way during a *performance?*" He took a terrific grip on my wrist and forced me to the ground. He tried to hold me down out of sight with one hand and his feet while he played the next number, but in an allegro passage I twisted free and crawled along toward a sound like that of trombones.

I got lost again and crawled out of the band to one of the snow-fence borders. I had no idea what the band was playing— neither what Lothar Swift was conducting in his faroff center nor what any of the divisions *thought* he meant for them to play. I was terribly ashamed of myself for getting lost. I sat there playing "Barcarolle" softly, because at least I could do that better than anything else.

A kid smaller than I came up outside of the fence and jabbed me with a toy whip.

"Who're all those?" he said.

"Corn State Southern Band."

"Boy," he whistled. "There's sure a lot of them."

"They're the biggest band in the world."

He turned his head in an arc wide enough to take in the nearer and farther edges of the multitude, spat, and admitted, "Could be."

"What's that they're playing?" he asked.

"The 'Corn Song.'"

He began to look slyly skeptical. "Why ain't you in there playing with them? You got a horn."

"I can't find where I belong. I ought to be with the rest of the trombones."

"I saw them ten minutes ago," he said, "when I was around on the other end of you all by the Skyride. *They* was playing the 'Corn Song' then."

If Lothar Swift had been as ambitious as my mother thought, or if he'd counted on the band's creating a sensation that would lead to the redemption of his debts, he was sadly corrected. The Chicago newspapers didn't even bother to comment on our size. There had been some talk that a beer company or a farm implement manufacturer was going to sponsor us, but after our poor showing on that first afternoon no one believed it any more. The crowds on the Fairgrounds walked *around* us, because they had to. That was about the limit of the attention we got.

Our second concert, on the following day, was scheduled for the dinner hour, when the grounds were mostly empty. They put us out behind Machinery Hall, where the ground tapered visibly into the garbage fill on which the Fair had been built. There weren't even enough folding chairs provided us for all the band members to sit down, let alone anyone who might have come to hear us. I wondered where the critics were that Lothar Swift had worried so much about the day I had played through the seven-measure rest.

Most of the band members I was acquainted with were talking cynically. Lard got a letter from his parents with the rumor that the band had barely managed to get out of the state before the sheriff pulled in Swift for his bad debts.

I tried to ignore this general gloom as much as I could. I'd taken some pictures of the *Akron* coming in over the lake. I'd seen the Ripley show, the marionettes, and a lot of other educational things. But I'd let myself be so excited by the idea of the band's triumph that this gloom scared me, like the fog I'd seen edging in over the lake when we played behind Machinery Hall.

There was still the Midwest Concert to play. It was scheduled to be in the Court of Nations. I sent off to my parents a picture postcard of the clean and modern pylons that surrounded this court. The picture was full of flags in bright, primary colors against a sky the color of laundry bluing. "We're going to play HERE," I wrote on the card.

In my stupidity, I had been slow to catch on that the Midwest Concert would only be part of the joke of our coming. We were scheduled to play it at six-fifteen in the morning. No one would be out at that hour to hear us.

When I finally caught the insult implied by this scheduling, I knew I'd taken more than enough. I canceled my promises to be good in Chicago.

That night I let Lard Williams and his older buddies ditch me, as they'd tried to do on the previous night. Sneaking through the Fairgrounds by the less crowded walks, I marched —dry of mouth and trembling—to the Streets of Paris where Sally Rand would turn me into a swine with those adroit fans. I even meant to stand at the side of the pavilion, from which vantage Coach Douglas had said you got a choicer view.

They wouldn't let me in. I ran at the entrance stairs with my quarter steaming in my hand, and the barker dropped his cane across my chest to block the way.

"You came to the wrong place, didn't you, sonny?" he said. He raised quite a laugh from the crowd in turning me back. "I expect you thought this was the puppet show, didn't you? A-dults only. A-dults only," he bellowed. "Why boy, you couldn't stand the breeze them fans make when they go into action."

To top off this humiliation, when Lard came back to the hotel room we shared with twelve other Bandsmen, he claimed he had seen her. Spiritlessly I asked him what she was like, and he shuddered in a pretense of disgust. "I don't think it's right to permit that kind of indecent show," he said. "Personally, I wish I had my quarter back. I'd rather have a ham sandwich and a bottle of coke."

Most of our roommates were in bed or asleep on the floor.

Fortunately the room was too dim for him to see my face plainly, though enough light refracted in from the metropolitan beacons, traffic, and the street lights for me to see him yawn as he started to take off his shirt.

"You fat idiot," I said. I swung with all my strength at his chest and felt the blow glance from one of his moving elbows.

"Here," he said good-naturedly. "Don't run amok just because you've ruined your mind with dirty thoughts. Relax. Sally Rand is probably like any other woman, though not so decent."

"I've never seen any woman," I said.

"You will," Lard comforted me. "Everybody will. There's just as many of them around as there are men. Be logical."

"Sure," I said bitterly. "I'll see one *sometime*. Like when I'm too old to care." But the worst of it all was that I had discovered you couldn't even count on a profit from being bad in a world like this one. I went to sleep on the hotel room floor feeling the misery of those who have tried to sell their souls and have found no taker.

Naturally no audience came to hear the band at six-fifteen the next morning. For our climactic Midwest Concert only about half of the band members showed up at the Court of Nations. And perhaps it is merely a sad irony that we played better that morning than ever before.

In that morning's program was the "Semper Fidelis Overture," and this time even I knew which number we were playing. I was close enough to Lothar Swift to see the sun flash on his swinging baton. During the seven-measure rest, I looked at the nearly empty balconies above us where the crowd might have been and thought how pitiful it was that only a handful of early-rising janitors should hear what we had made such an effort to bring. But when the rest was over I hit the first following note as hard as I could, feeling oddly free to do my best now that it didn't seem to count for anything.

This unattended concert was the end of the band. Naturally,

it dissolved without leaving permanent traces when we went back home. Lothar Swift was never publicly charged with any of the frauds he was said to have perpetrated to get us there, but he lost his share in the instrument store in his efforts to appease the band's creditors, and he disappeared from the state not long afterward. My parents were contented to think that I had profited somehow from the excursion, but after I quit practicing on my trombone they were very hard put to explain just what the profit was. Mrs. Packer died in the Mayo Clinic toward the end of that summer, and I might not then have had the courage to discuss the trip with her even if there had been an opportunity.

In all the years since the Fair, I have told the story of our band a number of times, for laughs. This monster that Swift created has come to seem like one of those kindly, vegetarian dinosaurs that once roamed but never ruled the earth—an altogether preposterous blunder committed against nature and a fine art.

But, if in some imaginary circumstance I should tell the story for Mrs. Packer, I would want to emphasize that last dandy morning in the Court of Nations. I would want her to believe that the lake behind us looked broad as any ocean; that the clear sky looked a million times as big as the patch of ground we sat on. The flags of every country were up in the early morning breeze, and on their rippling fields twinkled the mysterious symbols of authority and fidelity—stars, crescents, crests, hammers, sickles, heraldic beasts, and the proud gold lilies of the forgotten wars. From their staffs over the national pavilions the ultramarine and lemon and scarlet pennants streamed out like dyes leaking into an oceanic current. It was only the empty sky that watched us—but my God, my God, how the drums thundered, how we blew!

The Inland Years

"LAKE ARTHUR—round as the world" it said in the public-ity folder we received from the Arthur Chamber of Commerce, and the folder contained a map which truly showed the lake like a blue globe in a green surrounding atmosphere of mid-western prairie. The town of Arthur sat on top of it like an ex-aggerated polar cap, and it was ringed with the traces of high-ways and the indication of beaches where summer cabins clustered like sham cities. But Ellen said in amusement, as she had ever since I first met her, "It's square as a bear."

Before her family dispersed when she was fifteen she had spent several summers at Lake Arthur with them, and of course from the time she and I began talking of the possibility, one of her motives for vacationing there was to make a nonsentimental pilgrimage—like going back armed and disinterested to see something you have loved and been deceived by.

In the time when we were first married, nine years ago, and were trying to give each other our childhoods for sympathy and safekeeping, she had told me a lot of stories of Lake Arthur's summer Society, and her mothers' adventures and preoccupa-tions with it. From Ellen's insistent presentation Lake Arthur had come to stand for a bogey of the past that we were fleeing together—a world without more roots than were required to make it viciously rigid, not particularly rich except on a Mid-western scale but still wealthy enough to base its behavior and tastes on distinctions of ownership, outrageously provincial in its belief in its own cosmopolitanism, and as capable of dictating the path of error to those who fascinated themselves with it as the bigger Society that Edith Wharton wrote about. This last was classically demonstrated by the nonsensical marriage and divorce of Ellen's parents. So Lake Arthur, as Ellen used to speak of it, was a well-understood point of reference from which we could orient the departure of our lives.

Of course I had not the same personal recollections of it that Ellen had. When I was a child I saw pictures in the Sunday paper of people boating on Lake Arthur, the governor holding a pike and embracing a UP official from Omaha on the amusement pier at Arthur, this or that family breakfasting by the lakeside with their guests from Minneapolis. It hadn't made a great impression on me until I heard Ellen talk of it. Then I took over, perhaps with some sentiments of gratified snobbery, Ellen's resentments toward it.

I felt, though, that I knew Lake Arthur well enough so that for me as well as for Ellen going there would be a sort of return, however partial and qualified. She and I were much too poor to take better than a cabin on one of the newly built-up beaches where there were only marsh and forest the last time Ellen had seen it. That would be close enough to spy, from a removal of years and circumstances, on a landscape and a way of life which were reminiscent of "some baggage we checked somewhere."

Of course there were more definable reasons for choosing to go there. In anticipation we spoke of the coming week at the lake as our "bourgeois vacation" because it was to be the first in our nine years together when we were going to give up ambitious plans for trips and lie back resting in a lakeshore cottage. Some years when we had no money or I was in the Army there'd been no vacation at all, and again we'd made hectic and too extravagant trips to Mexico, Canada, and California in unreliable cars. This was our year to rest, and be damned to all that might be interesting and far off. Also we had no car to go junketing in. We were both thirty-one that year, and in the spring we'd put all the money we could raise into a down payment on a house. I had a job on a home-furnishing magazine which looked as though it would be the one to last unexcitingly forever, so buying a house had at least seemed justifiable.

For my part I was wonderfully content with our plan. I couldn't have faced the idea of traveling, which always manages to concentrate my interest in myself. For me it was a great thing to lapse entirely, so that what I saw could become more important than I, even if that was no more than the banal perimeter of the lake and the static weather of early August.

For the first couple of sunny days there I had an orgy of dissolving myself in favor of whatever I could see without rolling too energetically from a prone position on the beach or the pier. Such effort as I made was like taking a bit of plain bread and concentrating fully on how it tastes. I would squint over the lake and think, How round it is, and, because I wasn't in any competition to prove myself smart, could be pleased with such a perception. I got the same kick out of the straightness of the light rays that made the chiaroscuro of the diving tower at the end of the pier. With the little girls who went out to dive I could enjoy either the color of their legs and suits against the blue sky or their adolescent shapes without feeling the slightest interest in them as people. I watched the boats tick and sway against the pier and sometimes fixed in a dumb way on the pink house directly across from us on what was currently the "best" beach.

Built as it was down close to the water it looked like a tunnel mouth or a bomb shelter except for its vivid color. Really it was impossible not to look at it. It would seem to be in my eye, just as it was in the natural colors of the lake and woods, like a metallic grain, an annoyance, however beautifully modern it might be. Sometimes in utter childishness I would hold up my little finger to blot it out. It was an irritant that made me think —about bomb shelters and modern architecture and home furnishings and what they each cost—and my sun-softened body protested against thinking.

I made some querulous jokes about it to Ellen—this was her lake, how did she account for this monstrous piece of candy cluttering up the shoreline? All she knew about it was that it had been built since her time, as any jerk ought to know. "At least it's better than they used to build," she said. "We'll go across to Arthur one time and I'll show you the Swiss chalets and English half-timbered houses they threw up in the twenties." I began to argue that sometimes irrational structures like those fitted ideologically into a landscape—I may have said "timescape"—even though aesthetically they were grossly out of place.

"I don't know what you mean," she said shortly. I admitted I didn't either and said I certainly didn't intend to argue about it.

Ellen laughed. "Then the vacation is paying off already. Let's row over and see the pink house. Want to?"

The rowing put me in an odd state, seeming about to wake me up but never fully succeeding, as though I had been deeper immersed in sleepiness for the last few days—or maybe much longer—than I had realized. The afternoon wind on my chest and bare arms and the slap of waves on the boat bottom were so insidiously insistent on my relaxing into sleep that I had a period of silly panic in which I would keep glancing over my shoulder at Ellen to be reassured that she was actually there.

"You're huffing and puffing, old boy," she called. "We don't have to go this fast."

"Pretty big waves," I said. "I want to get in closer to shore." Frightened by something I couldn't name I was trying to cover it over with a more ordinary fear.

Ellen said, "Relax. If we swamp I'll hold you up. But this is nothing."

Idling to a stop forty yards out from the pink house, dropping the oars and turning to look squarely at it for the first time, I saw why it might have made me think of a tunnel entrance. The lower story was all open to the lake, an austere concrete cave overhung by a deck and the rooms of the second floor. I had not been able to make out these details of construction from my view on our beach, but I suppose they had registered and called up that particular comparison.

Everything about the house looked groomed, polished,

stripped for action. A beautifully varnished speedboat hung on davits at the house corner which thrust a little way into the lake —it could have been the lifeboat hanging at a ship's side. There was no sign of any inhabitants. I assumed—projecting my own state, I suppose—that they were sleeping through this hot part of the afternoon.

I asked Ellen how she liked the house and she shook her head. "It's a machine for living. I'm not for it, are you?"

"It's very Walt Disney," I said. "I personally believe that the people who live here are all enchanted. Look, not a creature stirring. Want to land and look in?"

"Oh no. But let's drift here a minute. You tuckered yourself out with that speed coming over."

We bobbed there for a while without saying anything. After a while a dumb-looking boy in a sweatshirt with the legend "Athletic Dept. U of Minn." appeared on the second-story deck and leaned on the rail, peering at us in the same dull way we peered at him. He had a drink in his hand from which he gulped occasionally, but he made no sign of recognizing us as human beings. It was like being with someone in a dream and feeling as though you knew him well and being at the same time unhappily doubtful that you would know him if you saw him again. The few yards of water that separated us from him might as well have been an ocean.

"Screech at him," I said to Ellen in a low voice. "See if he's real."

The boy up-ended his glass, worked for a while to get an ice cube into his mouth and pointed the glass at us. "Oo. Dayox oh eh."

Ellen said, "That's right, I remember now. He says there're rocks over there. Swing us with your left oar and then pull out farther. I thought I knew this place."

Once I had turned I kept going. We had seen the house and I felt enough anxiety, however unwarranted, about the crossing back to want to get it over with.

"You know about those rocks?" Ellen said. "There used to

be three frame cottages up above them on the hill and that's the way I had them located. Well—those rocks were where the eighteen high school kids drowned once."

"Shipwreck?" I said brightly.

She began moving in the most oblique ways toward her story. It was perfectly simple in essence, but in her memory it was confused with a lot of recollections of the way the shore-line had looked to her when she had first heard of the disaster, what her father had said to her about it, and how, year after year when she returned to the lake, she had felt when she looked at or passed near that point. For her, clearly, this personal recall was of the same material as the incident itself.

"It was the whole senior class from Rhinebeck," she said finally. "Rhinebeck's a little town about fifty miles from here. There were eighteen in the class. I think it was eight girls and ten boys. They'd come up here and rented a couple of cottages for their senior sneak day. As far as anyone knows they must have gone wading out on those rocks. Then one of them fell into deep water or got panicked and the others tried to help and the consequence was that every one of them got drowned."

I can't say what it was I didn't like about her telling that story. Perhaps part of it was a lack of satisfaction with its realism. As she told it, it didn't seem quite true. "Couldn't any of them swim?" I asked. "Surely one or two of them could have got out."

"I didn't know them personally. Maybe they couldn't swim," she said. "I think I'd seen some of the boys because Rhinebeck had a whiz of a basketball team and they used to come down to the state tournament nearly every year."

"Who saw all this to tell about it if everyone was drowned?" I demanded.

"I don't know," Ellen said doggedly. "That's the way it happened and there were people who knew."

The reason for my resentment of the story began to clear. In her tone I had heard something of her love for the lake, a new revelation of an attitude that seemed incongruous with the person I had felt sure of knowing, a revelation of something she had never wished to share with me, pretending to share everything. And yet, it was too silly to argue straightforwardly over her repetition of a story she once heard.

"Wasn't there a chaperone with them maybe?" I asked.

"I suppose so. Either they'd stayed overnight or were planning to stay overnight, so there must have been a chaperone."

"No chaperone," I said. "That explains it all to me. Whew. These eighteen kids had the greatest orgy Rhinebeck ever produced, so they made a suicide pact and drowned themselves for shame the next day. Kids then weren't as nice and well brought up as they are now."

Our rowboat grounded gently just about this time, and that seemed to me a lucky termination for such a pointless argument. I hopped out briskly and tied up the boat. Ellen was looking back over the three miles of water to where the pink house squatted at the shore, frowning toward it as though it might be the memorial of those drowned kids she was remembering or imagining.

She said, "It was an accident and one of them wouldn't desert the others."

"Be realistic. Maybe some of them tried to get away and the others dragged them down."

"I don't know why you have to have it that way."

"I merely happen to think it could have happened that way."

"I suppose so," she answered somberly.

Later that night we were wakened in our cabin by a rainstorm that beat loudly on the roof and blew in chilly drops at a couple of windows. I closed the windows and lay comfortably, feeling protected against the wide, noisy attack of the rain. I could smell our wet bathing suits in a far corner. The smell of drying wool and of dust enclosed me peacefully enough. I knew Ellen was awake but we did not speak for a long time. I thought she must have fallen asleep again when all at once she said, "There was a pair of twins on the Rhinebeck team. I remember them as plain. They were tall and shy and everybody that saw them play said they were the greatest ever. I guess that must have been the year I had my little red coat with the rabbit muff. I thought how fine it would be if one of the twins noticed me. I was so little then that of course they wouldn't have. They seemed like real grown-ups to me, though they were probably only sixteen or seventeen."

"Were they in that bunch that drowned?"

"I think so."

"I never heard of an orgy involving twins. Must have been quite a gathering."

"Oh, funny," she said. "Go to sleep."

"Are you going to sleep?"

"I will pretty soon. You go ahead."

In the morning, well rested, I went with cane pole and sunglasses to fish from the pier. Arthur was the kind of lake where any dope or child could catch perch by dropping in a baited hook and where good fishermen, given luck and patience, could bring up some pretty fancy pike and lake trout. I only wanted to be idle and perhaps get enough perch for dinner.

The beach's population of adolescent girls was out in force by the time I took my station. I ought to mention that from the time of our arrival Ellen and I had been aware that there was no one else our age renting at this beach. There was one generation ranging up from about ten years older and another one ranging from sixteen down. This latter included an unaccountably large number of daughters fifteen or sixteen, probably spending the last vacation they would ever have in the bosom of their family. These girls were addicted to gum, fluty cries, fancy sunglasses, and to giving sultry glances to every passing male except their respective fathers. Impatiently they lay tanning, and sometimes, rolling over to expose another slope or muscle to the sun, they stared out with fierce virility at our little lake as though it should have been a thousand-mile stretch of sea. It was these teen-age girls who gave our beach its one quality beyond comfort and quiet and made it seem worthy of looking out on something broader than the 1950's and the mediocre tremor of inland waves.

Pretty frequently, in late morning or late afternoon, boys came in speedboats from other beaches to raid our beach for these girls. You'd hear sooner than see the speedboats. They would blast a high note out beyond the pier end and settle to a halt almost within the waves of their own wake while four or five boys in sweatshirts and trunks studied the display of girls. The boat would creep in to be tied up at the pier with flourishes and self-conscious horseplay.

In the morning while I was fishing the boat came from the pink house. I recognized first the boy with the U of Minn. shirt. There were three others, and after tying up they strutted with more than the ordinary raiding party's arrogance among the blankets where the girls—and a few parents and wee ones—were whiling the morning away. While they went up the beach like a party of slavers a sort of hush ran along parallel with them the way it will when a visiting general passes groups of soldiers not yet at attention. It occurred to me that the mothers, fathers, and tots as well as the daughters were holding their breath and waiting for the choice to be made. There was a twitching of little tan thighs and shoulders and, I hope, a clenching of little jaws on the chewing gum.

I missed the actual selection because Ellen had come down from her housework in the cabin "to see what I was catching," and I turned my attention to chatting with her. Presently I heard the speedboat start and looked over her shoulder to see the boys.

When the aristocratic blatting of the motor died, the beach sounds dropped to normal, though they seemed clarified, as though the addition of an intense chemical precipitated out a certain former murkiness. A little kid was yelling, "Daddy, float over to me, over to me." The little boys playing shuffleboard on a floor among the trees resumed their clatter. I tried to communicate to Ellen the total impression this raid for girls had made on me. She snorted and accused me of exaggeration.

"You make it sound like Pluto coming up to steal that girl, whatever her name was," she said.

"That's it," I said. "We won't have summer again until he brings her back."

She scratched my belly with her knuckles. "You big fake. Here you are broiling in the sun and still pretending it's not summer enough for you. Look"—I heard the motor noise grow as she pointed—"they're bringing them back already. It's just an innocent young people's way of getting together here. It's always been done that way, my lad. When we used to come up here there were motorboats too, and the boys bummed from one beach to another in them to get acquainted with the girls."

"I wouldn't let a daughter of mine go out in one of those hell boats. I'd sooner see her dead at my feet."

"It's probably just as well you haven't any daughters."

"All right," I said. "I'd let them go. They could do what they pleased."

"Look, there are your little girls back safe on dry land. Not hurt a bit and they've had fun."

"And the boys line them up for hanky-panky later when it's dark."

Ellen was sitting with her knees folded up to her chin and her arms locked around her knees. Above her knees she gave me a secretive, happy smile that clung a long time on her mouth. "You caught on. The girls will take the steamer over to the amusement pier tonight and the boys will meet them at the dock there and they'll go up for a dance at Roseland. At intermission they'll bum down the Midway and eat cotton candy or something else awful, pick up a kewpie doll, and get kissed a time or two on one of the benches at the dock while they're waiting for the last steamer to bring them home."

"Well, happy memories," I said. "After all these years I get confessions. Who was the man—boy?"

"Mmmm—no one. None in particular. A kid named Charlie Fox one time. Someone—I can't remember his name—that I thought was the smoothest dancer."

"Did he have a speedboat?"

"I don't know. Listen, let's take the steamer over tonight. Will you?"

"It would be fun."

"Lots." She stood up suddenly and prepared to leave. "Catch fish," she said.

The steamer was the grandest relic left at Lake Arthur. I suppose it must have been about sixty feet in length, and, put-putting solemnly around the shoreline as it did five times a day, it appeared to be almost as high as it was long. I'm not sure whether there was a lot of grillwork and gingerbread around the upper decks or if it merely gave that impression. It was completely white, and against the color of the lake it always struck me as being phony and nice—the white and blue were just as starkly innocent as something you'd see on a postcard. For all its height the steamer had an absurdly shallow draught and could pull into water you would not think deep enough to float one of the speedboats. It stopped at any pier where someone hailed it, chuffling and whistling and being a great delight to the children as Ellen said it had been for as long as she could remember.

It was as much fun to ride as to watch. Our trip around to the amusement pier at Arthur was probably the nicest hour of our vacation. Ellen had dressed for the occasion in a fresh and billowy print—one she'd debated bringing, since we'd been dead set on the principle that this trip was to be as uncomplicated as possible—and she seemed to feel how pretty she looked. In the dusk she seemed suddenly shy and withdrawn from me, yet happier to be with me than on any occasion I could remember of the recent past.

Mounting the steamer we leaned into the half-enclosed engine room set slightly below the main deck to see the old machinery hiss and slide like a dinosaur breathing. We read the 1897 in raised letters on the steam cylinder and suddenly looked

at each other as though we'd shared an insight, but also as
though neither of us could say what it was.

We climbed to the top deck to sit alone while the steamer
backed away from our pier, and we remained alone up there
until it had made two more stops. Then a family of five came
up and took benches ahead of us.

I was surprised by how few lights seemed to border the lake
as we went around. Those few appeared weak and almost desperately isolated. It was then, I suppose, that transitional hour
when most of the vacationers were hanging on to the last of the
day's outdoor pleasures before going in to light their cottages
and begin the evening.

Underneath us—it seemed very far down—the lake was a
steady and yielding blackness. Now and then a solid wave
would collide with the bow and split away hissing. I remembered being frightened the day I had rowed Ellen across to see
the pink house and I was ashamed that I had permitted myself
that fear.

Ellen touched me and said, "You know, I'm happy," and I
answered that I was glad of that. For the time of the trip we
seemed equal to the cold neutrality of the lake, balanced, and
owing it neither fear nor gratitude for what it might be.

When we landed it was still not time to go dancing, so we
turned along the Midway, trying with a little too much eagerness to be excited by the music from the merry-go-round, the
smells of popcorn, and the thin crowd. After I'd tried the
shooting gallery and Ellen had thrown hoops at a peg floating
in a water barrel our good judgment suggested that we not
spoil the evening by trying to eat either cotton candy or any of
the other confections available and there was nothing else to
do. Ellen was sure that there were some bars up in the town,
and we left the pier to find them.

The one we picked at random—choosing it with no special
reason—was called the Orchid Room. It was small, which we
could tell from outside, and expensively furnished, which we

discovered with some uneasiness once we had entered. I was afraid the price of drinks would not suit us.

At that time we were the only customers, though there was a green-faced fat man on a raised platform between a piano and a Hammond organ and a middle-aged woman behind the bar. It was fairly dim in the room, but not so dim that we missed being impressed by the white orchids painted on all the walls.

As we sat down the fat man played a run on the Hammond and asked if there was anything we wanted specially to hear. Ellen said "These Foolish Things" would be fine. He shook his head comically and answered, "That one was before my time." Then he began slowly picking it out on the Hammond and presently was playing it confidently.

"How about the piano?" Ellen asked. "I'd rather hear it on the piano."

Obediently he swung half around to face the other instrument. "The old songs are corniest, aren't they?" he said. He played marvelously well. We relaxed to listen while the little place began to fill with customers. Presently those who came in were moist with rain, and Ellen, noticing this, said, "Anyway we can't go to the dance until the rain's over. How about that old 'Running Between the Raindrops,' Zach?"

"Zach"—because by now she had discovered who the piano player was, and in the general fondness she was feeling for anything that echoed from her past she was insistently overusing his nickname. Sixteen years ago Zach Winthrop and his Rhythm Boys had been very popular in this part of the state, she explained to me. She thought it probable that once when she was at Roseland his boys had been playing there, and she meant to ask him in some break between numbers if this might not be so.

But presently when she went to the toilet she found Mrs. Shaw, and Mrs. Shaw kept us busy for the rest of the evening. Mrs. Shaw—who had been Rita Chase before she married and had spent summers in the cottage next to the one occupied by

Ellen's family—struck me as being drunk as a pig when she wobbled to our table with Ellen. However, she went by waves, apparently ready to pass out for a period, then, recovering herself, was remarkably, bitterly, and suspiciously sober, while we went more steadily downward.

"Well, murder, kid," Mrs. Shaw would say to Ellen, "we've certainly got to do something about this. You know I had no idea that you or any of that silly family of yours was in this part of the country any more. I really hadn't thought of you for years and then"—turning to lay her round, moist little hand on the back of mine—"I go in to daintily powder my nose and who says 'Hello, Rita' over the partition to me but silly little Ellen Park."

"This isn't home country any more," Ellen said. "Harvey and I are only—"

"What do you know about that?" Mrs. Shaw marveled. "That is, what do you *know?* Hey, Sally." She was calling to the woman behind the bar and beckoning her over. "Sally, guess what the rain druv in. It's stupid little Ellen Park that used to live next door here at the lake when I was fresh and young." She put her arm around Sally's hips and hugged her with an immoderate shiver. "You kids know who Sally *is,* I'll bet, don't you? Why, you're sitting in her *intime* establishment. Sally, they never heard of Sally Racine."

"Of course we have. Hello, Sally," Ellen said. I rose and shook hands.

"Hi," Sally said. "Everybody having a good time?"

Mrs. Shaw wiggled her finger at me. "Who is Sally?" She tightened her hold on Sally and leaned in my direction. "You don't know, you silly ass. Well, you can just go over there and look." She flung her free hand toward a glassed display panel on the opposite wall. "Go on and learn something."

"Don't pay any attention to her," Sally said, breaking free.

Ellen prompted me nervously, "Miss Racine was a *Scandals* star."

"She was the goddam White Orchid of 1921," Mrs. Shaw

said. "Get over there and look at that picture." I did as I was told and found that the glass covered a two-page spread, in color, from a 1921 magazine. On one page was a picture of Sir Harry Lauder looking rosy-cheeked as a Boy Scout. The other page carried a full-length photo of Miss Sally Racine, the White Orchid. She too looked healthy and plump and, in her weird costume, about eleven feet tall. I stood for some time studying the pictures, trying to assemble an appropriate comment to carry back to the table.

Fortunately Sally had gone—to mix us drinks, as it turned out—and Mrs. Shaw was on another line by then. She was talking about Ellen's grandfather and then about Ellen's brother, who was killed on Saipan. She remembered his building a tree house down the bluff from the cottage and calling it the Park Hotel. She rubbed some tears away. "Then the silly little jerk got himself shot boom, boom in their silly war. Isn't that the way it goes, Elly? Tell me, isn't it?"

She went on, "I remember The Champ—I call my husband The Champ and God knows why—used to play catch or toss a football with him sometimes when he'd come around to pick me up for a date. Thought he was the swellest little guy in the world. He really did, Elly. When he heard about him getting shot he really took on. I can't remember all the things he said."

"What's your husband doing now?" Ellen said. "I remember him very well."

"He's doing all right," Mrs. Shaw said. She yelled for Sally. "Give us another round, Sally, and God bless us every one."

I protested against any more drinks, not very vigorously, I suppose. At any rate they paid no attention to me.

"What's become of that insane grandfather of yours that had the fish farm?" Mrs. Shaw demanded. "He must be dead."

"He wasn't insane," Ellen said laughing. "He was the smartest one of the Parks, anyway. You know there's a bronze plaque for him in the town hall here for what he did in conservation."

Her glance flickered in my direction and she said, "I'll show you sometime if you're interested."

"Why sure," I said.

"He was really a professor, wasn't he?" Mrs. Shaw asked.

"Yeah. He taught at Creighton for just dozens of years before he started the laboratory here. How I loved that old man, Rita. You remember the way he and Grandma were with each other? It was always 'my love this' and 'my love that' with them." She coughed suddenly with laughter. "You know that old Hupmobile he drove for so long. He'd get it out to drive into town here, then the two of them would be standing by it and Grandma would say, 'Darling, hadn't you better, if you want to, change your shoes before we go?' 'Well, honey,' he'd say and balk like a ten-year-old and sulk till she made him go neat up. They were so great. And I remember . . .'"

I felt chilly and cheated and again commenced to argue that if Ellen and I were going to the dance at all we would have to leave soon or risk missing the last boat back to our beach. My argument wasn't solid. Then there was still plenty of time, of course. I became further irritated that the two of them could so easily refute me. "It wasn't entirely my idea to come to the dance," I pointed out.

"Relax, then," Ellen said. "We'll finish this drink and by then you may be in a better mood for the dance."

Mrs. Shaw said grimly, "You're not going anywhere while we're having fun. If the boat's gone I'll drive you home. Where you staying, Elly?"

"Gorsky's Beach," I answered. "It's a long way around by road. We won't trouble you."

"Drink up and be quiet." She pinched the skin on the back of my hand with her red, dirty nails. "What are you doing around at Gorsky's? It's no fun clear over there."

"We can afford Gorsky's," I said. "We can't afford to have fun." In my agitation I had gulped my drink and was waving at Sally to bring us another one. I still didn't mean to get drunk that evening, but in some irrational way that felt like a revenge for the mesh of weakness and accident that had involved us with Mrs. Shaw I wanted to get just a little higher. There seemed to be something waiting to be said that would solve her—I remember thinking in those terms.

Ellen said, "We have fun in our own way, Rita. We enjoy quiet things. I read a lot and Harvey fishes. We row in the afternoons."

"Huh," Mrs. Shaw said, "that sounds dull as hell. What do you read? You mean he *fishes?*" She crawled half across the table to peer at me.

"He watches the little girls, too," Ellen said.

"Like your papa did."

"I don't either," I said. "I'm interested in people, that's all."

The two of them laughed absurdly, as though they shared a vision of my motives so secret that I could never hope to guess it.

"He is interested in people," Ellen said. "He's gathering material for a play. He wrote a play once, right after the war, about his experiences on a Liberty ship."

Mrs. Shaw studied me with a momentarily sober and perfectly hard amusement. "I know that one. *Mr. Roberts.*"

"You've got it," I said.

"Well, he almost sold it," Ellen said. "I told him he should go on and revise it or write another one. That's been four or five years now."

"I didn't almost sell it."

"Anyway the people he showed it to thought it was very good. Of course *Mr. Roberts* had come out by then," Ellen said. I could see she was wobbling in her chair. I thought perhaps I ought to grab her arm and drag her out of the place— even give her a swift punch and carry her out, the way you do in rescuing someone from drowning. I let the moment of good intention pass and dissolve in sulkiness and resentment.

That my quiet Ellen was drunk is true, and that fact explains exactly nothing. Of course the alcohol and our encounter with

Mrs. Shaw were necessary to start her talking, but they merely released something which had a dynamic of its own and was in motion below a level that the alcohol could reach. For a little while longer it was not apparent that Ellen was pouring out a monologue. Mrs. Shaw interrupted with questions or irrelevant attempts to change the subject or turned frankly and drunkenly to start a separate conversation with me, and from time to time I made my own bitter additions.

But as an hour passed and another after that, Ellen kept talking, piling up more and more of the whole story of her life. She kept smiling apologetically and abstractedly, and while she appeared to be watching Mrs. Shaw—she certainly wasn't telling it to me—perhaps she was looking past Mrs. Shaw too. It was, I suppose, like listening to a medium, though here it was Ellen talking through herself.

There was a long part of it which was given over to an account of her life with me. At some point she mentioned the way we'd married in haste in 1943 when I was being drafted into the army and how that hectic time had been brightened by the promise of the life we'd begin when I got back. Then there was the leave spent together in San Francisco. She'd just heard of her brother's death, but we'd been able then to keep a good heart because the war's end was at least visible. Then came the year in the trailer while I was finishing college, the year I'd written my play and we'd talked of how great it would be to get out with jobs of our own and our own apartment. Then how I'd got involved with Larris in promoting his cartoon books and how we'd traveled all over the country on that scheme. How we'd saved money on different occasions to buy a house, had spent the money and started saving all over again.

She said at one point that now we were really about to begin some of the living that we'd postponed so long, but this observation was given in passing. There was no end. Her story kept lapping back over itself as though a while before she had passed over too quickly—or missed—a key episode on which all the rest could hang.

I don't know what the ugliest point of her monologue was, whether it was her pathetic eagerness to get it all spilled out, or Mrs. Shaw's drunken, uneven attention, or my own resentment of what the story implied. The details of the story were ordinary enough, yet among the three of us we managed to qualify them so it seemed to be an endless record of failure. The same incidents might have sounded different somewhere else. Yet I hated Ellen because I thought she was using an unbearably strict measure to account for our lives, a measure strict as the edge of a knife—and then offering this knife edge to Mrs. Shaw to use against us in whatever capricious, drunken way she wanted. I thought it was as though Ellen refused to judge Mrs. Shaw in some desperation to submit us two to judgment.

I remembered, without wanting to go there any more, the dance at Roseland. I imagined that the dumb-looking boy from the pink house would be there with one of the girls he had found that morning on our beach. Later they might go to the steamboat dock and kiss while they waited for the last boat. I was afraid that even if we went now, I couldn't stand seeing those kids.

I shook the table and said, "Let's get out of here." To Mrs. Shaw, "Come on, you said you'd drive us."

"Lay off, Harvey. We're having a good time, aren't we? There'll be a lot more interesting people in here before it closes. A lot more interesting than you two, I might add." She put the back of her hand beside her mouth and stage-whispered to me, "What's your wife telling me all this crap for?"

"So we've bored you," I said. "Okay. Take us home."

"Christ, if you've gotta go, call a taxi. What's the matter, can't you even afford a taxi?"

As a matter of fact and among other things, I was not sure that I could. After the first round I had paid for everything, including a pack of cigarettes for Mrs. Shaw. The drinks hadn't been cheap, and here I was left with less than two dollars.

"Never mind," Ellen said dreamily. "We'll take a taxi."

I said, "I'm not sure we have taxi fare. Get this old bag in motion. She's your friend, remember?"

"Sally," Mrs. Shaw yelled. "Sally." The music from the organ stopped and everyone was watching us. When Sally arrived Mrs. Shaw said, "What class of people you catering to these days? These two latched onto me and now they want me to drive them home. I'm afraid of them. Tell them to get out and leave me alone."

Sally winked at me to show she was not taking this quite seriously. She beckoned me to come with her to the bar. "Look, Rita's drunk," she said.

I heard Mrs. Shaw wailing, "They get me off on a dark road and God knows what would happen to me."

"You don't want to ride with her anyway," Sally said. "I'll have a taxi here in a jiffy. You have money? Never mind, I'll fix it with the driver and get it from her tomorrow when she's cooled off."

"But she's a friend of my wife's," I said.

Sally, not bothering to try to understand that one, grinned wisely. "Rita's nobody's friend. You and your wife can wait in the entry if you want to."

While Ellen and I waited Mrs. Shaw came out to us. "You know how it is," she said. "If I left here now I'd be all sobered up before I got back, and my whole evening would be shot. Besides, I'm afraid to drive that far by myself. I've only got this silly little Pontiac and I don't like the way it drives. You see how it is, Elly?"

"Sure, honey," Ellen said. "Stay and have a good time."

"Oka-a-ay," Mrs. Shaw said reluctantly, as though we were forcing her to an action she would undertake only because we wanted her to so badly.

"It was nice running into you," Ellen said. She was swaying and looking pale. I could not tell how sober she was.

I said to her, "You might at least get your fat buddy to kick in for cab fare. Or for one round of drinks, just as a sign of affection."

"You bet I will," Mrs. Shaw said uncertainly. "Wait, don't move. I must have left my purse at the table, or I can borrow something from Sally. Don't go away. Wait. Wait now."

Who knows whether she came back with the money? The cab honked in a little while and Ellen and I went to it quickly, agreeing on that without having to speak to each other.

We sat on opposite sides of the seat. It was raining a little again, and the windshield wipers seemed to be cutting even pink slices of the neon lights from the bars bordering the road.

"You had nothing to gain by that last byplay," Ellen said.

"It did me good. Why take all that guff without answering?"

"You couldn't make allowances, could you?" She hiccuped gently. "Rita used to be such a quick, wonderful girl, I thought."

"You wanted to be like her when you grew up. I know."

"Yes, I did. Yes. To hell with you."

"That's a good reason for telling her what a crumby life you've had with me."

"I didn't tell her that. I told her where we'd been and what we'd done, like— Don't quarrel with me any more, just for tonight, please. I'm too tired of it, and I don't know how much longer I can take it."

"So I'm always at you," I said. "I never give you a minute's peace. If you'd just realize sometimes that it hasn't been all roses for me either. Then, while I didn't spend my childhood in this paradise, I have my feelings about it, too. Why am I excluded? Why do you have to talk to a drunken pig like that instead of me?"

"Yes, why?"

"I give up," I said. "I merely thought we were going over to dance at Roseland. Just like old times. Was it my fault we never got there?"

"No. It wasn't your fault. You win the argument."

"At least you admit—"

"You always win your argument."

"Then what—"

She interrupted me by turning abruptly against the side of the cab and crying, knowing that I knew my own answer, knew that she knew, knowing that neither of us could ever hide from the other again the commitment to betrayal that time had forced on us by the subtlest and most kindly-seeming frauds. I knew that it was nothing so easy as a particular or personal sin that she was accusing, and in the dark cab the longer I thought this over in silence the more it began to seem to me that she was weeping really for those children from Rhinebeck who had drowned once in the lake, holding each other's hand in a faithful line and never letting go.

When Old Age Shall
This Generation Waste

"SHE LOOKS like you," David Swift said to his hostess about the eager-eyed blond girl Ed Maroon had brought to her party. Because his mind was lean and limber, as it habitually was on the second drink of an evening's program, he registered this resemblance less as a fact inherently significant than as a fact on which playful and imaginative significance might be built up—as in a child's game a coincidence of sounds or numbers can begin the invention of fabulous lives and relationships. "Like one of the first times I ever saw you. At that party in Mick's room."

"She's Midwestern and exopthalmic," Joy agreed. "In what other way?"

"You both intend to have the world."

"Stop promoting me," Joy said. " 'Grant me an asylum for my affections.' " Absently she surveyed the menagerie of her single oversized room with its clumps of standing, sitting, and reclining figures composed uncertainly in silhouette against the fireplace glow or in the goldfish bowls of light from half a dozen wall and floor lamps. "Sweet narcosis is more my line, David. And she shows a good fifteen years younger than I— look at that skin. What makes you talk so funny, sweet man?"

He smiled fondly and patted her bare shoulder. "I was cuing you in on the origins of my lust after her. So you won't take it as disloyalty if I back her into the kitchen."

"Do," Joy said. "But gently. Ed's been making noises about marrying someone. Maybe this one."

" 'I don't hear no golden bands—' "

" '—settling on them soft dumb hands'? Maybe not," Joy said. "Make what you can of it. I want you to be happy. What a dull party this is going to be. Will it go?" Again she looked hungrily, like a witch tainted with scientific heresy, at the still-civilized behavior of the others in the room. Then with her trademark giggle of a girl catching herself in unbecoming solemnity she added, "You can still hear the piano and it's going for eleven-thirty, waaaaaaaaaaaat?"

"It will go. You've got the quartet here. For fragmentation."

"Oh, those boys."

"If you want to draw blood just keep having them around."

"They're kicks," Joy said. She patted his sleeve and, as though he had reminded her of a mingled duty and temptation, found a path toward the piano where the boys of the quartet were playing. They were a unit here because they ordinarily showed up at parties in the Village together (though they cruised separate bars), because they had once been employed together carrying spears at the Metropolitan, and because each of them found in sympathizers like Joy a diffusing medium that permitted them to be socially together without falling on each other with either lust or jealousy.

Now in their fortress corner of the room one of them hammered softly on a martini pitcher with the mixing rod. Another accompanied him on the piano, picking out with one finger the melodies of old show tunes. The other two leaned in, waiting the moment to sing or make funnies that would draw into the square of their loneliness at least a few stragglers from the dialectic around them.

As Joy came to them they turned to welcome her, David thought, like naked squabs greeting a parent. As so many have for so long, he thought. But what loaves, fishes, or worms has she really delivered?

.   .   .

For the next hour he moved from one group to another around the room with selective detachment. It was understood —by the waspish self-consciousness that had long ago fought the censor in his mind to an armistice—that he was a pilgrim on his way to Ed Maroon's girl, but it was a part of the terms that he must come at her indirectly.

He left a group discussing Indochina with a restatement of his warning, made twenty years ago, that the Communists were pretty Red. "And their children dance," he added, swept by a momentary shock of compulsion to expound on this text, but rejecting that in favor of leaving Job to be enjoyed by them as nonsense. He said to Gail Hunter and her new husband that it appeared to him modern artists took a lot of liberties with nature. That had to be categorized as a vice, he said, and if vicious were horses no one would ride. But they honestly did want to make a point, between themselves, about Motherwell, so he went to a far, secluded alcove off the room to confide in Mimi Hawk that even before he had read Kafka he had suspected people were not what they pretended to be. Mimi's escort, an instructor from Columbia, challenged him to explain this or get off the pot, but he would only leer and say that Kafka was deep. Terribly. Could anyone deny that and still pretend to intellectual responsibility?

Then, sick with himself for having only a mustache and an equivocal reputation as a wit to show how far he had come in thirty-eight years, he turned directly to the search for Ed's girl. He was fairly sure that now or presently she would be drifting unclaimed, since Ed's young and pretty girls were chosen to signify a pre-eminent manliness in him, and he did not really require them to be attentive once he had found his subject and begun to talk.

She was sitting by a tree floor lamp that cast one beam to the right and one to the left, spotting her and Joy equally, and again David was struck by their resemblance. The girl would pass for Joy's daughter, he thought, if it were not for some felt, intenser likeness which persuaded one that something stricter than a blood kinship had meant them to appear the same. The two of them sat in awning-striped chairs and naturally neither of them paid any attention to the other. From twin postures of relaxation their blue eyes watched the party with the same rapacity and the same need; and, at this moment, from each leaped a terse, female derision against the men who were foolish enough, for the moment, to ignore them.

But much as they look alike, David thought, the girl doesn't look the way Joy *did* fifteen years ago, and out of loyalty to Joy he could have added that she had looked then like the believer she was. She had believed in politics (a synonym for Roosevelt), in art (that is, Gustin, Kollwitz, and Picasso), and in the supremacy of personal relationships (or her first husband and himself, the important single weekend when she had dragooned him into going to Boston with her "to find out what we really have").

Now she seemed to believe in very little except parties like this one, in the expense of spirit, alimony, and the trivial surpluses of her pay from a trade magazine to gather this team whose very presence in one apartment was like a ceremony to the failures of promises. Once he had suggested to her that she ought to paste a partyful of her friends onto a collage and call it "The Death of FDR," and when she had simply nodded, said, "Fair enough," he was sure she knew as well as he how deeply she had chosen to commit herself to the impossibilities her collections represented.

There had been a time when he wished this could be a sufficient reason for breaking with her once and for all, for never coming back to one of her parties. What prevented him was knowing too well what she had wanted and what she had looked like, with her eyes so bugged out and blue, at twenty.

When he "hummmmmed" beside the girl's chair, both she and Joy glanced at him. Then Joy looked back toward the quartet's noise, more desperately strident now.

"We need refills, don't we?" David asked.

The girl swished the contents of her glass experimentally. "I really oughtn't. I really ought to get Ed out of here." She studied his face and found him sympathetic enough to permit her adding confidentially, "I guess you know how hard it is to break him off when he's enjoying himself. I could get *loaded* if he decides to stay too long."

Together then they looked across at Ed, saw him lean into his conversation, hitching at his belt as though he could earn money that way. In full voice he was saying, "She hadn't even read it well enough to know what I was talking about and she sits there telling me to search my soul. And I said, 'I've searched my soul and now I know what I want to be. I want to be an earnest, liberal, voted-for-Stevenson career woman who don't know from owl turds about fiction, so I can get a keen editorial job and throw the blocks to writers.' She gave me the whole Smith class then, two hundred and sixty-nine of them, all being superior to a hick that writes what she for Christ sake is supposed to have sense enough to know how to buy, pulp fiction. Anyway, she was bigger than me and when I saw that old left shoulder go up over her chin, I died. Man, I died."

"A cube of ice would *freshen* it," she said. "O.K. I'll join you."

In the white illumination of the kitchen that reflected in the same wavelengths from cupboards, stove, sink, walls and refrigerator, some of the girl's prettiness came apart like ribbons peeled down from a gift. He saw the excess of fat that blurred the definition of her nose and brows. Both her eyebrow penciling and lipstick looked more humorous than witching, and seeing this he felt something like gratitude to her. He promptly kissed her, but the contact was lukewarm as a daily thanksgiving.

Gently she disengaged herself and said earnestly, "After all, David, I came with Ed."

"Yes, Pat."

"Well, that's the way it is."

"Are you going to leave with him? What if he never finishes kicking down the—uh—enemies of light?"

Pat shrugged her full, childish shoulders. "Don't say that. I like him to find someone he can discuss with. I worry that I'm not much companionship since my mind doesn't work like his. You know. On abstract things."

"Like money? Like contracts? Isn't that what he was so impassioned about?"

"He talks about everything. I'm willing to wait through what I can't understand."

"It's love?"

Pat seemed embarrassed by the naive word and lowered her head. With a fiery, short fingernail she bobbed the new ice cubes in her glass. "I respect him a great deal, his being a writer and all, and what he stands for, his sense of fair play."

The ribbons are really unloosed now, David thought, and this little package wrapped a touching decency. Once more he could not help a comparison of her with Joy, who used to say the same about Ed, but who now was apt to call him "the fellow-traveling bore" or a hack, clutching him probably for that reason in her circle of misfired painters, musicians and heterosexuals.

"Don't you think his writing is fine?" the girl said. "The way it shows all this sympathy with the underdog?"

Her blue eyes demanded that he help her keep faith, and tolerantly enough he said, "Yes."

Then some trick sprung by the earlier identification of her with Joy, which he had considered purely intellectual and therefore under control, surprised him into saying, "Yes, but . . ." And the fat was in the fire. The very strictness of her honesty (which had been Joy's once) demanded that he try to be honest too.

"It's fine, but it's only a pocketbook formula. Ed himself

would tell you that about his books. I can't believe that every thug and hoodlum rapist who gets caught is Christ crucified. Neither does Ed believe it."

"What do you mean?"

"I like Ed. Ed's my friend." His hands flew wide in a testimony of good will, a gesture that might convey the absolution which he was giving Ed's *soul*. It annoyed him that he had made such a gesture and he tucked his empty hand under the arm with which he held his drink. "Ed's one of my oldest friends, so I can say this. Taking him seriously isn't the same thing as taking him seriously as a writer. You know—hasn't he told you—why only two of the novels he's written since the war got published?"

"People are reactionary," Pat said. "They don't like his message."

"It's not exactly that, dear."

"What is it, exactly?" He saw that she was disturbed, perhaps angry now by what she must think of as a disloyal attack on Ed. And he wanted to tell her, I'm only explaining this because you're more precious than Ed, younger, better than any of us, so you have to know where we all went wrong.

"It's *exactly*"—a humorously self-deprecatory inflection there which she would have to take as a promissory note, the token of inner humility—"it's exactly that Ed is half a step off each time he sets his foot inside a publisher's door. Look, dear, he's written eight novels since the war. I've read them all. Like I say, I'm his friend."

"What do you do?" Pat said suspiciously.

"Photographer's agent. I scoot around town and find jobs for them with magazines. But this is no qualification here or there. I'm Ed's *friend*. We were in college together. I always wanted him to do the great good thing. More and longer than you."

This last appeal seemed to work on her. She nodded humbly and licked her lips. "I guess probably. Go on."

"He wrote one about Hiroshima. It came a little bit late, just before the Korean war. He wrote one about the Commie general in Paris but left out the part where he behaves sadistically with the boys in *La Reine Blanche*. One about a veteran on the trail of killers but couldn't think of anything for him to do for kicks except shoot naked blondes with his forty-five. He wrote one about a homosexual who wanted to get well. Another about a cripple who masturbated on the pad of his crutch, but everyone told him it was too dirty to print. Then he did a summary of the life of King Saul for the Bible Sex trade, but he couldn't patiently dig a gimmick on it because he can't stand to read the Bible. All that work and . . ."

She had suspended listening some way back to corner a thought, holding it in a passionate suspension, waiting for him to be through so she could lave him with its overwhelming sweetness.

She said enthusiastically, "All right. He doesn't think all his characters are Jesus, but don't you yourself think there's a lot that needs saying for people who never had a chance?"

"Lots."

"Yes." She glowed with her triumph, forgiving him, it appeared, for anything he might have said, since clearly he too was pure at heart in spite of all his talk. "That's why I love Eddie's position. I know I may be talking like a schoolgirl, but that's not the awfulest thing in the world, is it?"

"By no means," he said, believing. He drank on that, feeling both purged and, now, forgiven.

A flush of heat had spread upward from her throat like a further and this time conscious sacrifice of prettiness for a higher cause. She shook her close-cropped head. "Besides his books, Ed and I have discussed things enough so I know how he feels about life. He's helped me *so much* with my own thinking." Earnestness half-choked her voice. Prettily she coughed and smiled at this fault. She said waifishly, "You may know him better than I. But I know he *means right*. I guess you can put some more stuff in my drink. Then we'd better go back. Ed doesn't like me to wander off."

·   ·   ·

He lost track of her for a while then, except by some inward contact with the sustenance of that healthy error she had offered him as an antidote for the rest of the party. To be as wrong as she was, as innocent of complications, was tonic, he thought, and justified a faith in the eternal renewal, which in turn justified him in taking more drinks than he had meant to allow himself.

He heard the tall Welshman to whom Ed was talking cry out, "Let them call me before a committee, and believe me, fellow, I'd stand up to them. I can't understand you chaps. Is it your country or isn't it? Isn't it, after all?" He knew Ed's answer down to its last polished evasion, and he felt with quick wonder that the polish didn't matter. Those who don't know what it's about will save it, he thought.

They come on, he thought, the innocent and ruthless young, gathering us up with them as they sweep over our mistakes and cowardice with each other. The image of Pat (and the others, this shouting Welshman with the twist of ears hardly emerging from his curls, all the others) sweeping on in an undamaged tide, unspoiled, moved him almost to tears. He almost wept then for the young man who, somewhere, might be for him the fresh counterpart that Pat was for Joy. David Swift without the holes in his head or life.

" 'You think I'll weep,' " he said to Gail Hunter, apropos of nothing but his own thoughts and the fast metabolism of alcohol. " 'No, I'll not weep. This heart shall crack into a hundred thousand flaws or e'er I'll weep.' "

"Why weep?" she said to this nonsense. "Look."

She was pointing to the quartet, on the floor now, more or less under the piano, which a while before they had been on top of. One of them, kneeling by the piano's side, was pantomiming two people kissing goodnight. He had wrapped his long arms around his back and was fingering his spine while his three friends tinkled and screamed with laughter, shilling for a more attentive audience.

Pat tucked her skirts primly and sat on the floor with them. Her round face shone willingness to be delighted, and David, watching, envied and blessed her once more.

It was much later, a little past two, while he was climbing the stairs back to Joy's apartment, that he encountered Pat again. At this hour he was content that the party's peak was over. He saw the rest of the night diminish away like a drooping plateau down which he could roll comfortably and effortlessly as a rubber ball. Already some of the guests were gone. He had walked down as far as the corner with Gail Hunter and Matthew. They had said a few things indicating that this might be the last of Joy's parties they would come to. Not that they were revolted or indignant—no, it was hard to describe, but there didn't seem to be any *use* in her parties. They didn't *mean* anything. Matthew had seemed like a good fellow. Maybe old Gail knew what she was doing this time, after three grueling and patently doomed efforts to stay married. He hoped so. She deserved a replacement on the scene, too. She'd done her stint.

Above the first landing of the stair, Pat bore down on him like a furious stranger. The brindle light of the hall reshaped again the personality she wore in his eyes, and seeing her in such expressive motion he thought, not displeased at all, she's told Ed Maroon off. She's leaving the sunken ship, too. A young fate on her way. Then he realized that she was going without her coat.

Clearly she was angry, and though she stopped to speak to him, her pause had some quality of illusion, the camera's arrest of a body in flight, a static lie without influence on the real forces that shaped trajectories in the physical world.

"Where on earth?" he questioned.

"It's *those fellows.*" It was almost comic how precisely her emphasis identified the quartet.

"Don't let them grind you down."

"I'm mad. They really got my Irish up. Let me go. I'm going to wait at the front door for Meredith Stark. We'll see about this."

"Stark?"

"You know. The movie star."

Suddenly alerted to the grotesqueness of what she was saying, feeling an initial compassion, David put his hand on the duckling plumpness of her shoulder. He turned her toward the stair light to examine her, believing that she was out of her mind from drinking.

"I've just spoken to Mr. Stark," she said. "When I explained the situation to him he agreed to come over." She was very close to crying, but except for the peculiarity of what she was saying, she did not seem to be drunk.

"Do you know Stark? Mr. Stark?" David asked cautiously.

"Of course I don't, but I think he has the same rights as anyone else. As you or me."

"Sure. But who—"

"Those *fellows*. One of them is even his agent, but when they began to say those ugly things about him I saw red. Honestly red. That's a dirty thing when he's not here to defend himself."

"Said—"

"Said he wasn't *normal.*" The last word came as from a dutiful child who is reporting a forbidden term strictly in the line of duty but who feels nonetheless the imminence of punishment.

"Oh." The reason and the method of her duping became clearer than why or how she had impressed herself enough on the quartet to make them choose her as a victim. As he began to shape a soothing explanation for her, though, a sound like the breaking of phonograph records, glasses, and the toppling of table lamps came down the stairs from Joy's apartment to remind him that Joy set up her parties to cause such improbable chances for involvement.

"You shouldn't mind what the lads say," he told her. "You don't care what they think. Besides, Stark is a public personality, and don't you think everyone in such a position *will* be smeared, now and then? It can't hurt him because he'll never know."

"He *knows* already," she said in a martyr's whisper, pulling herself free, without a show of anger toward David, but with the air of one who has heard the whisper of treason. "I told him what they were accusing him of. Naturally he resented it. Can't you see? I merely want him to be able to come into that room up there and defend himself like *people*. I don't know anything about him being a public personality. I think he's got a right to state his case."

David sighed. "Well, dear. You believe all this? Well, if he's coming over—and of course he wouldn't—he can ring. You don't have to wait for him at the street door."

"He's going to get his break," she stormed. "He's going to be *heard* if I have to smack them all down to do it."

David persisted. "I doubt that you really talked to Mr. Stark. None of these boys is his agent. They're hooked up with a theater crowd, but what probably happened is that they called one of their pals for you and he pretended to be Stark. Isn't that likely? Did you dial yourself?"

"You're very persuasive," she said in bitterness. "Telling me all that stuff about Ed and now about Mr. Stark. So were *those fellows,* and I gave him my word I'd meet him at the door."

With a quick lunge she was past him, fatal and certain and unamused as she went to keep her word. She gave no sign of hearing when he called after her, "Don't wander off."

But she must have been drunk, he said to himself, even before his concern made him report the incident to Ed. She wouldn't have taken those four clowns seriously if she hadn't been.

Ed confirmed it. "Certainly. There're two things about Pat. She drinks like Hemingway and she can't hold it. God, she's not quite so bird-brained as to think Stark would come across the street to answer a charge like *that.* I hope." Joy approached, led by the amused roar of his voice, and he flung his arms around her. "Joy, this will tickle you. My chickadee has come through with the best comedy of the evening. Hear this." When he had sketched in the story he was gasping and the tears coursed down his leathery face as he said, "Imagine, only imagine, what Stark would say if he did come. She'd ask him, 'Mr. Stark, are you normal?' and he'd answer like Mistress Quickly, 'No one ever accused me of *that.*' God, I wish it could really happen."

"You don't know anything about Stark except gossip," David said, amazed that he could feel reasonably pure anger as he spoke, could feel himself share Pat's pure anger.

"Whaaaaaaat?" Joy said, delighted to see him exposed like that.

"We don't really know that Booth shot Lincoln," Ed said loudly. He reached under his jacket to scratch his back defiantly. "Tell me, Davey, did Booth shoot Lincoln? No, I'll tell you. It was theatrical jealousy that fingered Booth. Gossip."

"Aren't you ever wrong about anything?" David asked, and through the pounding of pulse in his ears he heard Joy's admonishing and surprised voice—"David"—and he knew he was being in their eyes foolishly, childishly emotional. Very well. He accepted their judgment with pleasure. Their very contempt intoxicated him enough to swell on in righteous indignation. "Are we always to be so sure that there's a dirty story about everyone? Oh yes. Oh yes, dear ones, we're always sure, and the reason for it gets pretty hideously plain finally, doesn't it? We can't afford to believe there's anyone better than we or anyone who might, for his talent or even for his luck, deserve more than we've got in the way of recognition."

"Big. You're being big," Ed said. *"We.* The generous soul includes himself with us, Joy."

"Quit it," Joy said. "Come watch the boys."

But David couldn't stop. A wide anger and a sense that he had been too long their creditor drove him on. "What have you got to be so snotty about that girl you brought tonight, Ed? And you are being. You are. If she has a decent impulse you've got to snicker and feel superior. Why, Eddie? Feel a little insecure about the prospect of bedding with her? Think you might not be up to it? So you've got to beat her down before you get her there, is that it?"

"Not before," Ed said. "She has nothing to complain about there." His face was flushed, but he was staring fixedly into his glass so that there was something fortlike and rigid about his exterior, as if thought and even anger had retired to a redoubt deep inside.

"Why fight?" Joy said. "Come on, Davey, let's go read *The Magic Mountain*. I do love you both, and if you either hit each other something might break. David!"

He turned to her, mastering the pitch of his voice but feeling the clear blade of his anger swing as if in open air above him. "Now you've heard the gentlemanly boast," he said to her. "A while ago I happened to—in a disinterested way—happened to ask Miss Pat if she loved our friend. She blushed over the word *love*. For which in return she gets from him public statements on the course of their sexual congresses." Again he turned toward Ed to ask, "How was she, Ed? You won't mind telling us. How was she?"

He had put Ed to flight. At least, with a grimace like a tic in his right cheek, Ed turned, shrugged and walked to the kitchen.

"Proved your point?" Joy said acidly.

He took a deep breath before he could meet her eyes. He felt a kind of nausea, as he had once when he had been in a real fist fight—very long ago, certainly close to twenty-five years ago—and had won, by the sheer expense of adrenalin. He was not a person who could easily or often take the loneliness of victory.

"I was offensive," he said. "I offended you, but that doesn't mean I was wrong, Joy."

"Oh, you'll weigh it out on your little silver scales," she said. "With charity and justice for all."

"Don't *you* fight me, Joy."

"I never fight. I read *The Magic Mountain*." Their eyes met in a long contention. She dared him to name her and her party as he had named Ed—and at the same time pled with him not to.

Then one of the quartet screamed ticklishly. His friends were lifting him by arms and legs. Half of Joy's remaining guests followed them as they carried him to the bathroom. When they pulled the shower curtain closed in front of him and turned on the hot-water tap, one of his friends explained to Joy in the polite tones of a grade school boy justifying a game to some stuffy aunt, "He was awfully drunk. He had begun to say things that he'd be ashamed of and he'd've thrown up in a little bit. He *always* does, y'know." Smiling, he wrinkled his nose to underline the cuteness of this circumstance.

Through the shower curtain the errant one thrust his head. His eyes under his plastered-down hair were pink and certain of their woe. "I loved her," he squealed.

"Who, Kevin?" the spokesman said.

"I was only teasing her about Stark."

"He means that deevine little girl," the spokesman explained.

"She was the only girl I ever loved except my mother," the boy said and everyone who heard him tittered uneasily. "I wanted to marry her and settle down."

"Don't be *boring*," the spokesman warned him, like a ventriloquist pretending anger at his puppet. "He always talks like that," he explained at large. "And it's so basic it's *boring*."

But the boy with his head through the curtain had twisted his face into a real wad of agony, and all at once he bellowed gutturally, hopelessly, with such genuine horror of himself and the world that it seemed to David only cruelty to him even to listen.

"Now, Kevin," the quartet spokesman said, "you were unnecessarily rude to your friend on the subject of Stark, besides getting Maurice to impersonate him, and no one is surprised that she left you. No one."

Another of them tried to put a drink in Kevin's dripping hand, but the glass slipped through his bony fingers and smashed inside the tub. "I want that girl," he howled. "Want her to know I love her even if—"

"Don't say it," his friend warned him. "Do you want me to be ill?"

The boy clambered out onto the bath mat and began toweling off his face and his clothing.

"Revolting, isn't it?" Joy asked David with a thousand-times distilled and qualified enthusiasm. Her blue eyes twinkled with the self-punishing smile of Circe grieving.

He nodded with an honest agreement that she could hardly have guessed, as though he knew some final, stubborn suitor in his heart had said goodbye to her, as though the impulse which had made him quarrel, for the first time openly, with Ed had gone on now to its natural consequences. Sadly he knew it didn't matter any more that Joy had her reasons for being and for staying where she was.

Free now, he would go down to find Pat by the door or on the nearby Village streets. He would find her chilly and lonely now, he thought—probably at last convinced that she had been tricked by her own generosity of spirit, but maybe too proud to come back and be laughed at until she had lost that generosity in the vortex of denial that Joy presided over.

He would take her arm and they would walk away from it like two Chaplins—the old Charlie, that is. Maybe they would go no further tonight than to some coffee shop where they could sit and talk while he explained his claim and right to be with her rather than with *them*. And the explanation, now structuring itself like a law in his mind, would be the bridge on which the two of them, recognizing a mutual need, could cross. *When we came out of exile, we were as those who have dreamed,* he would say to her. Nothing could matter less than her failure to spot the source of the quotation.

He would explain how he had felt after the quarrel with Ed —not that he would quote Ed's painful remarks to her, of course—and quickly divert this explanation to the episode it reminded him of. I had a fist fight once, he would say. Only one in my whole life; for better and for worse I've not been the physical type; rather an egghead—and that was before you were born. I was fighting for a girl at a dance—she was one of my eighth-grade classmates who had danced all evening with one of her cousins I despised—and afterward on the stairs down from the American Legion hall I hit him with the heel of my hand and called him "a rotter" and told him "to keep a civil tongue in his head" when he answered in the lovely and wholesome vulgate that I was a bastard. Then I beat him up and ran twenty blocks home through the moonlight, thinking I could do anything, since I'd won my fight, I could go everywhere. I think I've got that confidence back now. Some interior season has changed. I can do anything. Can't I? Can't I?

But when he had sneaked Pat's coat from the hanger, folding it inside his own so no one would suspect what he intended, he found it hard to assemble the right words for saying good-bye to Joy—since it would be dishonest not to hint at the finality of his going.

"Don't go yet, lamb," she said when he approached her with the coats on his arm. "Tomorrow's Saturday, you know. Well then, you have to." She leaned against him tiredly when she kissed him, and he understood that she had counted on his staying to the end of the party. It was in the later hours that she needed him to help sort out the living souvenirs, so to speak, of the smashed bric-a-brac left around her then—he the knowledgeable audience for her loyalties and the one who remembered as well as she the true Eden, those days when all their painter friends were on the Project, those train trips down to Washington where the war was, Sally's play, Mick's affair with a two-star general, the major called Snow White, and Ed's first book.

She needed him to watch with her, in the New Testament sense, while she played out her caricature of the Passion.

Well, he was tempted to stay with her, even then. But while he fingered her shoulders fondly he heard Ed, again in his argument with the Welshman, pleading the Fifth Amendment for his being at such a party among alcoholics and perverts, for his lack of reputation, and for the quality of his prose. Mimi Hawk was necking on the sofa with the instructor. The one of the quartet who cared had turned on TV for the Late Late Show. The wet one sat huddled in one of Joy's dressing gowns, explaining in an awed voice that he was a clown because his male parent was a brute.

"It's been a big evening," David said, dragging the coats between himself and Joy and turning. "Spiritually enriching."

Pat was not inside the street door as he had expected, and when he did not see her he was momentarily chilled by the idea that she had gone without him.

The street door was still open in his hand and he was peering timorously, molelike, out of the shelter of the building when he saw her a few feet to the right of the steps. With her, soldiers.

So afterward he had this to bear on his conscience: That if he had merely had the physical courage to let the door slam behind him so the spring lock could snap fast, no one would have been hurt except perhaps himself.

He held the door open, though, because his first glimpse of her among the soldiers set his heart pounding and choked his breath. He thought of jumping back inside until he could understand what she was doing with this uniformed crowd, two of whom were holding her in their arms as if to keep her warm that way. He wondered if he would have to save her from them and instinctively rebelled. He looked beyond them for a policeman but saw only empty streets. It was as if the soldiers had been sent here, as a unit, on purpose; but of course it was Pat who had stopped them or attracted them to this door.

"Hiya," Pat called to him in a not unfriendly voice.

He heard one of the soldiers ask her, "Is that one of them?"

She shook her head. "Not exactly. David," she called, "I've found these boys that are all of them from the anti-aircraft or anti-something."

"Aircraft," one of them announced in angry pride. He drove his fist into his palm and bounced on his toes.

Pat shook the soldiers' arms from around her and stepped toward him. The soldiers followed her in a crowding phalanx, not noisy, just attentive and ready.

"They're ready to help," Pat said. "When Mr. Stark comes they're going with me to make sure he gets a chance to defend himself."

"No," David said hopelessly. He slid back a little farther into the open door, thinking that Pat was having her joke too, but that she had gone too strangely far with it. "You know Stark isn't coming," he said. "Don't you know that yet, Pat?"

"I don't care," Pat said.

"Then how could he defend himself if—"

"We all like him," Pat said.

"Of course you do," David said. "I like him too, but that isn't the point, since he's not coming."

Pat climbed half of the four steps. The soldiers didn't follow her, though two of those in the lead put their feet on the lowest step. "Do you want me to go up there and listen to *those fellows* rub him in the dirt?"

"We'd better go back up," David said, clearing his throat. "Ed's worried about you and you'll get cold down here without your coat." We can straighten it out later, he thought. When the soldiers are gone. He wondered whether the soldiers might be drunk, but that did not seem to make much difference.

"Ed . . ." Her lips curled in an unmistakable, knowing grimace of distaste. "I don't care what Ed worries about. I'll go back, though, if you want me to."

There was a kind of querulous muttering among the soldiers, but they still made no move. Pat climbed another step, her eyes square on David's. He lifted the arm with which he held the door to let her pass under it.

The first blow came from her shoulder hurled against his ribs as she thrust him aside. The next several blows were light, merely the passing stiffarms of the leading soldiers as they swarmed in toward where Pat was screeching for them. David glimpsed her mouth open in a red zero and heard her shrill instructions melt into a high, quavering, vindictive scream before one of the raiding soldiers paused long enough to knock him down.

From the sidewalk he watched the running tide of them go in and begin to climb toward a door that would not be locked against them. For some reason he tried to count them as they went, but he could only be sure that there were enough of them to get a hearing for Mr. Stark.

The Goldfish

PROBABLY IT was the light of the intensely summery afternoon which exhausted me initially, for, after a shower and a
shave, I had felt very fit when I left my hotel room in the Loop.
Sometimes I develop headaches or dizziness on days as stun-
ningly blue and luminous as this one was, even when I am
strolling on the campus or in the countryside close to home. I
am sure that there is some unusual type of photophobia—a recognized disease—which inclines me to these symptoms, but
neither doctors not optometrists have been quite able to pin the
condition down for me, though they admit that it must have
an organic basis.

It could hardly have been any anxiety about seeing Linda
that was playing hob with the way I felt. I had not the
slightest reason to doubt that she would be glad to see me. I
knew from recent letters that she was happy and well. Perhaps
I was responding, in some delay of reaction, to the outdated
fears I had once had for her and had fought down too brutally
for my own good. Perhaps— But I was truly bothered by that
sunlight coming in among the increasingly rotted buildings
that lined the street, and I had been hanging for thirty blocks
on a porcelain strap that was positively mucilaginous with a de-
posit of sweat before I gave in and asked one of the Negro boys
beside me for his seat. Without any questions, with a perfectly
natural politeness, he rose and nodded for me to sit down.
Before I could make it, a fat white woman had slopped herself
into it. Well. The eyes of the Negro boy met mine; he lifted his
shoulders in an amusing way and thrust out his lower lip
in an expression that spoke volumes. I smiled back to show I

understood perfectly what he meant, clenched my teeth and hung on. It was only a few more blocks to my stop then, and I made it all right—covered with chilly sweat, though.

It occurred to me that perhaps I shouldn't rush on to Linda's feeling as shaky as I did. Wouldn't it have been silly to knock at her door for our first encounter in more than two years and then practically collapse into her apartment calling for water or smelling salts? Worse than silly in the circumstances; it would have been a downright disaster. That's why I permitted myself to go into the bar on the corner, where I quickly had a shot of whiskey.

Of course, it was a Negro bar and not at all well kept, but I must say that I felt more at home there *at once* than I had on the streetcar among members of my so-called race. If they'd like to know, their blue eyes had made me distinctly nervous, or perhaps defiant is a better word. I'd felt if any of them wanted to question my leaving the car in this colored neighborhood I might have said quite rude things to them.

Leaving the bar, I passed two incredible blocks. It would be good to have photographs of such places to show my rather easygoing liberal friends at the college, who admit, of course, the plight of the Negro, but who do not seem to be able to keep the image of actual conditions before their eyes. If they could have seen this neighborhood . . . well, it looked certainly as if these blocks had been bombed from the air.

Right in Linda's front yard, as you might call it, there were tottering brick walls and open foundations and basements. There was untouched grass growing over and through the ruins, with paths cutting it that could have been made by either animals or neglected children. At the entrance to one path I saw a discarded diaper and a candy-bar wrapper, meaning nothing perhaps, but shocking to find under your feet.

Happily, the apartment building where Linda actually lived was a sturdy old place. It looked bourgeois and homely at the far side of the ruins and grass, and if it hadn't, I might still have lacked the nerve to go in.

It was like coming to shore to find her card and doorbell button in a row of others beneath polished mail boxes. The instant I rang I heard a door open above me. Probably she'd been waiting nervously since I called her from my hotel.

Her face, in my first glimpse, appeared both whiter and more mature than I had expected. Worn a little, yes, but finer.

"Hello, friend, come up," she said and gave me the precise, square smile which I remembered from the time she first walked into my class one September day four years previously, and I wanted to bless her for appearing so—thank her, that is.

A great deal had happened in these four years. That is, a great deal had happened to Linda. To me, nothing at all. Nothing. There's the ultimate grief of being a teacher. One sees his students come in from a past which lies behind them straight as a string, watches them change and grow for a time, then go straight away into their lives while their teachers must slip back year by year to begin the process which comes to seem—and I shouldn't say this—like a misconceived attempt to go somewhere oneself. Sometimes one feels like calling out to a departing student, "For heaven's sake, take me with you. Help." Perhaps I was not meant to be a teacher, and made a foolish choice of profession somewhere a long way back. At any rate if it were not for my wife's example and steadying influence, I've no doubt I would have bolted before now—my wife's health has always been uncertain, just as her courage and cheerfulness have always been completely certain. Maybe I've remained a teacher because that's one way I could pay the doctor bills. I am not—at least no longer—suited to earning a living outside teaching. It could be put that way.

Perhaps with Linda more than with any of my other students, I had felt a real compensation for being caged in my profession. It was as though I *had* gone with her in some way, I had been so close in sympathy with all her struggles.

She left college after her sophomore year to marry, and you

can readily imagine the fireworks it caused in a staid school like ours when the word went around that she had married a Negro. "Not Linda Harris!" they said. Just that way, "Not Linda Harris!"—as though they knew anything about her beyond the superficial facts that she was a beautiful girl and a more than usually popular one. The idiots had known nothing at all of her inner self, and hearing them rant and take on as they did always gave me a tiny thrill of satisfaction—of satisfactory complicity perhaps, because it was I alone of anyone at the college who knew her well enough to understand what she had done and appreciate the nobility of it. I just could have said plenty to them on the subject of their bigotry, but it contented me to keep quiet and exult with the notion that Linda Harris had shaken them up in a way they weren't likely ever to forget—and that I perhaps had been the catalytic agent, so to speak, which had precipitated from her the essentials of character that permitted her to leap over the false boundaries of race in fidelity to her true feelings.

I was Linda's adviser as well as the instructor of her freshman composition class. I remember—like touchstones representing all our association at the college—two conferences with her which seem to justify me in feeling as I did about my influence on her. Once she'd gleaned some academic prize or other and while I was congratulating her on her intellectual growth she suddenly broke in with that sudden and startling frankness of hers, "Why is it, though, Mr. Mansfield, that the more I think I'm learning, the more I feel like breaking and running for it?" Well, that was a devastating question to come from a girl who seemed to have everything in the world to give her confidence and assurance of the future. I didn't bat an eye. I understood what she was trying to get at, and starting with the concept of *delaissement,* I tried to explain that this was perhaps the condition of mortals who attain a certain degree of self-consciousness. I insisted—what I've always clung to for myself —that courage alone was an adequate response to what everyone must finally discover himself to be. I gave her something to read then which could explain this better and more poetically than I could hope to.

The other occasion of importance commenced with her bringing me a paper which she had handed in to her political science professor—a Mr. Wiley and an old goose if I ever saw one. Her subject was intermarriage, and she'd made some comments which evidently had upset him. Perhaps he was afraid someone might think she'd got such courageous ideas from *him!* Well, not in a million years, but then one should never underestimate the timidity of a teacher at such a college as ours, which might be considered way down the academic ladder, but where some people cling to their jobs like living death. Linda was really hurt by some of the catty little reactionary comments he'd penciled in the margins, and she was so innocent of pedantic cowardice that she couldn't see what had motivated them.

I explained the vicious mechanism to her, straining to do it in such a way that her still-fresh confidence wouldn't be replaced by cynicism, of course. I can congratulate myself on a good job of expression that time. It hit and we ended our conference—it probably lasted a good two hours—laughing hilariously and eagerly like a couple of kids in the pantry. That was one of the most rewarding moments of my life. We achieved a moment of shared insight, I have felt, that nothing could ever take away from us. Altogether good. It was a spring evening, the first day of that season when I'd been able to open my office window, and I remember glancing out with surprise when we were through talking to discover that it was almost dark outside. There was a dead, mellow calm in the air. The campus lights were coming on. With all this it seemed to me that Linda and I—a little like Swift and Stella, a little—had escaped from what people think—and they're right—is inevitably a characteristic of colleges, into a knowledge that was half sympathy, half rational comprehension, and altogether lively, a living thing. We stopped even laughing and sat there awhile without needing to laugh or talk. I sometimes thought that just then in some unplaceable moment before I grabbed my briefcase to go home I gave Linda some supplement of assurance that enabled her to go courageously to what she did later. And by being just what she was, a student willing to receive the best I had to give and carry it out into life, she gave me something that has made my own problems endurable.

While the substantial look of the apartment building where Linda lived had quieted my anxieties about her, my minimum of complacency was quickly enough stripped away by the quality of the apartment itself.

The rooms were large but grossly misproportioned; very narrow, as though they might be only half of what they were originally built for, divided quite ruthlessly after the design was finished. There was layer over layer of poverty, like layers of wallpaper, and I tried in vain to find on top of this something that Linda might have brought to it that would have redeemed the whole thing.

She used to paint very nicely when she was in college. Perhaps I had set myself to expect that her talent for colors could have touched up anything—with drapes, or paintings, or something.

What actually caught my eye, though, was a pile of laundry in the seat of an old green sofa. From it the arm of a man's shirt hung into a puddle of sunlight coming from a window up behind me. There was an odor of cookery and staleness that I had not noticed in the hallway. I must report the truth that, finding Linda in the midst of this, still looking and seeming as beautiful as ever, I could almost hear myself saying, as the college people had, "Not Linda Harris."

She was from the first instant flexible, lively, and full of chatter. "Ralph's not home yet," she explained. "He won't be for a while, but you've got to stay till he comes. He wants to meet you so much. I've told him you were God." She was mocking me with a freedom and friendliness which was new, and which I found quite attractive. I had thought of her as being, perhaps, a trifle oversolemn except on rare occasions.

"He's going to school now," she said. "He's a talented guy. You know, he is, honestly. I'm glad he's getting his chance. You know you got here a little faster than I expected." I took this to be a carefully shaded apology for the condition of the apartment, but if it was an apology it was in no sense a lowering of her banners.

"Don't you think we have a cozy place here?" she asked. "It's pretty ratty, huh? We think we have something lined up on the South Side, come fall. It's a better neighborhood."

"I'm glad of that," I said. "This is spacious." She had led me by this time through the first room into their parlor, which was not quite so bad as the other, though furnished like it with heavy and worn-out pieces representing the taste of Sears-Roebuck customers of the twenties. There was even a huge, very old-fashioned aquarium—a square glass box sitting in its own wrought-iron frame—which I took to be one of those inescapable monstrosities dear to the hearts of landlords. Really an atrocity, besides obstructing any rational distribution of the rest of the furniture.

"You're right," she said. "It's eighty feet long, stem to stern, and that's all one ought to claim for it. Don't be falsely hearty, huh?"

"I hope not," I said.

"Not you, Wilson." She shook her long hair in a suddenly vigorous gesture, as a small girl might to rid herself of an annoyance. "I get heartiness in gobs from the family," she said. "That's the new phase. They've long since stopped threatening or praying, or weeping or fasting maybe. I'm not sure it's an improvement. I'm not sure. At least it's easier on my nerves."

I held her hand a minute. "It's been a long war, hasn't it?"

"You don't know," she said. "Yes, you do, don't you? I wrote you so damn much about it all you must have felt that you were right here in the middle of it. Poor old Wilson. I pictured you sometimes as being all soppy with Papa's tears and—I don't know—squeezed bloody with Mother's embracing me. I tell you it was just the funniest thing I've ever seen in my life. That woman embraces like a python. They'd come in our place over on Harmony—that was even rattier than this—and be polite to Ralph for about ten minutes and then he'd leave. So they'd start talking annulment and pretty soon Pop would have used up his arguments and would pound his knees. Mother would be more ladylike than you can imagine except that every three minutes she'd be up hugging me. Ooooh. But I wrote you all that."

"Not quite."

"Not about Mother's hugging. It didn't seem as funny then as it does now."

"But they're finally reconciled to your marriage."

"They're hearty. Can you imagine another phase after that? I don't know. I wait and marvel. It's kind of funny the way they run their heartiness. They *ignore* me practically. Everything's Ralph. 'Isn't it wonderful Ralph's putting on weight? Isn't he looking well? Wasn't that a witty thing he said the other day?' And he kind of likes it. Why don't they just stay away?"

"Now, now." I felt very cautious about commenting at such a delicate point. I tried to make my expression count for the things I couldn't risk in words, and I think it did, for she replied, "I know, Wilson. I know, I know. The trouble is they can never do anything right together. Pop would be all right by himself, I know he would. He's kind of like you, Wilson, in a lot of ways, really. That woman always manages to cross things up. What a talent."

"At least the big battle's over, and you've won."

"There's a fact," she said. "Oh, look at us—right off the bat gabbing so fast I haven't even asked you to sit down. Sit down? And you do drink, don't you? We'll have one and get down to serious gabble. I'll only be a second. Relax, and think of dozens of things to tell me about school. I'm tired of talking about

Ralph and me. Or you can sit peaceably and watch the gold-fish."

I wasn't quite sure whether to laugh at that remark, and she gave me no clue. I looked at the big old aquarium with a faint smile that could be interpreted as she wished.

"The fish are Ralph's," she explained. "I'm not a great friend of fish. I have been meaning to do a watercolor of them, though —been going to for about a year—the way they move like flags in a jungle. See, they're just blocks of color against those green plants. Be right with you, sir."

So I sat staring at the aquarium and seeing the gold banners Linda had set in motion for me—the brave banners of her vision and courage, if you like, or her youth. Those had never gone down, I understood, and it seemed to me very clear that I had not come on this visit to bring encouragement to her, but to get it for myself, however I might have thought of things previously.

I thought those gold blocks of color were the banners of an exiled queen and, paradoxically, of a girl who could only be-come a queen by accepting her exile. Actual tears came to my eyes just then, and I caught myself whispering, "I'm so proud of you, Linda. You've won." Well, that's just the sort of thing I might have wished to whisper to a daughter if I had been a person destined to have one. And she had said I was something like her father. Maybe—I toyed with the idea, turning it to the light—her words meant more than she knew. I allowed myself to think that in the world beyond appearances I was her father. Why should it not be so? With my soul I took her for my wished-for own.

In that sentimental relaxation I also recalled that she had been calling me Wilson. This was new, and a symbol, I thought, of the fashion in which our relationship had grown closer since we had last seen each other. While she was in school we had always been Miss Harris and Mr. Mansfield to each other, and though I had signed the many letters which I sent her during her hardest trials "Wilson," her replies had always come back to "Mr. Mansfield." I had wondered why, but had attributed it to a delicacy of feeling in her. Perhaps Linda had felt that my wife would not have understood the familiarity, though I am sure she would have, if I had felt justified in burdening her with the really shattering problems of which Linda wrote. My wife suffered a great deal during the war with the general sufferings of humanity. I did not believe that was entirely necessary and perhaps have more and more sheltered her from news or knowledge of suffering.

Sitting there, letting so much flow through my mind, undammed, I realized how tired I had been for a long time. From far at the other end of the apartment came the sound of Linda's movements in the kitchen and the sound of water gushing into the sink. I *let* myself realize how tired I was, for in this moment it seemed to me that finally I could afford to. It's all right, I thought, *she's* all right. I can testify that I'd had some grim visions of what might have happened to Linda—the crime rate is high in the submarginal districts to which she had been forced—and I could let these go now, forever. The worn and tasteless parlor seemed more like home than home was. Linda might have found me asleep if she'd taken two more minutes with the drinks.

Too soon I heard the agitated tinkle of ice in glasses and turned to see that Linda had been stopped at the parlor door by an enormous black cat, which was entangling her steps and forcing her to pay it attention. She kicked it lovingly and tried to step around. "This is my old Lucifer," she explained. "Let go, you dumb old goof. Ignorant wretch."

In spite of her gentle kicks the cat wouldn't let her pass. Its claws were in her stockings, and with slick, strong movements it clutched around her ankle with a foreleg. I never have liked animals much. It has always annoyed me terribly to see them occupy the attention of people as though they had a valid claim to our precious time. So the note of affection in Linda's voice as she spoke to the cat came to me as a minor annoyance—it was almost as though I were annoyed with her—but I caught myself up with the reflection that the kind of isolation to which society has subjected Linda might well force anyone to turn some of his affection away from the human species. I have no difficulty understanding why Swift found horses more virtuous.

"Here," Linda said, "take the drinks a minute, Wilson, please." As I did so she picked up the cat, lifted it over her head with both hands as I have sometimes seen people lift babies, then lowered it to her shoulder, and rocked it a moment before she tossed it to the couch beside me. "Sleep, you old mutt," she said softly. "He's Lucifer because he's the proudest of the angels. What arrogance, but I love him. He's convinced Ralph and I belong to him. On top of that we've discovered that he eats Ralph's goldfish. I don't know what we're going to do about him. Anyhow, I'm afraid to plot against him."

"You could throw him out of heaven," I said. "That neat solution once occurred to the Supreme Intelligence." She was momentarily more concerned with watching the cat settle than with my joke, then she wanted all the news.

Was Charley Watson still teaching painting at the college? She'd read that a picture of his had taken some prize in a show at the Art Institute and had meant to get downtown to see it. Did I know that Joan Wiley had married a forest ranger and that they were living in Wyoming? Imagine Joan on a horse. Kevin Rice was living in town and had called her once. He was an interviewer for some company that surveyed public opinion. She told me about her own employment—occasionally as a salesgirl, now and then as a model for one of the big stores, right now she was making out bills for the gas company. I kept nodding approvingly and hating more the drudgery that confined her.

Her best friend at school, a girl named Evelyn Wright, had passed through town not so long before on her way to Baltimore with her husband, her new husband. "Evelyn came to see me *alone*," Linda said. "So that's fine, if she wanted to; why not? But we never really got beyond that point. She kept sneaking in apologies for not having brought her husband. Isn't it funny? You know it was through Evelyn that I met Ralph in the first place, and she wouldn't stay long enough to see him. I guess that comes under the heading of ho hum, doesn't it?—or 'Should a wife be jealous of her husband's past?'"

Hastily I inquired if Evelyn was still painting.

"Oh, sure. She brought along a portfolio of little things to show me. She's good, you know. She was at Cranbrook last summer and they're going to Mexico this winter. Her husband has work there and she can study." I want to make it perfectly clear that there was no tone of envy in Linda's voice as she spoke of the good fortune of others. Of the two of us, it was I who was having the difficult going.

Trying my best, I said, "That's fine and I certainly hope she goes far, but I hope you do too, you know. I hope you're still finding time for your work—your painting—in spite of all your work."

"No. I mean I do a little. Not much," she said. "Ralph's been doing quite a little."

"I didn't know he was a painter too."

"He isn't. That's his watercolor over there against the baseboard, poor thing."

"It's quite good."

"It's not. Painting makes him happy, though. It's another thing he's taken away from me, and that's why he likes it." She set her jaw stubbornly and almost seemed to dare me to argue with that interpretation.

I couldn't have argued. I was too much bound by loyalty to her for that. I thought round and round to find an oblique way of reply, some way that might turn away the unhappy implications she had spoken without striking at them.

I said after a while, "Let's agree that I can't guess what all your troubles have been. Perhaps I was dull enough to think they all came from the outside and the things people put in your way. Forgive me, but let me tell you something. Perhaps

you don't know how much it did for me—really did for me—
to get your letters and see the courage you displayed all the
way along. There have been times when I don't think I could
have gone on if it hadn't been for your example. What you
proved for me was that love was possible, by you and Ralph
finding your way through. So you've given something crucial
to at least one poor mortal. That's bigger, isn't it, than . . ."

And all the while I was talking I felt that things were twisting farther from what I wanted them to be. All our sympathy
for each other seemed to be blunted. It was almost as though
there were an active, evil presence in the room twisting what
I meant and what I hope she meant.

"Why did you have to make that speech?" she asked.

I sat stiff and looked at her until she went on, her voice a
kind of hiss, "Wilson, were you in love with me that spring
you encouraged me to marry Ralph, and didn't have the nerve
to say so? Was that what it was all about? Because I was in love
with you. I know because my psychiatrist told me. I *was,* I
mean, and it was pretty silly both ways, wasn't it?"

It's hard for me to recollect what we said next afterward.
I've honestly made an effort to piece it together. However painful it may be for me, I couldn't live with myself if I didn't make
the effort to see things exactly as they are and face them that
way.

I think I convinced Linda that I had never felt anything for
her except the deepest kind of admiration and respect, that
there had never been any question in my mind of loving her
as a man loves a woman. I tried to give her terms to see how
a young, beautiful girl with a passion for what is good and right
and possible in this world of ours can seem to a teacher—a
rather discouraged one—the most valuable creature the world
can produce. Yes, in that way I loved her, of course.

I don't know if my means of expressing myself then were as
good as they might be. I cried a little and that may have dis-

credited some of the things I meant. I might have done better if her husband had not arrived when he did.

He came in all handsome and jovial, carrying a white cardboard carton of the sort that ice cream is packaged in. It was, as a matter of fact, impossible not to notice he'd brought it, because he held it with that kind of ostentation that goes with a slight pretense that something is or should be concealed. After kissing Linda perfunctorily he placed it on an end table beside the couch, chuckling, half-embarrassed.

He removed the cat and placed himself next to me on the sofa, leaned his forearms on his knees so that he addressed me over his shoulder, though with a great deal of affability and respect.

"Why don't you get us all a drink, Linda?" he asked. "I, for one, have a real thirst, and I suspect that Mr. Mansfield wouldn't be averse to having a refill, would you, sir? For myself, I've been in the academic mill today and nothing exacerbates my thirst like the application of the old brain."

"Linda told me—"

"Yes, I'm enrolled in Northwestern University this summer," he said. "Law is my field. That is to say, law may be my field. I'm, you might say, exploring my capacities this semester."

I was trying to like him. It's not hard to see that I had a great deal staked on being able to like him. I never expected to have so much staked in such a way. He was, too, in many ways more charming and impressive than I'd dared, in the years just past, to expect. And I hated him.

The worst of the remainder of the afternoon was the line of talk we fell into when that ugly black cat began pestering us again. It ran across in front of Ralph and me while Linda was in the kitchen, then began playing with us, attacking our feet with arrogant stupid leaps. Ralph dragged it by its tail from under the end table. He began to caress it and slap it playfully, mastering it, one might say, by paying it this undue amount of attention. "Are you fond of these beasts, sir?" he asked. "I don't care much for a cat, but my wife has an obsessive attachment for them. I point out to her that this one goes so far as to eat my goldfish"—he gestured toward that horrid, jungly aquarium—"but this only amuses her. That's quite true. I've formed the theory that women are fond of certain animals and men of others and that's all there is to it. Does your wife like cats, sir?"

"I suppose she hasn't much time for pets," I said stiffly. I heard Linda come back into the room with the drinks, but even when she offered me mine I couldn't meet her eyes, feeling, as I did, embarrassed for her. "My wife is not very well."

"That's right," he said patronizingly. "Linda explained that to me, too. But other women, women ordinarily, I've found that most women like cats, and I'm almost tempted to the study of psychology to determine why. Can it be for aesthetic reasons?"

"He *is* beautiful," Linda said from across the room, speaking with a strong voice. "Furthermore, he keeps the rats away. That's necessary in most of the places we've lived."

Ralph chuckled. "You see, sir?" He dropped the cat between us on the sofa and turned his attention dramatically toward Linda. "But he eats my goldfish," he shouted at her. Then he spoke to me in a sycophantic tone. *"They're* beautiful too, wouldn't you say, sir?"

"Well . . ."

With a queer nervous excitement he stretched himself upright, and, as though the dramatically appropriate moment had arrived and been recognized, he took up the cardboard carton and opened it for my inspection. "I thought I'd better pick one up to replace the one he got last night," he said to Linda.

"Sure," she said. "They only cost a quarter."

"You begrudge me that quarter?" Ralph demanded in a hard voice. "You don't want me to have my fish?"

She tried to laugh away the foolish insistence of his challenge, but he was not going to let himself be distracted. It was as if he felt some clear necessity to show me how she could yield. "Aren't you glad I got the fish?"

"If that's what you wanted," she said, reddening and turning her face away.

"Yes?"

"Yes."

Ralph suddenly thrust the carton in front of me so I couldn't avoid looking down at his goldfish hanging in exquisite detachment between the white cardboard walls. As I stared I felt the cat crawl familiarly against my leg. I can't explain what possessed me just then—it was as though I knew what the cat was thinking better than I knew my own thoughts. The cat understood what was in the carton and was moving toward it hungrily. In a kind of premonitory horror I sensed the fishy taste and the crunching of spindly bones.

I laughed sociably. Both Linda and Ralph swung to stare at me and then I *heard* myself. It was the ugliest laugh I had ever heard.

"I'm not feeling at all well," I said. I did not know how much longer I could be responsible for what I said or did. "For pity's sake, help me downstairs and get me a cab. Meow. Ha ha. I'm sorry."

And in My Heart

THEY CAME across like a flood when the traffic light changed, the girls in sweaters with books shelved in their folded arms and the wind fiddling with their hair, the young men in shirtsleeves or field jackets, bareheaded or wearing canvas hats. Toward the time when the campanile bell would ring two o'clock they had loitered out as couples or little groups from restaurants and rooming houses until they jammed the corner opposite the campus with a nearly amorphous concentration of movement. Except for linked arms here and there and a few couples holding hands, the bodies in the crowd did not quite touch. Nevertheless, when the light turned green, they moved as a single mass and carried Orin Corrigan with them over to the diverging campus walks.

A girl in a plaid skirt shouldered into him, looked up with innocent, hard eyes. After she had reasoned that such an old man must be a professor, she said, "Par me." Then she trotted ahead of him as if she counted on pure hurry to bring her up with friends sooner or later.

Corrigan took the same walk as she and watched the distance between them increasing. He saw her fat little hips work comically under the plaid until she was screened from sight by a crossing flow of students. I wasn't really laughing at her, he thought, turning right to avoid the crowd—nor at any of their genitive fashions. He was laughing because to his eye all this had never changed.

Once again the drying elm leaves and the autumnal brassiness of the sky kept a silence for him over the babble of the students surging toward their first classes. Under the changeless

sky their rhythm and tone seemed exactly what it had been
when he first came along this walk in 1921. He was a student
himself then, but had been no more a part of them than he was
now. Then he was, if you please, a cowboy from western Ne-
braska who had never been farther from home than Fort
Riley, where he served a short hitch in the cavalry. He had
come to the university with a new black suit from Denver
wrapped in paper at the bottom of his suitcase, wearing that
same black suit nearly every day through his first three years.
He had worn it on this very sidewalk, his hands hanging raw
and big and awkward from the sleeves like the token burdens
of his separation from the others. He was older than they, even
then, almost thirty when he enrolled as a freshman here. He
was also taller than most and had the habit of walking with his
head thrown back a little—partly from shyness, partly to catch
the air and the overhead sights, and partly because it had
seemed a poetic stance.

His unaltered habit of alertness let him hear and see—no
clearer after all these years of expectancy—the murmured harmony the unknown students made with such a day. The emotional part of his imagination transposed it to an entity
crowded with wings and horns that blew the failing seasonal
magic, the dignity of youth, and the dignity of their faithful
ignorance as it clattered on under such a sky.

Well, well, well—he had caught this much of meaning before,
many times. He had come to the university first because he
caught—like a tall snowman catching snowballs in the face—
many things which beat up his emotions and which he meant
to write out as poetry. And when you came right down to it, he
had stayed too long because he had never quite managed to
find the verbal shapes for what he knew. There had been no
failure of initial vision, he thought soberly, but a failure of language, a failure to convert. The passage of thirty-odd years
had clarified and then accommodated that failure.

Quite a lot of years ago he had published two volumes of
verse—*Ranger Ballads* and *Days West*. Nice things had been

said about the books when they were new. For a little while in the late twenties he had been a figure on the national literary scene. He was one of the "younger poets" compared rather favorably with Sandburg, Masters, and Lindsay. That was fine —worth what it was worth. His wife had been proud of his position, though by the time he had married Gail, his little bit of fame was already fading into the past. To the end of her life Gail believed that he had "contributed something" to American poetry, and he was glad she thought so. But for him the illusion that his published work mattered went with everything else.

It was not in his nature to be bitter about his failure. The effort to write had carried him high enough to see life better than if he had not tried. If there were no words of his own for *all this,* there was, like an armory open to him, poetry to borrow for the expression of his reverence. He might have "gone farther," as some of his colleagues said, if he had not learned here so awfully much of the poetry on the library shelves. He thought what he had learned worth the price of ambition. He had got what he needed most.

For two steps he limped as the shock of remembered words met the shock of his straining senses. "And in my heart how deep, unending ache of love . . ." For every detail of it all, he thought—for these kids, the weather, the disastrous neoclassic buildings of the main campus, the postprandial mellowness of his bowels. Armed with verse he could confront the mystery of the day without a shadow of dread.

A workman on top of Sedley Hall threw down a handful of leaves from a choked rain gutter. They fell separating and flashing yellow from the height of the building. A few struck among the vines on the wall and then tumbled after the others like a shower of notes from stringed instruments. "Beauty is momentary in the mind . . . but in the flesh it is immortal." Stevens' paradox might be a game of wit for some of his younger colleagues. As for himself, he believed it. Leaves fell and his good young wife was dead and their beauty for having been was immortal. What had been was the unchangeable and everlasting.

In truth—through the truth of poetry—what *had been* was enough for a man and left no room for anguish. He had lived close to despair when Gail died two years before. She had so much wanted not to die and she had gone before he had taught her that neither of them quite needed to be what she had always wanted and sometimes imagined them to be. "A little too soon," he had thought in a terrible sacrilegious rebellion against her death.

But finally he knew better. In the very incompleteness of life was its immortality—a tricky and worthless enough immortality without poetry to illuminate it, he supposed. But there *was* poetry, and in it the whole story was told, finished, rounded to completeness. The true aspiration was not to alter or add to it, but to rise through emulation to the point at which it could be grasped. That was all he must slyly teach his students. He must nudge them on to accept gladly the loss of the world.

His beginning class in writing was waiting for him in the room directly above his office. He knew two of the boys from the spring semester of his Chaucer class. Good boys, and he had seen some—well, uh—*promising* verse that each of them had done. The others were all strangers to him. The leavings from Moore Tyburn's class, he supposed. He had not gone to registration this year, but it did not require bitterness for him to believe that most of these—provided they were really serious about their work—would have preferred to leap right into Tyburn's advanced class and probably would be there if Tyburn had accepted them.

The girl sitting next to the door had the library's ancient red copy of *Days West* on the arm of her chair where he could not help seeing it. She bit decisively at her nails as he walked past her to his chair.

"Now then," he said, swinging his chair to face them and

crossing his long legs. "I want to tell you how glad I am to have you with me this semester. I'm a little surprised, though, on a day like this that you would come to class. Perhaps I'm a little disappointed. Independent spirits ought to spend a day like this inviting their souls and confounding academic conformities."

The nail biter giggled and nodded to show that she was going to be fast on the uptake for his humor.

"Bu-ut, since you have accepted the yoke, here we are in what I want to be a very, very informal circle. We're here because we want to learn what we can about writing. Naturally I include myself when I say that. The university says I am your teacher. But you know how universities are. They like to set up chains of command, like the army, while literature is maybe not even a republic but an anarchy . . ."

The boy to his left, the Jewish boy in a field jacket and suntan pants, was watching him cynically through the fingers on which he rested his face. Obviously he was thinking, What a lot of horsehockey. Clearly this boy was one of Tyburn's rejects, doomed to miss—and to resent missing—Tyburn's incisive explications. Noting the boy's disrespect for what he had said, Corrigan liked him at once.

But he went on evenly with his familiar banalities. ". . . only eleven of us altogether, and we want to speak with perfect frankness with each other about our work. We'll take turns reading our work aloud in class. I've been working on some verses that I'd like to expose. And I hope we'll all put aside any feeling that an honest criticism of what we write is, ah, an equivalent of an assault on anyone's chastity."

Again the nail biter giggled helpfully. From under his lids Corrigan glanced at the other three girls. Two of them were smiling with ordinary tolerance. The beautiful girl in the corner sat as though she had not heard—in fact, as though she were not listening to anything he said. Her face was as perfect and lustrous as china, and except for its excellent shapes seemed just as expressionless. Her pale hair was drawn back with a lavender ribbon so that her ears were exposed, and these, Corrigan saw, had an extraordinary translucence. Glass ears and glass eyes, he thought, wondering why she had come to his class. It was part of his belief that beautiful women never wrote much or well, nor wanted to.

". . . I have no lectures for you. Rather than ramble on like this through the period, I'd like to make a game of having each of you write a description of—well, of a tree. That sounds trivial for your talents, but it will serve for a beginning. Write about any tree you've seen or imagined. We don't want to admit that only God can make a tree. Everyone shall put forth his own leaves in this class. With hints from nature, of course." He waved his hands in a coaxing signal for them to get ready, set, and go.

He gave them a quarter of an hour, and when they were finished the papers were passed around the circle of chairs to him. He leafed quickly down through the pile, his eyes alert for something that might set them arguing. The top paper began, "My tree is a friend . . ." Oh, oh. From the nail biter, he guessed. Perhaps when she felt more at ease in the class she would do better.

"Here's something interesting," he said. He extracted the paper and held it up. "Whose prose?"

"Mine." The boy in the field jacket flipped up one finger from his chair arm to identify himself.

"Mr. Forest. Steve Forest," Corrigan read. "I'll read Mr. Forest's description of a tree to the class and the rest of you will be preparing to criticize it as I read. Now," he said, hitching his feet back under his chair, readying himself for the sport.

" 'The tree looked like a broken hand. Every branch had been cut by shrapnel. Some of the branches were ripped off clean, but most of them hung by fibers like tendons sticking through skin. The stripped trunk looked like a patient idiot who had been beaten a long time and doesn't understand why. There were ax marks on the trunk which were still bleeding a clotted sap. The ocean clouds behind it looked like scabs floating in a bucket of mucus.'" As he read the last simile, Corrigan let his voice rise up theatrically. "There!" he said. "There we have something to talk about. What do you think of this bit of writing . . . Miss Emery?" He had picked a name at random from the class roll.

The nail biter answered. "Why—why—*goodness!*" She had expressed herself so adequately that all of them laughed. "It doesn't sound like just a tree, I mean," she said, and the laugh went around again.

"Mr. Kelsey."

"Mmm. I liked it. It's kind of Wastelandish."

"Mr. Jost."

"I think it has its *own kind* of power. I think you *see* this. I think he gets you to sort of *know* what kind of tree it is he means."

"I don't *see* it," Miss Emery said, bold from her previous success. "Is it an elm or a maple? Ha. *What* kind?"

Corrigan saw the blaze of Forest's contempt leap toward the girl and diverted it by saying, "Mr. Forest, you might like to tell us—"

"I think *this girl* simply doesn't want to see it."

"I certainly don't," Miss Emery snapped. "There's nothing objective about it."

"Let's have another opinion," Corrigan said. He swung his glance around the circle and picked out the beautiful girl. He indicated that she was to speak.

"I . . . I . . . I don't feel well," she said. The class roared its delighted approval.

But the girl got up and raced for the door. She was barely past it when Forest jumped up and followed her out. The others watched with various shades of amusement and sympathy.

Corrigan dismissed them all soon afterward, diverting their thought from the little episode as well as he could. He anticipated the problem the girl might have in forcing herself to come back. Like an animal trainer quieting his beasts, he called up the tricks learned from many years of teaching to blur down and unfocus their curiosity. By the time they all left, he felt that he had been successful in his attempt.

But his own curiosity was caught on the spike of a single question—why it had been Forest who had followed her. Forest and the girl had been sitting on opposite sides of the room. He had caught no sign of familiarity between them, and, granting that Forest might be the kind of rambunctious boy who would try to shoot all the quail in the class, still following a girl when she is about to throw up is an unpromising approach. Maybe it was pure compassion or even guilt on Forest's part.

Half amused, he thought of Forest following the girl with remorse and saying to her, "I'm sorry I wrote that tree for you. Look, I'll write you another, with unspoiled green leaves and a little toy wind monkeying around in it . . ." He had liked Forest, and he rather hoped this was the way it might turn out.

As he dawdled in the classroom then, Forest came back. The boy seemed to want to say something, and Corrigan waited. Forest gathered up his books and crossed the room to gather those the girl had left.

"We must grant a certain *power* to your prose," Corrigan said gently. "Is the young lady all right? Or did she vanish? She seems a very ethereal creature. Not quite of this world."

"Of this world, all right," Forest said bitterly. "I told her not to come in this class. But I'll be damned if her being here is going to keep me from writing the way I please. And to hell with all the other bastards, too."

"Why—why—"

Corrigan saw the boy's brown eyes fixed on him with reckless begging. "Why, they all mean well," he assured Forest. "They may be sort of amateur in their standards, but they mean well. They— I take it you know this young lady?"

"My wife," Forest said, his beggarly eyes shifting now as if he could not meet even Corrigan's gentle gaze.

"Wife? I didn't see any Mrs. Forest on the roll," Corrigan said. "But then I miss things."

"Elaine Biddle," Forest said. "The two-day bride. We're not

living together. She only came into this class because she's
damn sure she's going to get at me. If I could've got in—"

Forest stopped with clumsy abruptness, but Corrigan finished the sentence for him. If Forest could have got in Tyburn's class, the wife, parasite, nemesis—what was she, then?—
would have been kept out where she belonged by Tyburn's
standards. Kept out of the realm of art where this boy was
scrabbling for a foothold. But in Corrigan's catchall class, open
to all comers, she was very much a presence to be reckoned
with.

"I'll be glad to hear more about all this," Corrigan said en-
couragingly. "But I don't feel we can exclude her from the rolls
—if that's the problem."

"It isn't that," Forest said. "It isn't that. It's so goddam much
more than that."

"If I can help—"

"You can't help," Forest said. "Only I may drop your class,
too. Nobody can help." Abruptly he turned and stalked out.

But he's taking her books to her, Corrigan noted. He sighed
as he started back to his office. He felt a faint, undefinable dis-
appointment at Forest's outburst. He liked the boy so well that
he wished him beyond self-pity.

Moore Tyburn was doing the talking. It seemed that from
his strategically placed easy chair in the corner of the Frank-
lins' living room he had been talking for a very long time; his
speech had the quality of a monologue that must have had its
true beginning not only hours or days but years before this little gathering of professors and their wives had assembled in
the house of the head of the English department.

He sat under a modish floor lamp, drinking from time to
time from a glass of milk that the wife of Professor Peltus kept
constantly refilled for him. He finished a story about Dylan
Thomas and the old days "at the Horse" with a contemptuous,
final remark about the degeneration of this tavern in the Vil-

lage since Thomas's death. "No one goes there any more," he said.

"We were there just two weeks ago," Mrs. Peltus said, with a half-defiant, half-apologetic snicker. "Just to *see* it. It seemed to be quite full of tourists and phonies."

"Oh?" Tyburn asked her coldly, pondering her qualifications for distinguishing phonies from genuines.

This was Tyburn's first year on the faculty. He had lectured here at the university once during the past winter, had thereafter been considered as a possible colleague.

When it came to hiring him, the executive committee of the department had gone along enthusiastically with Corrigan's recommendation. "We need somebody who's in touch with the new things. A writer from New York, preferably," he had said. Among Tyburn's qualifications was the fact that he had been on the staff of a famous literary review and appeared ready, like some of its other editors, to move up to *Life* or *Time*. He was a real catch for the department. Their formula for accommodating him was that he was hired not so much to supplant as to extend the writing program that Corrigan had run for so long. But they had greeted him with lively expectations and no little awe.

Physically he was a fascinating little figure, with an aggressive, blue-stubbed chin that flashed metallically when he spoke. His slightly protruding eyes never met those of the person to whom he was talking but swung with quick anxiety to that person's face as soon as his gaze was distracted. His wide, curving brow was in constant perspiration this evening.

He repeatedly "denied intellectual responsibility" to this or that writer of national reputation and had several times referred knowingly to Trotsky as "the old man." An air of barely suppressed wrath charged nearly every one of his sentences. And these mannerisms of his speech exerted a hypnotic fascination on the listening faculty wives.

Corrigan sat there almost as rapt as they. For several years he had admired Tyburn's poetry and his critical articles on Joyce, Thomas, and Lowell. He was happy to see the young wizard in action, to note with sleepy irony the adroit corrections he was administering to Mrs. Peltus and the liberal Mrs. Thorne, whom Tyburn quickly exposed as "Stalinoid," denying her intellectual responsibility between two sips of milk.

But before long Corrigan began to sense his error in coming to sit at the young man's feet. (Figuratively at his feet; actually he was clear across the room, in shadow, being as quiet as an old man can who has taken enough good Scotch whiskey to scramble his senses.) In his earlier talks with Tyburn there had been a tacit fraternal ease, the complicity of two practitioners isolated, as Tyburn seemed to see it, among the mere merchants or middlemen of literature constituting the rest of the staff. But as this evening progressed Corrigan began to hear in the passion of Tyburn's monologue a probing scorn that he could only take as personally directed at him, whatever the others made of it.

"Our great curse at the *Review*," Tyburn was saying, "was that absolute legions of contributors failed to realize that Whitman is dead. The old beard is gone. For my money he's back at Paumanok where he started. And yet, though it's past midcentury, there are still these highly emotional sodbusters and sodbustresses who go on trying to extend the Whitman catalogue of American goodies, busters who feel that coming from west of Chicago is, in itself, qualification as a poet. You can't imagine how many man-hours the staff wastes reading poems in praise of Lake Michigan and Abraham Lincoln. It's perfectly true—so what?—that every American hamlet is a Spoon River. Go read the gravestones, feel deeply, send the results to the *Review* with—by all means—return postage included. Maybe it is Edgar Masters they don't know is dead.

"Maybe the new leisure is going to continue the explosion of yokel poets, but it's the duty of responsible local and state officials to head the stampede off, stamp it out wherever it shows its dowdy head. I've seriously weighed the possibility of putting poets on reservations like Indians and prohibiting the reading of Whitman and Masters in the same spirit that fire-water is prohibited our red brethren. The sheer increment of defiled paper coming from the hinterland is enough in itself to delay the building of a literature. And Europe's gaining on us again. We've got to clear away the crud. Obliterate." For a moment he dropped his face into his spread hands as if to weep. Then he shook himself and hissed, "I do blame it on Masters more than poor old Whitman. If the sonofabitch were here I'd hit him in the face. *I'd hit him in the face.*" He struck his knee with his clenched fist. "Once I went to the trouble of finding out where Masters was buried, and I made the pilgrim-age there to spit on his grave. Pork-barrel poetry is killing us."

Mrs. Peltus, her face aglow, poured him another glass of milk. "Masters was one of my favorite poets—*when I was in high school,*" she confided naughtily.

In the center of the room Professor Peltus shuffled his feet and coughed. "That's very interesting. You would agree with James's remark in, I believe, *The Art of the Novel,* in which he says he sees no reason why the acceptance or rejection of a duke shouldn't be more interesting than, say, a lady with a cicatrice or, say, the adventures of Jeeter Lester's daughter. Not of course that James had read Caldwell. In merely using that as an illus—"

"People aren't talking so much about James now," Tyburn said ominously. "But exactly. The smell of horse dung does not automatically make it literature. But what a long time that theory rode in the saddle. Hey. You see I'm using the regionalist lingo myself. Help. I'm drowning."

Belatedly sensing that the stage had been set for a debate between Tyburn and Corrigan, Peltus said, "What do you think of that, Orin? Your interests have always been more or less re-gional. Not that Professor Corrigan as a poet *was* a Regionalist," he said with a castrated chuckle.

"I've read his books," Tyburn said sharply. He was not going to allow quarter.

"Bu-u-ut," Peltus said, oblivious, "he was something of a forerunner of the Regionalism that developed here—in the thirties. Never a part of it, but—"

"I think . . ." Orin Corrigan said slowly, setting his empty glass on the rug and pulling his legs under him—then, in a moment of terror, he did not know what he thought. There was an absence, as if the growing nausea and resentment with which he had been listening to Tyburn had brought him to the edge of a precipice and pushed him over. Recovering with a burst of anger as if adrenalin had been spilled into his bloodstream, he thought, This tormented little bastard has always from grade school up had to assert his superiority by running something else down, and doesn't even know he's doing it. He's got his little yellow teeth in the butt of something marching to power and he doesn't mean to let go. He'll hang on for the ride the way ten years ago he would have held onto Henry James and twenty years ago to Regionalism. And he's got enough teeth to hang on tight. More than enough. If you heard—*heard* what he said about Masters and still think he's a fit person to discuss things with, then nothing I can say or have ever said in the years you've been my students and been on the staff with me will make any difference.

He said, breaking with his thought as the thought had broken angrily with the darkness beyond the precipice of surrender, "Will you pass me—or, no, would you fill my glass, Mrs. Dillon? Scotch and water. Thank you. I think that Regionalism had its weaknesses."

Did they—did any of them—realize how baldly Tyburn's remarks about Masters had been meant as a thrust at him? Evidently not. And in a smeared moment of self-pity he stared a Tyburn and asked, silently, Why? Because he had written and published a few poor poems a long time ago? If they were so bad—and no doubt they were—then they might be allowed to die out gently, as such things always would. But he knew, intuitively and with a fear he could not wholly understand, that Tyburn did not mean to let them die quietly. They would have to be ridiculed and hounded from the minds of men. He did not, just then, hate Tyburn, but with despair he recognized Tyburn as a pattern of things to come. He would be the new power on the English staff here. His sharp tongue and his hate would mold these opinionless men and women—these Peltuses.

Blind among enemies, Orin Corrigan thought as he drank his Scotch and water down swiftly. Then the corrective intelligence in him changed this modestly so he thought, Only, I am the one that wrote *Sweet Grass Bend* and *Crazy Horse Is Dead*—not either *Lycidas* or *Paradise Lost*. That's not my line. I didn't write it, so it's not my line. Great Jesus, men who were not poets (practicing) could claim, in their anguish, the great things Milton said. But once you went in the ring, you had to fight there with your own.

"Now in your class in writing . . ." Tyburn said challengingly, sensing his advantage, meaning to pin the old man to the wall. His voice was exultant, triumphant as a steel rasp hitting pith.

"It hasn't been awfully successful," Corrigan said. "None of my students ever published much." He groped his way to his feet, nodding and smiling and thinking that he might have acquitted himself better if he had not had that last Scotch.

Outside the maudlin, red moon shone on the streets and through the frames of branches. There was an extravagance of longing and of inhuman loneliness in its color.

But don't write about that, Corrigan thought. He felt giddily drunk and tired and ashamed of both these things. Don't write about that moon, or the seventeen miles of grass that lie between Emerald and Dumont or the way young men used to ride it (before that war, before that Strange Thing, Phelps Putnam called it, when the talking rats of Europe came and carried us all off from what we were), singing and passing back and forth a bottle of corn whiskey on a night like this, or how one of those got killed the next day in a Regionalistic manner (by the brother of the girl he fooled. Who said they would marry in a month and a day?) Don't write about such things or some sonofabitch from New York will ridicule you for it sooner or later. Maybe he ought to pass that bit of wisdom on to his writing class.

I could go back and sock the little bastard, he thought, bumping against the wall of a building and recovering himself.

Without knowing how he had come there, he was downtown in the traffic of the little city that lived off the college. He saw the door of a bar which was as purely anonymous to him as any could possibly be. A platonic bar. He went inside and had two more drinks while his suppressed rage against Tyburn swung tormentingly against himself. It was no one else's strength but merely his own weakness that was hard to face. It was hard to endure the change of things where the best that you had known and done became, in the metamorphosis of time, the unmistakable sign of what you had missed. Some devilish spirit of justice impelled him to think that Tyburn must be right. What had been the truth was changed. Then it was but now it wasn't. . . .

Suddenly he realized with shame that he had slid off the seat of the booth and was sitting on the floor without strength to raise himself. The waiter was supporting him so that he would not fall flat.

"You got to watch that forty rod," the waiter said. "Work up on it more easy, Professor."

He knows me and I ought to know him, Corrigan thought. But as far as he could tell he had never seen the waiter before in his life. When the man helped him shakily to his feet, he managed a small laugh and said, "I'd appreciate it if you'd call me a cab."

Looking around now, as he had not when he came into the bar, he saw that two of the young men from his class, Forest and Kelsey, were watching him with a sort of skeptical compassion. He grimaced and waved to them before he waddled out. He did not think they had been laughing at him, but that made very little difference. They had seen. He had lost something to them that he could probably not afford to give up.

At the door of his apartment he thought miserably, If Gail were here the whole smeared evening could still be made all right and its misfortunes be given the quality of an ultimately joyful farce. I'd go reeling in to tell her how beautiful the night is, he thought, and that all the sonsofbitches in the world don't count. But she wasn't there and they did.

For the first two months of the fall semester, the beautiful girl, Elaine Biddle, handed in exactly nothing to Corrigan. He made no formal demands on any of his students for any particular volume of work, preferring to let them go at their own speed, concentrating his critical assistance on the best of what was brought to him. He hoped the encouragement and examination of excellence would do all that could be done to lead the stragglers.

But the Biddle girl—or Mrs. Forest, whichever might be the truer name for her—gave no sign that she ever meant to hand anything in. She came regularly to class and sat always in the same chair. Once she had found her place she sank into a beautiful remoteness which isolated her like a bell glass from the rest. It was not that she was utterly speechless or expressionless —when one of the other students had read aloud his production, a poem or a short story, and Corrigan called on her for comment, she would open her pink lips to deliver a brief cliché of praise. When the rest of the class laughed or grew excited in argument, an extremely faint smile or furrowing of her sleek brow indicated that she heard and was acknowledging from far away the concerns that the others met so frankly.

It was clear by now that Forest—her husband, in a legal sense at least—was a storm center of the class. When Miss Emery read a story of her own about the adventures of two girls on a bus, Forest announced immediately that it was "crap." Whereupon Miss Emery fled the classroom in tears and Forest tried to cover his real consternation over this result by an impassioned attack on all stories that had surprise endings. When

Forest read his own work—he had read two stories thus far—Miss Emery got her own back by saying they were certainly very much like the stories of James Farrell, if *that* was what he had been aiming at. Scabs in a bucket of mucus, *indeed!*

Well, it certainly was what he was aiming at, Forest told her, only he meant to write a better prose than Farrell's. And the whole class—except his wife—slam-banged into an argument about realism, naturalism, and the happiness of most human beings.

She only watched from her china-blue eyes, as though she were looking in at the rest of them through the bars of a cage. She had no opinion to offer.

And finally Corrigan concluded that she was not in the class because she wanted to write—whatever her motive for being there might be. It was largely curiosity that moved him to keep her after class one day when the others had left.

"You haven't handed anything in to me yet, Miss Biddle," he said gently.

A quizzical expression showed on her face, as though he were giving her some odd bit of news. Then she nodded in agreement, but she said nothing.

"Well, when can I expect to see your work?" he prodded.

"You mean," she asked slowly, "that I'm supposed to write something?"

"That's the general purpose of this class," he said. As he watched her, trying to see through the mask of her withdrawal to the real person within, it suddenly occurred to him that maybe there wasn't any. This manner of hers might cover an incredible vacuity, an absolutely interstellar emptiness onto which most observers might project an image of themselves. As on the first day she had come to his class, he was struck by the inexplicable peculiarity of her beautiful head. Now, as then, her hair was held back by a lavender ribbon. She wore a lavender cashmere sweater on which he saw a pearl-rimmed sorority pin. She seemed to shrink inside the sleek, furry black coat that she had thrown over her shoulders.

"All right," she said faintly. "I'll write one." With the faint grimace of one who tries to remember something, she turned and left him.

The next morning he found her story on his desk when he came to his office. It was on ten faultlessly typed pages, the pages themselves conveying some of the quality he had sensed in her person—aloofness, a sort of nonpresence that still left a physical track to dissemble its lack of reality. And the story— the story was wonderfully, or horribly, more of the same. As he began to read it he had no sense of its quality. In terms of language it had none of the awkwardness or straining for effect that he was so familiar with in the attempts of his students.

On the other hand, he had the sense that it might have been written at top speed in this single, perfect draft, with no pauses at all for reflection and no conscious concern except for an awe-inspiring neatness. He was not sure that her story meant anything at all.

"It's not a realistic story," he ventured as an exploratory beginning on the afternoon when he called her in for a conference.

"No," she said. Her pretty head was inclined over the pages laid on his desk top, and it seemed to him that there was an unusual flush to her skin, as if she were afraid.

"But it's interesting," Corrigan said. "It *seems* interesting, though I have to admit I found it opaque. I read about the old woman and the girl and her doll, and I know that the old woman breaks the girl's doll. But I don't know what this all means, what I'm supposed to understand by these events."

He saw the coral-colored tongue touch the girl's lips, and she said in a small, thrilling voice, "My theme is the death of beauty."

The precise little sentence stung something in Corrigan's mind. His first—defensive—reaction was that such precision was comic. He was glad she had not declared herself with such patness in front of the class. He could imagine their nervous intolerant response. But as his mind repeated the silvery tone in which she had spoken he heard in it an unbearable candor—as if, he thought, a sibyl had spoken directly to him. It was at some deep level terrifying to admit what he had heard.

"Yaaaas," he said in his encouraging classroom voice, urging her to go on, to expand her explanation of this theme. But she sat as if she had told him all he needed to know.

He dropped his attention to the baffling pages. As he turned through them he began his own paraphrase, in the hope that his interpretation might unlock the frozen structure of it. "Yaaas, I see. The doll is the symbol of beauty, then. Something that the living little girl holds and loves in her naïve childish belief that because it is beautiful to her it is also eternal—or we might say indestructible. Then when the old woman wantonly takes the doll from her and destroys it, the girl learns that beauty is transitory. That's the main line of the story, isn't it? *Now,* what does this discovery mean to the girl? What does she do with it, for the rest of her life?"

"Nothing."

He laughed at the abruptness of her answer—hearing in his own laughter the bray of insensitivity, but puzzled as to how else he might proceed. "I mean, suppose that in life someone perceives things as this little girl has. Now, as we go on living this perception somehow gets carried into our lives. How would it affect her relations with other people? What's the human consequence of this rather abstract perception? Does this girl go on through life making her protest against the death of beauty? Is that her problem? I don't mean you have to write all this down in the pages of your story. I'd like to help you think around it, to see if we can't bring its meaning more out in the open—"

Now Miss Biddle was shaking her head. "The girl doesn't protest. She's glad the doll is broken. Here . . ." She reached for the manuscript, opened it with precision and put a sharp fingernail on a line near the bottom of the page. "She laughs because the old woman does what she wants in breaking the doll. See?"

"Go on," Corrigan encouraged. He had read the line she indicated. It said the little girl laughed—but there was a total omission of motive for the laugh.

"That's all," Miss Biddle said. "She's glad it's broken." She swayed back from his desk and the manuscript into a ramrod stiffness in her chair. Her exquisitely painted lips were open just enough to show the glitter of her teeth. "If it's broken no one else can have it," she said slowly.

Again it seemed to Corrigan that he heard a sibylline finality and inclusiveness in her interpretation—if that was what it could be called. Beyond any psychological interpretation that might be made of either her story or her comprehension of its meaning there seemed to ring a metaphysical knowledge. It was as if she said that beauty might act on men but had no intention of rewarding them, that it did not intend itself for life, but was a mischief there.

She knew that? Slowly, and with a certain fatigued resignation, he assured himself that she *knew* nothing of the kind. Any attempt to question her in the words at his command would only baffle her, he believed, would break like ocean froth against the stone limits of her vocabulary. And yet it seemed to him that the knowledge was with her, and he felt something of the ancient terror that might impel a man to lay his hands on an immortal and hold on for an answer that he must have.

He brushed the manuscript aside decisively. "Well, it's *interesting* work," he said in ironic bafflement. "Now there's one other matter I've been a little curious about. Sometimes I've wondered *why* you were in my class. I've had a chance to discuss their intents and aspirations with other members of the class, but you and I have never talked much. Now just what—"

Her eyes blazed fiercely. *"He's* been complaining to you about me. He thinks I'm just here to spy on him. But he needs someone to look out for him. He's got to be careful." There was no doubt in Corrigan's mind that she was talking about her husband, but the emotional outburst was thus far as opaque and inscrutable to him as her manuscript had been.

"Now, now," he said, trying to placate her. "No one's complained to me. Maybe if you'd tell me a little more what this is all about, I could—"

"It's none of your business," she said in anguish so unmistakable that he was stung to the heart by it. "It's none of your business." She snatched her manuscript and dashed from the office. She left behind a faint odor of perfume and scented soap. Corrigan heard the sleet rattle on the window of his office. Outside he saw the black trees motionless in the icy downpour, and like a child terrified to learn that others, too, are lonely, he suffered from the ache of mystery she had left.

"She didn't write that, you know," Forest said. "She got scared when you asked her why she hadn't handed in anything and went to the sorority files and found something, copied it, and handed it in." He ended his charge with a low-toned but almost hysterical intensity. Corrigan saw that his hand was trembling.

He had been walking along the street when Forest called to him—from the door of the bar in which he had collapsed that night at the beginning of the fall. There was something very important that he needed to know, Forest said, inviting him into the bar for a drink. And as soon as they sat down he began an impassioned revelation of how his wife had cheated by handing in a story she had not composed herself.

"It was quite an extraordinary piece of work," Corrigan objected. He squinted into the fog of pipe smoke that he was laying between himself and the boy. Since his interview with Miss Biddle he had permitted his imagination to wind around the meaningless—or uninterpretable—elements of her story until they had closed into a coherent structure. Her offering had struck its needling roots into his thought and his thought had nourished it, until by now it had become more a story *about* the sibylline Miss Biddle than a product by her—or by someone else, if he were to credit her husband's information.

He did not want to credit it. The story of the child and doll, the old woman and Miss Biddle, was now, in its growing, his property. "It's an especially unusual piece for her to find in the sorority files. I thought they were more given to storing successful freshman essays than this sort of thing."

"Maybe they clip literary magazines from other colleges," Forest said. "They're resourceful. They'll do anything. I don't know where *they* got it, but I know where she got it, because she told me."

"And you're telling me," Corrigan muttered into the cloud of pipe smoke. With his usual moderation of tone he added, "I'd have preferred to find this out—if I found it out—by myself."

Forest nodded somberly, "So I'm an informer. I don't care. I've got to do things the only way I can. With her it's kill or be killed."

"Oh, now," Corrigan cautioned. "It can't be that desperate."

Forest spread his hands in suffering exasperation. "For me it is. If she'd give me a little time, then it might not be. A few years. I know if I'm going to make anything as a writer I'd better concentrate all I've got on it now. I'm not so strong that I can afford not to." He peered down in dismay at his quivering hand on the table top between them. "I think if I can have as much time as Dostoevsky, and nobody gets in my road, then I'll be as great as Dostoevsky, because I see what he's talking about. You know what I mean."

"Yes."

"But she doesn't want to give me any time. It's *now, now, now* with her. Like her getting in your class and pretending to be a writer. Ha. *That's* why I have to stoop to informing on her."

"Mmmmmm." Corrigan was not, by any means, sure that he understood what he was hearing. Hints of a pattern from Forest's rambling seemed to spread sensibly across his mind, but it was such a pattern as only the imagination can credit, and not the sort which could provide a credibility sufficient for action or even advice. "How did you happen to marry this —this virago?" he asked.

"I hashed at her sorority house last year," Forest said toughly. He took a savage gulping drink and then, while his eyes met Corrigan's with beggarly frankness, the left side of his mouth sagged as if it were being pulled down by a hook. "I fell in love with her, with *them,*" he said, and with a resumption of his tough affectations went on. "That sorority was a heady brew for somebody who comes from PS 214. And the year before I'd been in Korea. No hero stuff. I was a clerk in Pusan. But it *was* Korea. And then you know how the girls smell when they come down for breakfast."

"I expect they must perfume themselves."

"Whether they bathe or not," Forest said, writhing with the memory of his temptation. "Every one of them smells like the big thing asleep upstairs."

"Thing?" Forest had made it sound like a hibernating female mastodon, drowsing in some gilded twilight where all mastodons are gray.

"The girl thing," Forest said impatiently. "The real thing. The most important of all. So you get to telling yourself if you could just get into one of them once it would be the moon. You'd have it. You get desperate enough you'd even marry one of them for it."

"Desperation indeed!" Corrigan said, but he was no more amused than impressed by this passion.

"Well, maybe it wasn't just as crude as that," Forest conceded. "Maybe I even loved her. I don't know any more. I really don't know why I married her or why she married me. But I know that even if it was made in heaven, now—this year— wouldn't be the right time for it. Do you see? And she doesn't want anything any more except to ruin me."

"I doubt that. I really doubt it," Corrigan said. It was his public duty to doubt, and his private, poetic and illicit pleasure to believe that he was listening to the simple truth. On Forest's hints he was visualizing the girl not as an object of love but as

Love herself, an emanation of intolerable perfumes from ta-booed regions that Forest called "upstairs." An implacable spirit whose purposes were no more charitable than those of a dy-namo or a forge.

And in the core of his being he could believe that Forest was the chosen victim of divinity pursuing its own ends, the crass youth who ignored all warnings of normalcy, who might have peeked on Diana herself and was now torn by his own hounds.

Against such belief, of course, his duty as a teacher stood foursquare. At the command of duty he must categorize the Forests as a fairly ordinary young couple agitated by the or-dinary discords of those who marry in college. It was his duty to submit as a listener while they needed one, to let them use his ear as a poultice drawing out the poisonous extravagance a literary temperament would stir up from the commonplace.

"One of her tricks was to be at me every minute," Forest was saying. "Sexually. She may look cold. Before we were married I thought she would be," he confided, only refraining from the probable truth that he had hoped she might be. "But when I got a lousy bronchial condition I didn't feel like doing it, and even then she wouldn't leave me alone. Not that she liked it—"

Corrigan gestured for him to stop such revelations. Of course it was for Forest's own sake that he wanted him to desist. Nev-ertheless, his old nerves had tingled as if in the presence of a sacrilege. Superstitiously he felt that *She* was overhearing them and would be revenged.

"Now, now, now," he said in a cautionary tone. He in-creased the density of the smoke cloud into which they were peering so profanely. "Now we needn't transgress certain se-crets."

"I don't give a damn about proprieties," Forest said. As if he had not already made that plain, and made plain that a blindness to the real nature of his antagonist was part of the means by which She was destroying him. "Christ, I've talked about it to other people—"

"And they all laughed," Corrigan said, laughing gently, feeling a superstitious shudder threaten his control, threaten to crescendo the laugh louder into an obscene hysteria. "She's a very attractive woman, and it's easy to see you wouldn't get much sympathy as long as she's pursuing you. No."

"They all laughed," Forest said. "Nobody else realizes what a bitch she is. Nobody can tell—like in class when I try to say something. She's there hanging on every word I say, so that I always mess it all up and sound *stupid*."

"She delivers you to your enemies," Corrigan mused. And it seemed to him that the other members of the class, who did not think of themselves as Forest's enemies, who in general admired him at least for his stubborn, headlong ferocity and probably for the glow of real promise they saw in his work (he the one they would most probably think of as an artist)—they were indeed the enemies of the biding, still-imperfect self that Forest staked everything on becoming.

"Perhaps because she loves you," Corrigan went on tentatively.

"I don't ask her for that," Forest said bitterly. "That's the last thing I'd ask her for."

"But more likely because you love her," Corrigan said, feeling with a certain relief that the clichés of verbal communication tempered and controlled the very paradoxes they might create. "You don't want her to see anything but the best. Yaaaas. It may be that I understand. I see it might be better if you weren't both in the same class."

"If she was only willing to *wait*," Forest said. As if the arrow flying at the heart could listen to the merely human cry that protests its flight. "See, I want to be generous with her—or anybody. I don't like what I'm doing to her. But before I could ever get quite set to give her something, she'd already asked for it and tried to get it."

"Well now, well now," Corrigan said. "I can't do a miracle for you. Alas. But now I wonder if I can't do something to relieve your situation. Let me try."

• • •

Because he would not and could not—given what he had glimpsed, being transformed thereby into a less than innocent bystander—expel Miss Biddle from his class for cheating, he chose another method of separating her and her husband. He went rather humbly to Moore Tyburn and asked him to take Forest into the advanced class.

"Why not?" Tyburn asked. His hurtling, insatiable appetite for fodder to hurl into the mill of literature had brought him past the point of setting standards for admission into his class. He would welcome new recruits.

"Actually this boy does pretty well," Corrigan said. "Most of his stuff has been fairly autobiographical, but melodramatic, accounts of his war experience in Korea. He hasn't much sense of organization, but if you'll read these things of his I've brought, I think you'll find a certain power."

"I don't need to read them," Tyburn said. "If you found merit in them, that's good enough for me. I'll be glad to get him. Sure, send him to my class. Do you want to handle the red tape of transferring him or shall I?"

Corrigan said, "There's possibly just one thing I ought to tell you, and that is you'll find Forest . . . fragile. No, that's not the word, but he's more advanced in his opinion of himself than his work will show. *He's* out ahead of his obvious limitations. He's the 'artist as a young man,'" he concluded awkwardly.

And admitting the awkwardness of his statement, he could not exactly blame Tyburn for laughing in response, "Oh. *That* bullshit. I've pretty well got my people over that so they look at the *work*. I've convinced them they're all Midwestern bourgeois anyway, who've been laved by the horn of plenty since the war, so there's no bloody use in them going around like the *poets maudits* or sobbing about themselves as if they came out of the *thirties*."

Corrigan waved a big, soft, freckled hand as if to erase an error written on a blackboard. He said, "I don't mean that Forest is full of self-pity. It's hard to state, but he sees himself as—well, as he said to me, as an incomplete Dostoevsky." He put one sausage-sized finger at one end of Tyburn's desk and one at the opposite end and said, *"Here's* what he actually is and *here's* what he *knows* he is."

Tyburn nodded in smiling complicity, closing his eyes. One staff man to another. "I already had one of those," he said. "I beat that bullshit out of him and now he's doing some pretty fair things."

"Well," Corrigan said. "Maybe you can beat it out of Forest. There's another thing. He's having a lot of trouble with his wife and—"

"Who hasn't had?" Tyburn said gaily. "Anguish and agony. We all get it. There'd be nothing to write about if we didn't. Good," he said, like a colonel accepting a junior officer from another colonel. "I'll be glad to get your boy. Look, Corrigan, I was going to call you. You know Randolph Markwell is coming here Tuesday. We're going to have a few drinks with him and eat at the hotel before he goes up to Old Main for his lecture. I wondered if you'd go with me to his train to meet him. And I *also* wondered if you'd introduce him instead of me. Franklin thought I should introduce him, but I have the strong feeling that since we *made* him at the *Review,* it would be fresher all the way around if you or someone else from the outside sort of summed up his work for the audience."

The direct consequence of Corrigan's meddling was that Forest's wife quit his class. She came to him in a quite unexpected burst of passion. Her translucent ears glowed like pink neon from a suffusion of blood. (Was it from the cold, which by then had gripped the campus in a pre-Christmas chill, he wondered when she came into his office? It was not. It was from sheer female rage.)

"I know all about it," she said in a shrill, simple voice. "I know you listened to him and believed everything he said to you about me."

"Now, now," Corrigan said in a fumbling, pipe-stoking

embarrassment. "You surely don't think I'd listen to anything too personal in nature. Or that he would divulge so much of your personal affairs as you seem to think." As he spoke he remembered Forest's telling how she would not leave him alone even when he had a bad cold—and her ice-absolute blue eyes seemed to be reading now the exact content of Forest's confidences to him. "He wanted to get into the advanced class. I felt it justified—oh, for a number of reasons. I have great hopes for your husband, Mrs. Forest."

"Don't you think he told me how he'd tricked you?" she said. "He's a lot more neurotic than you think. He's told me that you fell for a big old sob story he gave you."

Corrigan took the implications of this as calmly as he could. "You'll—both of you will—have to forgive me for not keeping your pace. I've never quite encountered a similar situation before. I wasn't aware that you and he were still in such close communication. Evidently I misjudged."

"Oh, he comes around to tell me when he thinks he's put something over on me," she said. Then in the exhaustion of her anger she said with a grave mellowness which in its commonplaceness might have been that of any girl, "I only try to do what I can to take care of him. I don't want him to hurt himself. He is a strange one. I knew that and Mother and Daddy knew it and everyone at the sorority house knew it. But everyone wanted to help him. If he could just accept anything. If he could just accept for me to be with him. At least I could keep him from killing himself. He's not such a genius as he thinks. But you encourage him."

"Do I?" Corrigan asked. Then, smiling and with half-closed eyes, he said, "I don't know that I do anything at all. You two seem to be using me for purposes I don't understand. I feel like the hall carpet. I sense a great deal of running back and forth over me."

Finally, more in sorrow than in anger, she announced that she would not be coming back to his class. Tacitly they both agreed there would be no point in her continuing now.

.   .   .

The visit of the poet Randolph Markwell went off rather suc-
cessfully. To begin with, his appearance brought the welcome
necessity for Corrigan to read all three volumes of the young
man's poetry, where he found, as he was prepared to do, an
excellence and a power that moved him greatly. One night as he
read late in his study at home, he let Markwell's book fall from
his hands and smilingly remembered the evening at Franklin's
when Tyburn had spoken of going to spit on Master's grave.
Yes, Corrigan thought, what these young fellows of Tyburn's
and Markwell's generation had done justified all the fury they
might feel toward their predecessors. "Drive your plow and
your cart over the bones of the dead," he thought. *They* had
obeyed Blake's injunction in these last twenty-five years, and if
they had ridden over many things that had been precious to
him (even Whitman, he thought, they had to grind into the
earth to get their foothold), here, in this book he had been
reading, was the warranty for their ruthlessness. It *was* better
than the poetry produced by Masters' generation; at least it was
alive now with that keening thrum of work that has matched
its hour, while the verses of Sandburg, Masters, Robinson, Lindsay, Jeffers—even Frost—remained alive in another sense altogether, like memories of joy or honor outlived.

He had been reading Markwell's long poem on Orpheus and
Eurydice, marveling at the rich progression of the structure—
the first section, in which themes, rhythms, allusive names,
hieratic words were strewn down with a profligacy approaching disorder, to be caught up again, expanded, connected with
each other, inflected by their new place in the constellation of
images, brought to an ironic halt, destroyed, and then resur-
rected in a final choral harmony where each held its properly
subordinated place so that what was partly a narrative of the
search through hell for the loved one moved not merely in a
narrative line but on a broad, devastating front. There was
something of Rilke's treatment of the myth in Markwell's poem
—none of the good young ones since Eliot were ashamed of

confiscating what they needed—but there was in the poem as a whole the honk and gibber of an emotion that exceeded the form. The hell where Eurydice was sought was real and no less mythic for being the contemporary scene and culture, Eurydice no less fabulous for being—as the literary gossips were well aware—the poet's first wife, now in an asylum in Massachusetts.

The poem lit up many darknesses, Corrigan thought, half-drowsing in his chair. It was in the glow of the poem, after all, that he had seen the propriety of hatred between a generation and its predecessors, a rigid necessity of rejection that was not without its beauty. And then—perhaps more important, perhaps less—there was a kind of morality in the very structuring of the anguish and separation that were the subject matter of the poem. If it did not, by its argument, justify God's ways to man, it did justify again his belief that art was not helpless before the sweep of time. It was strange how that knowledge satisfied a need primitive as hunger.

Of itself the story of Orpheus and Eurydice was unbearable. Not only the loss of the wife, but the mocking condition of the God—the *Thou shalt not look back* which demanded a faith that uncertain humanity could not bear. But the bargain was otherwise with art added. The loss was irreparable, but the looking back was not a hopeless glance into the void. Out of memory a song could be made, and the celebration of what had been defied the mockery of gods or things. She *was,* the poet said. I *loved.* And loss was not the void.

Why, I've moralized Mr. Markwell's very modern poem, Corrigan thought slyly, and I don't think he'd like it if he caught me pinning a tail like this on it.

But in the comfort of his study and his solitude, he did not care much what Markwell's response might be. The poem was his tonight, and he could dandle it on his knee and spoil it like a sentimental grandfather if he chose.

He looked out through the wide windows to where the street lights were shining on thick snow. He knew well enough that

that denying whiteness was hell, and he knew with a sort of total clarity how sick with love he had been for his wife and others who were lost in it. I can watch them go without howling, he thought, because I can look back and know that if we go, we have been.

Carefully withholding the private reflections that had come from reading Markwell, he shaped his other thoughts of that night into an introduction for Markwell's lecture in the Old Main auditorium. To which Markwell responded, as soon as he rose to speak, by saying, Goodness, he hadn't know there was *all that* in his l'il old poem about Orpheus and Eurydice—a tongue-in-cheek disclaimer which satisfied the entire, diverse audience of librarians, English faculty, graduate English students, writing students, and a scattering of out-of-towners who had driven in through a growing blizzard to get the Markwell word. It produced a yak, and, as a lecturer, Markwell was in business for yaks. His enthusiastic approach to modern poetry was of the golly, gee whiz, lookee how old Eliot juggles so many balls at the same time school. He was not going to be caught *solemn* by any quick throw rifled down the third-base line, he let it be known.

His talk was unflaggingly entertaining, Corrigan thought, and foolish. To which he had no objection at all. It seemed to him that anyone who had written *Orpheus and Eurydice* had every right to masquerade in public as a clown and a trifler. There was no safe audience for a poet to meet face to face. And yet he felt a qualm lest some of those he saw down there in the audience should think the stream of sparkling inanities from Markwell was the business of a poet. Loafing in his chair beside Markwell and screened from the room's attention by Markwell's pyrotechnics, Corrigan could watch the faces of his students lifted in the bright hypnotism of belief that the end of their efforts was to be, somewhere and sometime, as entertaining as Markwell was tonight. Of course, he supposed, it was part of the department's purpose in bringing "name writers" here to the campus to foster the illusion that a writer's career might come approximately to the same kind of success as that available to an actor or an automobile salesman. Given the hostile pressures of the world they would have to find their lives in, it was, perhaps, an illusion they deserved.

He saw Elaine Biddle in one of the front rows. She was watching Markwell's every move with a coldly carnivorous stare as if she meant to find, then and there, the secret of his success and appropriate it. At least so it seemed to Corrigan, sensing her ruthlessness, though he could hardly have said why she might want the secret. Surely not for her own use, unless she meant to make a career out of plagiarizing manners as well as manuscripts.

He was still wondering about her motives for venturing out on such a cold night when he saw her at the reception for Markwell that Tyburn had arranged to follow the lecture. "I'm not asking any of the old goats like Peltus and Franklin," Tyburn had confided to him, marking him sheep with the same opportunistic recklessness that had marked him goat on another occasion. "I plan to lay in a little booze and give the writers on the campus—maybe some of the younger people from the art department—a chance to take down their hair with Mark. He'll like that." For this proposed intimacy, Tyburn had rented a private dining room above one of the town restaurants.

The room was filled, an hour after the lecture, with the happily drinking young sheep from the writing classes and faculty. A bar had been improvised at one side of the room. Opposite it, on a couch that seemed to date from pioneer days, Markwell continued to play his role of Poet as Success. Corrigan made no immediate effort to join the group around him, but paused on its outskirts long enough to hear that the topic was basketball and the university's prospects during the current season. He saw that Elaine Biddle had found a place beside Markwell on the couch and was watching his face with that unwavering intentness that a careless man might mistake for an interest in what he was saying.

At the bar Forest was haranguing Kelsey and Jost. He had not taken off his green GI coat. His face was red and sweating and he was drinking very fast. "No," he was saying as Corrigan came up to them, "no, that's not my point at all. I'm not saying Markwell is no good. I haven't read his stuff, so how could I say that?"

"If you haven't read his work . . ." Jost said, shrugging and laughing.

"I have read *some* of it," Forest insisted. "Not bad. He's got some good lines. What I'm talking about, for Christ's sake, is why he's doing the kind of thing he's doing and how he's got where he is. I mean, what's the good of writing that kind of thing any more? So he does it very well. So he's learned *how* to do it very well and he knows all the tricks, and how to make it sound like it said something on three levels, and so maybe the quince is the emblem of love and happiness to the ancients *and* the symbol of European civilization. What difference does all that make? Who cares? Do you care?"

The rhetoric was addressed to Jost, who, more nimble socially than Forest, ducked it by stepping back to acknowledge Corrigan's arrival, at the same time passing the question to him as if it were a plate of cookies. Noting that Corrigan must have overheard the substance of Forest's question, he asked, laughing, "Do *you* care, Professor Corrigan?"

With Forest watching him from furious eyes (though he was laughing too), Corrigan considered the question with hmms and ahhhs until they had put a drink in his hand. Then he said, "Do I care about the symbols of European civilization? I hope I do."

The young men, Forest included, took his answer as a joke and respectfully ignored its feebleness.

"I don't care about them," Forest said. "I don't feel anything for them at all. They're a lot of junk jewelry as far as I'm concerned. One thing I have read of Markwell's is this long-winded pretentious business about Orpheus and Eurydice. No doubt it's a pretty story, but it's not important to us."

"Important as what?" Corrigan asked.

Forest seemed annoyed by the pedagogic demand for an illustration. "Well, as important as the things Dostoevsky wrote about, for example. Or the things that Lawrence wrote about. You see what I mean." His tone added the impatient postscript "If you seriously want to and aren't just wasting our time."

Corrigan said, "A colleague of mine consistently finds Shakespeare superior to all modern poets. Maybe that's not all there is to be said, though."

"I mean there isn't any point in second-rate work," Forest said. "Anything that there's something of it better than just clutters up—"

"'Something of it better than . . .'?" Jost giggled. But Forest was above any mere sniping at his syntax. He was plainly in the grip of his vision, which happened, as it had with more than a few from the literary pantheon, to be a vision in which he did not distinguish between himself and greatness, between the plant that does not grow on mortal soil and the imperious need for recognition he felt within himself. At this point he plunged on to another incoherent fragment from his reflections. "You read about Van Gogh at the time he and some of the others, Impressionists, had a show of their paintings, and you can see Van Gogh standing in front of his, waiting for people to come and look at it. How embarrassing he'd be to everyone else who'd kind of stand back and say, 'My little daub doesn't amount to anything,' when Van Gogh knew his did and no one else could see it." It was shockingly clear—to Corrigan at least—that Forest was talking about himself, that he saw himself here, among this crowd of dilettantes and poseurs, as the lonely and furious Van Gogh.

And would it not be, Corrigan wondered, an impertinence to ask, Where is your work? Van Gogh, Rimbaud, Joyce, or any other of the furious egoists must indeed have seemed as intolerably vain as Forest now, but couldn't Forest realize that

everyone else looked at that vanity through the justifying frame
of hallowed works, while only he presumed to look at it na-
kedly and share it with no visible sign of justification? To feel
oneself not only an artist but a great artist was a recklessness
that approached insanity—and he could believe that was exactly what Forest felt of himself. He did not want to deny what
Forest felt, but by his whole temperament and from the mel-
lowing that age had given him, he wanted to interpose a
maybe between Forest's reckless *I am* and the certain denial he
would encounter if he exposed himself too far.

"I have the weakness of liking all art," he said, seriously
wishing to take up Forest's argument. "For me the libraries and
museums aren't big enough. I like whatever is done in the right
spirit, and I don't always know how to put it in ranks—first,
second, and so on." It seemed to him at that moment he knew
what it was he had to teach Forest, if there were time and opportunity for it—the way to accept a scaling down from the
vision to the accomplishment. He knew what it meant, and the
boy needed to know, and there was the true valence of peda-
gogy. But as they were met here, he could not even find a way
of assuring Forest. While he was composing a way to lure on
Forest's argument, Forest's wife slipped between them and
took her husband's arm.

"Come on over and talk to *him*," she said to Forest. "He said
to bring you over."

"Go on," Corrigan urged. "It's not every day you have the
opportunity." He was lightly disappointed by her intrusion at
that moment, but ironically pleased, too, that she should be
demonstrating her usefulness as a wife. So now he knew why
she had braved the blizzard to come out tonight. The little
pirate wanted Markwell for her husband—not his scalp or his
money, but the Success of him, softened up and in a mood to
talk to Forest as an equal. She knew, he thought, what kind of
gifts were likely to touch this strange husband of hers, and if
she could not offer him her physical charms directly, at least
she knew how to use them in barter for something he wanted.

He had fallen into a banal, edgeless talk with Jost when he heard the shouting from the couch. It was Markwell's voice.

"Everyone's a writer," Markwell was shouting bitterly. "Paper's cheap, so you're a writer too." It was Forest at whom he was shouting, Forest planted on a chair in front of him, staring at the poet with the knowing smile of an inquisitor who has just exposed a phony. "Jesus Christ," Markwell shouted, "I know your type. The Village is full of them. Find them in every college, little sonofabitching pipsqueaks who have to bolster their ego by attacking someone. How I *pity* you. I didn't come here to be attacked. I thought I was among friends." He swung, as if desperately, toward Forest's wife, and, seeing in her eyes the sympathy of a mother cobra, twisted toward Tyburn as if Tyburn could exorcise these nightmare figures which had appeared to disturb his peace. "I'm leaving. Moore, I'm going back to my hotel. When's the first plane out of this goddam hick town? All I asked for was a reasonable amount of manners. Did I ask for anything more?" he demanded of the hushed group gathered around him.

"Take it easy, Mark," Tyburn advised. "Get him another drink, you. I don't know where this one crept in from," he told Markwell, pointing his elbow at Forest.

Then the voice of Forest's wife, piercing and memorable as the shriek of a seabird, cut its ice edge through the racket. "Well, it was stupid," she said. "Everything you said all evening was stupid. Did you think you were talking to a kindergarten?" she said to Markwell. She dragged at Forest's shoulder. "Come on, Steve," she said. "Let's go out of here."

As if he were intoxicated, or rapt in the continuation of the dialogue that Markwell had cut off, Forest, still smiling his fixed, catatonic smile, let her lead him from the room.

"My God," Corrigan said to Tyburn a while later. "What happened over there?" He held one hand over his eyes as if it were his own embarrassment he was hiding. "What brought on the fuss?"

"This kid attacked him," Tyburn said. "Mark was just talking about the Dodgers—perfectly innocent—and what's-his-name butted in and asked 'Who do you think you're talking to?' and Mark ignored that. But he butted in again with something about Mark sounding more like a traveling salesman than a poet. Wow. Where do you dig up characters like that? It's unbelievable. It was like some silly thing out of Dostoevsky. And then that girl with him, who'd been making big eyes at Mark, turned on him too. Christ, I don't want this to get back to New York. Now I'm going to have to get Mark good and drunk."

As he filled Markwell's glass again with shaking hands he demanded of Corrigan, "That's the boy you peddled to me, isn't it?" With a semitolerant laugh he accused, "You didn't tell me he was crazy."

"Ah, well now," Corrigan comforted, "the boy's just awkward. I don't suppose he meant to offend anyone."

"These bleeding little egos," Tyburn said. " 'Exterminate the brutes.' " There was a momentary flash of puzzlement across his face, a frightened wonder, as if some perversion of the optic nerves had given him a short glimpse of a chimera. But then he said, *"Otherwise* it's not a bad party. Mark's seen students before. He'll just have to lump it. But the kid must be a clinical case."

Corrigan bowed his head to this judgment.

It must have been that night when he caught the bug. When he left the party not long after Forest's bombshell, the snow was falling with soundless emphasis, as if it meant to finish things off here and now. It was falling on top of other snow and already had hidden the hubs of cars parked along the street. Under the street lights and the shop lights it glittered with a fluffy, malign purity, and its delicate texture muffled the sound of the few cars still passing on the street.

The air was not cold. After the wind that had blown all day had died, there was a sort of neutrality in the temperature. Corrigan was sweating under his overcoat as he came into the district where no tracks broke the snow along the sidewalk.

He had to wade with high prancing steps for the last few blocks before he came to his apartment building. He was panting when he came onto the steps, which the janitor had shoveled clear.

Then as he stood there looking back on the formless white that was already filling in even his own tracks, it occurred to him that he did not want to go in. Some rollicking impulse to go flounder in the inundation of snow held him awhile, staring back. Childish, he thought. Then he thought, Children hear it —the siren appeal of the snow that dissolves away the familiar forms and outlines of things so they know the intimate attraction of nothingness. Like a memory older than any memory of love he knew how falling snow and the night posed the question, "Do you care?" and what drunken delight it was for the child to answer, "No." Nothing in life was quite so keen as that presexual thrill of abandonment back to nothingness, the white center.

He heard the temptress' voice, oddly like Elaine Biddle's, and he thought, No one else I know would guess what lasciviousness it will be to yield. And then, as if he needed a conventional reason for staying out, he thought, I won't go far, and it is beautiful. To watch it awhile longer can't hurt. But the legs of his trousers were damp above the tops of the four-buckle overshoes his wife had bought him. All right, not tonight, he thought sadly, and went in to the comfort of his apartment and the precaution of his cold pills.

Nevertheless, in spite of caution, he had caught the bug. His first sign of it was an extremely nasty and literary waking dream of Forest's wife, in which she took the double role of the child and old woman in her story. It was nasty in its gross sexuality, and it was literary in its fantastic resemblance to the hunting days in *Sir Gawain and the Green Knight* when the Green Knight's wife comes to Sir Gawain's bed. Mrs. Forest had been to Corrigan's bed in a wintry castle and he had accepted her—if that was the word for the ugly connections they had made—both as prepubescent child and dripping grand-mother.

He woke with a heavy sense of self-repugnance, found that his eyes and all his muscles ached, as if from immense effort, and that his throat was painfully sore. Some strain of ancient Calvinism made him glad of the pain. It was a specific and merited punishment for having dreamed as he had—though at the same time, at a remoter level of awareness, he understood that the dream itself was a graver rebuke than the pain. He gargled and tried to stretch his muscles with some bending exercises. Finally he got himself in shape to go to his office long enough for conferences with Miss Emery and a doctoral candidate preparing a thesis on Chaucer.

By afternoon he had to admit that he needed medical attention. He took a cab to the dispensary at the university hospital, and there, after an examination, the doctor ordered him into the hospital "for a few days."

"Bronchial pneumonia," the doctor said. "I don't think it's going to be serious, but we want to keep an eye on you."

"Sounds as if the police were taking me in," Corrigan said, his little pleasantry reflecting a deep-lying guilty sense that it was not for his illness that he was being taken in but for the improper dream that had accompanied it.

"Yes, protective custody," the doctor agreed absently, already occupying himself with the formalities of ordering Corrigan's admission. "I'm not expecting anything serious to happen. But we have to think of your age."

The pain was still slight, and that afternoon began like a holiday for Corrigan. Lightly intoxicated with the fever, he submitted contentedly to the attentions of the orderlies helping him into bed. The neutral whiteness of the bed in which he lay seemed a wonderfully privileged substitute for the snow that had called to him the night before. This was like a child's pretense of dying.

He felt fine in the bed, he felt wonderful. He had needed, he told himself, this stage setting for his thought more than he needed medical attention. After submitting to having his temperature and pulse taken he let himself slide swiftly back into a rehash of his morning's dream. Let the doctor believe he had pneumonia, he knew he had caught the Forests—they were in his psychic stream like the cocci in his blood. When he was prepared to deal with them—lying flat on his back seemed the position of choice for doing so—then his blood would expel the hostile bugs quickly enough.

In the meantime he was close to enjoying the spectacle of his fight against the contagions. His hospitalization was like a warrant for digging back through the unconscious panorama of the dream to the conscious preparation for it. (Only enforced leisure could warrant the impracticality of such speculation. It could produce no valuable return.) Here he would speculate on the way his dream of Forest's wife had grown like a wild vine from his perfectly conscious interpretation of her story, the way that little stolen seed had gestated within his life as within a natural womb.

As he lay there looking out from his windows onto the white campus and the white hills beyond the edge of town, it seemed to him that he could see through arch beyond arch beyond arch and behold, almost diagrammatically, how the process of imagination worked. And it seemed to him, with an exuberance he had not felt since he was a young man, that he was about to begin a tremendous imaginative work. Little Miss Biddle had stolen a story, and that was a crude illustration of how the process worked. But he—well, he was going to steal Miss Biddle and her story, and the story of her stealing the story, and the story of his stealing, and . . . Contentedly he fell asleep.

Within a few days he saw how he had been tricked into this euphoria by his fever. *Something* strange was happening in his mental life, but it was not the beginning of a new phase of creativity. All over again he had to admit what he had long ago humbly concluded—that his ability to write had been exhausted. The lifelong accumulation of experience and insight from reading had been somehow tipped loose and was avalanching *as if* toward some point of concentration where it might be transformed into a work of his own. But it never quite arrived. Instead it seemed to exhaust itself in the fireworks of literary dreams about Forest's wife and—sometimes—Forest. He had tried imaginatively (using the same heavily equipped critical probes that he might have brought to a poem) to pierce their lives. And he had gone too far. He no longer had any defense against them. Whenever he slept he would find himself dreaming about them in one literary situation or another. They were everyone, from Popeye and Temple Drake to Dante and Beatrice, Gatsby and Daisy, Heathcliffe and Cathy, Paul Morel and Miriam, Raskolnikov and Sonia, Paolo and Francesca, Maggie and Jiggs. Sometimes he was involved in their relationship carnally, sometimes spiritually, but after a time these dreams became his chief source of discomfort. Then they began to frighten him as he recognized them not as promises of new insights but as signs of dissolution.

After a few days he complained of them to the doctor. "They're embarrassing," he said.

The doctor listened but was not greatly impressed. "They'll go away when we get your fever down. You're clear enough when you're awake, aren't you?"

Yes, Corrigan admitted, he was, but wakefulness had become increasingly boring. Now his days seemed to pass in an uneasy suspension between the boring winter whiteness that his consciousness perceived and the unholy medley of his dreams.

It was as if he had abandoned that familiar vantage point from which he could turn safely toward either reason or fantasy. He felt a great fragility in himself and a bitter impatience with it.

The upshot of it was that he stayed in the hospital longer than his doctor had expected. As the doctor had promised, the disease had taken no serious turn, but his convalescence was slow. After the fever ended, his horrid literary dreams disappeared, and that was a testimony to the doctor's acumen, but Corrigan believed they were still going on inside him, more and more identified with the secret processes of dissolution that his bout of disease had accentuated. It was a humiliation that his last spark of creativity had turned to ashes so quickly.

The Christmas vacation passed while he was still in the hospital and he remained as the first semester drew to an end. It was late in January when, one day, Tyburn came to call on him, bringing a bottle of whiskey and an issue of *Botteghe Oscure* in which some of Tyburn's poems had been published.

At first Corrigan thought irritably that the younger man had come simply because it was the season when promotions and salaries for the following year were about to be decided, and that Tyburn might be simply angling for his support and a good word to the head of the department. That support wasn't needed. This was Tyburn's time. He was on top. He could ride. His generation had secured their reputations, and the head of the department could count up the number of publications credited to Tyburn without any help from Corrigan. (The departmental secretary kept a chart of publications by members of the staff, a chart which had always reminded Corrigan of the stack of an aircraft carrier with its painted emblems of the kills to be credited to each pilot.) Tyburn would rise.

But evidently Tyburn knew that too, and something else was bothering him. In the little time since last fall he had passed from worrying about his security on the staff to a deeper concern. When he had drunk a couple of drinks from his present to Corrigan, he slapped the *Botteghe Oscure* against the bedside table and cried, "The poems I've got in here are *wonderful*. But as soon as I read them I tore up everything I've written since last fall. I've lost my ladder."

"That can happen," Corrigan said drily.

"You've been through it," Tyburn said. "You should have a perspective on it. You were doing wonderful stuff before you settled down to teaching. So tell me, is it worth it?"

"I don't know."

"I've got to decide. It's not going to hurt me to stay here another year, and Franklin knows the people at the Guggenheim foundation, so there's a good reason for staying next year at least. But I've got to make up my mind. I've got to decide whether what I can do for my students is more valuable than what I can do for myself."

"Well?"

"I don't know," Tyburn said somberly. "I can't get the score. Look, that kid you sent to my class. The nutty one. Forest. You were there the night he took off on Markwell. All right. It was a thing that happened, and I made up my mind that it wasn't a capital offense. So, I called the kid in and had a long talk with him and thought we had everything straightened out, really. It seems there was more to it than met the eye. Markwell had been pinching his wife, this girl Markwell had been pinching was his wife, and *that* is what riled him up to call Mark down. Which makes *sense*. Those things happen, and I've seen Mark in trouble before, but I didn't know it at the time. So Forest and I had this good talk and I thought we were seeing eye to eye. Then about a week ago the kid gave me part of a novel he's been working on."

He paused and shook his head ponderously and poured himself another drink.

"Did it show merit?" Corrigan asked.

"None," Tyburn said briskly. "Or I shouldn't say none, but it wasn't good."

Corrigan nodded slowly. "I'm afraid that Forest, after all, is a mute inglorious Dostoevsky. The fascinating question is whether or not that is a contradiction in terms. If mute, then Dostoevsky?"

"He *thought* he'd put so much into it," Tyburn said. "He thought it was the history of all the anguish he's had with this nympho wife of his, and there are some moving touches—uh, *moving*—when he describes how she made insatiable demands on him while he was suffering from the common cold and a

big dream sequence where he has her raped by a gang of hood-
lums in Chicago, but it's pornography at best."

"Oh my," Corrigan said, clicking his tongue.

"But when I tried to tell him this—"

"You didn't," Corrigan gasped. He could feel the spastic
twisting in his stomach now, fierce and undeniable and hot and
passionate as belief itself. "You didn't tell him it was pornography?"

"What's the point in criticism if it isn't honest?" Tyburn said.
"So I told him. So—"

Through the muffled, bombing bursts of his breath, Corrigan
gasped, "He swung on you." He saw Tyburn's eyes round out
in solemn saucers as he nodded.

"Thank God I didn't lose my head," Tyburn said. "I ran
down to the departmental office and the secretary and I held the
door on him while Peltus called the campus police to come and
take him away."

"Hooooo-ooooo," Corrigan shouted, the breath exploding
now from his cramped lungs, "Hooooo-oooooo, hah." Like a
leaping trout he flung himself up, scattering bedclothes wildly
as he turned in midair. When he landed, with his face half-
buried in the pillow, he was sobbing with helpless laughter.

"Tell me again," he gasped. "How you-ooo-ooo held the
door on him."

Happily—it might have gone otherwise—Tyburn began to
laugh too. When he could control himself Corrigan sat up and
grasped the whiskey bottle by the neck. Between fiery gulps he
said, "Don't talk any more about leaving, Tyburn. Where else
would you find it like this? Where else on earth?"

"It is pretty funny," Tyburn said.

When they had finished the bottle between them, Corrigan
was shouting for the nurse, demanding his clothes, swearing
that he was going home.

He thought after this that the Forests were through with
him. Just as the embarrassing dreams vanished—or went under-

ground—after the fever, the young people moved in the course of time beyond his purview. When the second semester began, he learned from gossiping with some members of his class that Forest had not registered. He had left the campus, and Corrigan's informants did not know where he had gone. And his wife? Oh, still around, still living at the sorority house where she had been all winter.

Corrigan saw her one evening when an unseasonable warmth had turned early March for a few days into May. He had taken a long walk in the afternoon and was coming home feeling hungry and fit. He had entered Fraternity Row a few blocks above the campus. The imitations of English country houses spread a theatrical setting down the street ahead of him, and into this setting, like a swan boat, came the largest and most chrome-laden convertible he had ever seen. Softly, swishingly, ponderously it glided to the curb a few dozen yards ahead of him and stopped. From a door wide and massy as a church portal, Elaine Biddle Forest descended. She was in a white evening dress and on her shoulders was mink.

At the instant of her descent a gold bar of sunlight flashed through the thicket of elms and fraternity plantings across the street to illuminate her almost to incandescence. As if she had been expecting it, she paused momentarily in the light and with mannequin grace, mannequin blankness wheeled slowly for all the world (or all the universe, Corrigan thought breathlessly) to see.

Then her equerry—tall, broad-shouldered, short of hair and clean of feature, dinner-jacketed and most evidently odorless as the stratosphere—leaped out behind her and with an athletic step led her up the front steps and into the fraternity.

That tableau was staged to mean something, Corrigan thought. No part of it was accidental—but where in the universe of accident was the origin of this theatrical purpose, and *whose* exactly was the discrimination that chose the details of costuming and light and arranged the tempo of this visionary scene so that fleeting as it was it should continue to vibrate like the persisting hum of a tuning fork? Mine, he thought with ironic arrogance. It was my little eye that saw it all. But whose eye was his? The wind blew acidly from the northwest as if to remind him that the false-spring blandness of the afternoon was an illusion made by powers who need not recognize his claims as a stockholder.

As the tuning-fork hum of beauty died out and he walked on toward his dinner he fell into a depression, as if it should be an automatic hangover from the exultation he had felt in the instant of seeing her. The depression moved through phases as distinct as spectrum bands. He felt a kind of groaning compassion for Forest that he had lost this girl, that he had let her beauty go by default into the hands of—of that Philistine, that embryonic hotel manager or corporation lawyer. It was one up again for the enemy. In this vein of thought the convertible, which had seemed a swan boat to his eye, became a vulgar bit of ostentation, a commercial virility symbol by whose authority (*in hoc signo*) the collectivized male should ravish away the Queen of Love herself. Not that Elaine Biddle was, in this discounting phase, worth likening to the Queen of Love in any way, shape or form. He had it from Tyburn's instructed epithet as well as hints that Forest had given him that the girl was a "nympho." Probably very little ravishing was required. But at the basest level she was valuable poetic property, and recruit writers should learn to cling to their beautiful women, just as recruit soldiers should learn to hang onto their weapons.

In the violet gloom of his depression he realized with a nauseated shock that it was not exactly for Forest's sake that he regretted the loss of Elaine Biddle to the others. Remembering those desperate dreams he had had of her while he was sick he admitted with savage frankness that in his decrepitude *he* was the desolated lover. It was his abandonment and jealousy he lamented now that she had been carried away by that gloomy chariot. He thought, raging, If I had it to do over again, all my life, I'm damned if I'd be a poet. I'd have her. Like a sign of the imminence of his death he felt a swift resentment against his dead wife—that good, warm, encouraging, wise, and loving companion, whose very goodness had tricked him away from the absolute abandonment to a single need which had been— he saw it now—required of him. Insanely, he hated her.

And then, of course, he neutralized the insane revelation with countervailing admonitions to himself. He had had a fit and was over it again, luckily, and able as he had almost always been to see things in proportion. He would go on to the end as himself—a limited man trying to make at least the holy counterfeit of salvation out of his very limitations. With his mouth he would not willingly or overtly deny the woman who had been so faithful and precious to him. But in his heart, in its despicable slime and fear . . .

To the end now, he supposed, that heart would be telling him that he did not care about the past with its measured successes and its limited failures. It was only the monstrous and chimerical future that he loved, the future in which he had so little stake, the true hell of exclusion from which no singer could bring back a credible image of love.

She came to him within three days after this, arriving at his office so demurely and so dully earnest that he would not identify her with the girl he had seen getting out of the convertible.

She had brought a package for him. She wanted him to read the manuscript of her husband's novel.

"Well, but if he'd wanted me to read it . . ." Corrigan began protestingly. "Mr. Tyburn's already read it, I think, and discussed it with your husband."

"Read it," she pleaded. "I want to know for sure if it's any good or not." Her pale eyes looked more guileless than she could possibly be. She had laid the swollen bundle of manuscript between them on the desk and, while he had not yet picked it up, his wariness conceived it as a bait that he still had the chance of refusing.

"Why?"

"Because as far as he's concerned he's thrown it away," she said. "He wouldn't even take it with him when he left. He would have burned it if I'd let him."

"I heard he was gone. Where?"

With a frown and small shrug of repugnance she said, "Back to New York. His brother-in-law edits comic books. He's going to work for him, writing stories or dialogue or something like that."

"Too bad."

"He had such high ideals."

"Too bad," Corrigan said, "but this isn't the end of his life. I have the hunch we're going to hear a good deal from that young man before it's through."

She, with that air of not seeming to hear anything she did not want to—rather, of testing with her need whatever was said to her and accepting into the realm of her concern only the useful—said, "I want him to come back here. I want him to finish this book."

"Why? A good many times it's wiser to put aside something that's badly begun and make a fresh start. I think you want me to advise him—encourage him—to go on with this, and I suspect Mr. Tyburn may have discouraged him rather sharply. But isn't it likely that I might have the same reservations about it that Mr. Tyburn had?"

She did not hear him. She merely waited for him to admit the folly of his evasiveness.

"Why?" he asked again, and because she did not answer he answered the question himself with a sign of resignation. "Because it's about you."

"It's about both of us," she said in a high, silvery voice. "And he doesn't need to think he can leave it like this. I know him. He won't ever do anything without me. He's got to understand that. He's got to face it."

It was no outward display of force that lent her speech its absolute certainty. She was not the kind to clench her lovely jaw or even to lean forward for emphasis. The certainty came rather from that tantalizing, centripetal glow of frailty toward which she expected force to flow as the normal pressure of air brakes in toward a vacuum.

"You mean *I've* got to face it," Corrigan joked oddly, picking up the manuscript and hefting it. "I'll read this. I want to read it. But I don't know if anything you want will come from my reading it. I couldn't possibly use it as a basis for intervening in your personal life—even supposing that I had means for doing so effectively. I feel that you've brought me this as if I were a lawyer and this was a document—"

"Just read it," she said. "You'll see."

All through that night he sat at home reading the story of the Forests. It was not the "true" story of what they were and how they had come, so strangely matched, together—for, as he had often admonished his class, truth requires form, and the intent to tell the truth is no guarantee that it will be uttered. After the glimpses and conjectures by which he had known the Forests during the past winter, here was only another glimpse and conjecture. The manuscript was—as Tyburn must have pointed out—formless to an extreme. Sometimes it was confessional in form and reduced painful scenes to comedy, and at other points it was so ponderously stylized and rhetorical that the tissue of dialogue and scene was squeezed to death by the language. It was a big manuscript, and it was tedious. As a literary effort it was quite unmistakably inferior to the Korean war stories that Forest had shown him (and Corrigan realized with a pang that this was the precious work going on behind the scenes, saved until it could be shown to Tyburn's more fastidious gaze, while the pieces on which Forest had staked less were being shown to him). If he were to answer as a responsible critic, he could only say that the work was a complete failure.

And yet as he read toward midnight he knew that there were images rising from the turgid brew and begging for completeness that were of more than ordinary power. Mangled giants struggling through a swamp, he thought, and it seemed to him that what the work needed—all that it needed, but that which a literary work must never need—was to be considered an amputated chunk of the reality which should have been its subject.

He read of the spring night in the sorority house when Steve Forest (called Sid Fleischer in the manuscript, with a transparency so futile that Corrigan ignored it) had been washing dishes alone in the kitchen. As the young man worked at the sink he suddenly began throwing pieces of china out through the open window beside him, at first fearfully and then, when no one appeared to stop him, in an increasing rhythm, hearing them tinkle in the lonely dark outside. If he had stopped to think he might have rationalized this gesture as an appropriately defiant resignation of his job as hasher at the house. But he was not even thinking of it as defiance yet—only as something he must do because he was young and it was spring.

Then he heard behind him, without having heard her footsteps as she came into the kitchen, the trusting, uninflected voice asking, "Why are you doing that?"

Not knowing yet and never to know, Corrigan thought, how she had heard the tinkle of destruction and had come down from her second-floor room because it was destruction she loved, needed, or chose. Because she would have recognized any splintering of windshield, crash of falling walls, smash of bottles as a call to which she must respond, faithfully hounddogging the sign of destruction because it would have been for her the sound of her prison door opening.

"That's a stupid question," he had answered. Frightened, Corrigan thought, because he had been caught, expressing his fright in aggression, ready to "walk out" then as always later with his thumb to his nose, but tolerating her there, waiting, because she had come down smelling of them, all her sisters, because in her person *they* all stood there obediently waiting to be snowed with any silly explanation he might make up.

Then under her nonaccusing stare Forest had panicked. He did not want to be fired for breaking dishes, but most of all he did not want to be fired for having done something that he could not explain with dignity to the housemother when she got around to firing him. So he had gone out into the back lawn of the sorority house and begun to gather the broken pieces of china up in his bare hands and carry them down the slope to the trash barrels. The girl, still in stocking feet as she had come downstairs, tried to help him and (with what meaning, purpose, cunning?) stepped on a shark-tooth fragment of a cup. She sat there with the faint light slanting down on her from the kitchen window above, holding her foot while they both watched the blood ooze out through the dirty nylon. She said tranquilly, "It doesn't hurt. I can't feel it."

This was the image of their recognition. Its felt load of significance was grossly disproportionate to the scene in which Forest laid her for the first time some weeks later. Perhaps the one moving statement about their mating in the basement smoking room of the sorority was the sentence, "She cried." Only that in twenty pages of prose that Forest might have memorized from the reading of spicy magazines during his lonely nights in Korea.

There was little enough to be made from Forest's report of the long-drawn-out conversations they had during the time they decided they were engaged. Except even then Forest seemed to have suspected—what never became more than a suspicion—that she wanted him because she believed that he was "lower" than she. Her father was a lumber dealer in a middle-sized Illinois town—Anglo-Saxon, Methodist, the owner of a Cadillac and a twelve-room house, member of the country club, father of two boys in the insurance game, and a Republican. It never occurred to his daughter that these attributes were not marks of superiority. It was merely that she did not want them. Forest was a Jew, a houseboy in her sorority, and —in his own admission to her—an artist. By these signs she recognized him as beneath her, and she wanted him.

Already by the time she had gone home to Illinois for the

summer vacation the horrid comedy in which she pursued and
he tried to evade had begun.

If it had not been for their separation, Forest might have
escaped her. He went with a friend in a battered car to Oregon
for the summer. He hocked everything and borrowed money
from his parents, intending in his own phrase "to jump off a
cliff and live." If he went too dangerously far in his self-
abandonment he would "knock himself off. A nice cool bullet
through the head didn't seem like such a bad idea sometimes."
But in Portland he got mixed up with a crowd of painters at a
beer party and had an affair with a coed from UCLA "whose
equipment was phenomenal." He could, or would, or should
have been content with her and have transferred to UCLA for
the fall term if it had not been for the letters from Elaine in
Illinois.

He quoted one of the letters. It was an utterly flat and dull
account of a weekend in which she had swum three afternoons
at the country club and danced three evenings with some boys
her cousin knew at Northwestern. She had been bored by it
all, she said.

But the point was that Forest didn't believe the letters.

Precisely because they were so void of content, he had believed in anguish that there was something glamorous going
on that she was not telling him. The hot prairie nights, the
band playing under the stars, the colored lanterns quivering
like live things in the palpitation of the air—Forest could imagine this and in the grip of his imagination could not conceive that in such a setting there was nothing going on that he
needed to know about.

But you should have believed her, Corrigan thought, involved like the ever-passionate hick who yells warnings from
the theater balcony, the sympathetic freshman who wants to tell
Othello not to believe Iago and doesn't give a wandering damn
whether Shakespeare made a work of art or not. You had to
believe that it was dull there because—well, because if you or I

or anyone else following us could just hang on to the literal truth of things we'd save ourselves this awful bother of fiction, poetry, pursuit of phantoms.

In the moment of his excitement, something banged Corrigan's chest like a stocking filled with sand. Palpitations, he thought. He poured himself a large glass of whiskey for a cure. It was not late yet. Not midnight. He was going to see this manuscript *through* before he went to bed, he told himself.

The memorable image of Forest's wedding was the present given him by his wife's parents. Because he was a writer—he took no pains to hide this from them when he suddenly appeared in their Illinois town and, with Elaine, announced what was about to happen—they gave him a Webster's unabridged dictionary.

But aside from the presentation of this ambiguous symbol the bride's parents seemed to have acquitted themselves rather decently under the shock of the marriage. In his manuscript Forest took pains to mock their staid Republicanism, and he had "bit his lip" to keep from laughing at the marriage ceremony performed in the Methodist parsonage. But the sheer fact that they had permitted it to take place at all stood mutely to their credit, as well as the clumsy attempts of the parents to make him (the dark, exotic stranger come into town hitch-hiking and carrying only one cardboard suitcase) feel that now he must look to them for help "if things ever didn't go quite right."

Justifiably, Forest contrasted the price of the dictionary to that of the Packard Sixes which the family had given his wife's brothers on the occasions of *their* marriages. Truly it was as if good common sense had told them not to spend too much for a marriage that wouldn't last. But again they had acted decently against this wariness in loaning the newlyweds the family Cadillac to drive to Chicago for a honeymoon.

The honeymoon was a horror. On the one hand he expected her to bring to the marriage bed in a cheap Northside hotel that glamour which she had so tantalizingly left out of her letters, that glamour of the upstairs in the sorority house—to bring him *the others* with whom he had so hopefully identified her. And she had lain there in his arms a single, naked, demanding self—not even as "phenomenally equipped" as the girl he had left in Oregon. He was too close to her, suddenly, to see that she was beautiful.

On the other hand, as soon as their first hasty bout on the rented bed was finished and even before she had commanded in that unworldly voice, "Do it again," he had glimpsed the immensity of her demand on him, the motive that had overridden parental objections and sorority platitudes about love and marriage as if they didn't exist. It was, Corrigan sensed, the depth of nothingness in her which had on the one hand permitted Forest to see whatever his desire could paint in her and conversely established her need for him. She must have someone whose imagination, whose occupation with her, would give her the reality she did not feel. From that first night when she had stepped on the glass and reported that she felt nothing, she had recognized Forest as the fabricator of her reality. She had watched him read *pain* when he saw the blood flowing. And if he had, in the proof, turned out to be an insufficient artist to turn her nothingness into existence, at least he was the only artist she had ever known. And she was determined that he must suffice.

Her demand emerged as a metaphysical one, and to call its expression nymphomania was at best a clumsy metaphor. In the same way it was clear what her ultimate motive had been in requiring Corrigan to read the manuscript about her. On the paradoxical bed in Chicago the Forests had failed the test wherein illusions and the need to be created might have fused in reality. Deserted, and as if feeling herself fading back to the nothing she had been, she had called out one more time, and this time not to Forest, but through Forest's work to him, "See me. Make me real."

The cursed honeymoon had lasted just two days before Elaine drove the Cadillac south out of Chicago by herself. And there

was only one happy memory of it which Forest, with "Dos-
toevskian" self-abasement, had put down. During an hour
when his new wife was out of the room he rifled her suitcase.
It was full of such splendid underwear as he had seen only in
store windows and advertisements before—a foundation gar-
ment of orchid-colored silk, a black half-bra and panties, a
cloud of white lace, and a crisscrossing of white elastic straps
with gleaming buckles—all that modern heraldry of romance
and woman cult suddenly, as he said, "his." Staring down into
this treasury, Forest confessed, he felt the one moment of
generous lust that he would know on the entire honeymoon.
This, and not the dangerous void of the woman, was what he
wanted. He had plunged his hands recklessly into the yielding
stuff.

(". . . arms closing on wind, lips speaking a name which
must be her name . . ." Corrigan incorporated this fragment
from Markwell's Orpheus poem to piece out the prose with
which Forest had described the episode. But he sensed, in an
uncontrolled impulse of compassion and humility, that he was
being called on for a belief greater than his belief in poetry. He
must not lament—and poetry was lamentation—on pain of
losing her. *Do not look back. Believe she is with you.*)

The Forests, he read, had made another effort to live together when they came back to school at the beginning of the
fall semester. They rented a tiny apartment, installed in it the
cloth of gold of her underwear, and his Webster's unabridged
dictionary, and within a very few days it had become untenable
for the two of them together. ("It was like having a body in the
house with him," Forest had written with unintentional comedy.) She wanted to cook for him, and he was used to cook-
ing for himself, a much better cook than she. She wanted him
to stay home in the evenings and read his work aloud to her.
(Since he was already deeply involved with this present manuscript in which he had so many derogatory things to say about
her—its composition seemed to have progressed like that of a
journal—he felt trapped by her request, dreading at the same

time that he might hurt her and that she was stifling his "honesty.") When he did read to her he had the feeling that she was not listening "critically." She seemed to bathe in the sound of his voice with no interest in its meaning. When he tried explaining to her that he wanted to be like Dostoevsky, she smiled a catlike smile of satisfaction with him, as though he were *announcing* to her that he already was Dostoevsky. This made him wild. Couldn't she understand how goddam lousy and imperfect his work was *now*, while he was learning his craft? To which she would reply maddeningly that she could understand that *too* and at the same time. In her oceanic emptiness she drowned his attempts to organize his life and his work logically. She cared nothing if he choked on his own inconsistencies as long as she could have him with her—"In there with her," he wrote, referring to the hated apartment.

("'You're trying to make a doll's house out of this,' Sid Fleischer yelled as he walked out. He was going downtown to get drunk. He was going to get damn good and drunk. Let her fester there in the festoons of the bourgeois respectability she had brought with her. He thought of how she would be in bed waiting for him when he got home. The covers would be pulled up to her eyes. Her catlike eyes would be watching him when he came in reeling drunk. She never seemed to sleep. If he woke during the night, she always seemed to be awake before him. Let her stay awake tonight. He was going to get drunk and he was not coming home.")

This must have been about the time I first saw them, Corrigan thought. He wondered with a sort of tense fascination if he would presently appear as a character. He thought not. He would have seemed too unimportant, too neutral, to Forest. (And now he felt a queer, repentant impulse to accept Forest's judgment in the matter.)

It's only now, this way, as a reader, that I can belong in the story at all, he thought. Then he thought, They need me. If I weren't here, what Forest thinks of himself and her would be true, and if it is, he's already lost her. Or what the world thought of them would be true. And if it were, Forest had never loved her at all. It *must not* be true that the boy was a spoiled piece of slag from the Age of the Wars, an egomaniacal piece of waste who had blundered into marriage with a nymphomaniac. But if I am not real in this story by reading it and holding it all in my heart, then whatever game we've all started to play when we play at writing is lost, he thought. He was very tired now from the effort to compose the Forest story, but for the most important of reasons he would not let himself quit and go to bed.

He read on into the dream sequence that Tyburn had mentioned to him and discovered what Tyburn, with his psychological insight, must have discerned—that it was a wish-fulfillment fantasy, in which the imagined rape of the wife was a hope of diverting her frightening attentions from himself. But it had another correlation, too, which opened out like an exploding fireworks bomb. Placed against it with a perhaps unconscious cunning was a passage describing her confession of her first sexual experiences. Forest had overcome her reluctance to speak of them by making love to her, and in the very tempest of their embrace had paused to whisper, "Tell me all about it" —delighting to learn that it had been "a fraternity man, a real Joe College" who had deflowered her after a homecoming game.

Voyeur too, Corrigan thought with a groan, recognizing the dream as a means by which Forest saw through his wife to the multiplicity of experience that could never be his. Voyeur . . . that term must be justly added to the long list of other truths about this—this *writer*.

Yet, conceding impatiently the depravity involved, he relived in an overlapping revery his own recent glimpse of the girl. She was again in front of the fraternity house, descending once again from the swan boat with the twentieth-century trim. The sun struck her gold. She turned with a hungry smile toward the light. Then, between submission and rapture, took the arm of her escort to let Joe College lead her up the stairs and in through the secret door of the fraternity house to her destiny among the lives of strangers. As she disappeared— out of memory, out of conception—Corrigan felt his own lips shape to the begging question, "Tell me."

But the door was closed behind her. She had come to them —not reluctantly, but pleading to be made alive. They had lost her and this was the way the story ended.

He finished the last pages of the manuscript. There were no surprises left to come. He looked up at the mantelpiece clock. It was almost three now. Of what night? Of what reality? He was an old man fondly wishing—and not for the first time, of course—that experience could be as coherent as desire. Then would I have held her—held them—in my heart.

But time was again the clock's time, and the story would end there as it must end. "Arms closing on air . . ." and "lips that would kiss form prayers . . ." while "love that robbed us of immortal things" gave nothing, gave nothing that time could not take back.

How could the Forests' story—which was his, now—end in time except with Forest going off to forge in the smithy of the comic-book trade the uncreated conscience of his race? While little Biddle, Eurydice of the expensive underwear, dropped back into the social millpond from which she had so maladroitly and with such wasted expense tried to raise herself.

In time the story ended with time's ending, and there would be neither occasion nor need for him to say the one thing that mattered. Precisely there was the unavoidable terror—that he could never say to her with the imperial emphasis required to establish all it meant, "I saw you."

In defeat he rose from his chair and started toward the bedroom. Tomorrow he would return the manuscript to Biddle (half-regained, lost on the instant of discovery), and he would try to be socially kinder than Tyburn when he discussed its weakness and its merits.

It is a terrible thing to be kind when you want to love.

He would, out of kindness, refuse her any encouragement

she could pass on to her errant husband. What could he say except that time would have its way with them and their stories, fictionalized or real; that on either side of its narrow course remains the same primitive wall of darkness that has rimmed it from the beginning?

We cannot speak the living truth to each other. That was *so,* he thought furiously. But must not be. In the middle of the living room he stopped, feeling all his limbs tremble.

Suddenly—involuntarily, he thought—he spun on the toe of his right foot, kicking his left heel in the air. His left foot crashed down on the hardwood and he whirled on it. Around and around the room he went in a dizzying circle. Beyond all reason (but also beyond all wish to stop) he yielded to the necessity of the dance. Bones creaking and muscles twinging he rioted on his way, an old man refusing to die until he heard the Forests' story come out right and clear, dancing in the face of its tragic fragmentation, dancing because in the circumstances it was the common-sense thing to do.

The Father

THIS BEGAN many years ago. Since its origin was from an accident and since many of the consequences would never be duplicated, it may stand as a unique little history without much relation to the fated march of public events or the destinies of most people.

It began on a March morning when Cory Johnson was shelling corn in the crib on his farm. He had a rattletrap old sheller that he was rather proud of. Some of its parts—the gears and the rust-pitted flywheel bored for a hand crank—had come from a machine in use on this farm for longer than Cory had lived. But he had rebuilt the frame and replaced the shelling spikes inside. He had rigged an electric motor and a system of belts to run the apparatus after the REA brought the wires out on this mail route west of Boda.

The sheller worked well enough. When there was no load of corn hitting the spikes, the rising and falling hum of the motor and the sibilance of the belts on the pulley faces were reasonably quiet. Of course, when corn was actually being shelled, a deafening racket filled this solid-walled room in the corner of the slatted crib.

Cory thought he was alone on the farm at this hour. His wife had taken all three children with her in the Model A. The two older boys were in school and would not come home until late afternoon. His wife hoped to drive into Boda to see her parents if the roads had not thawed too badly. She meant to take Bobbie, the youngest boy, along with her. Probably those two would not be back much before noon.

Cory liked being alone on his place. The job he had laid out for himself this morning was not pressing. At midmorning he would go to the house for coffee and cold pancakes with jelly. While he ate the snack he meant to listen to a science program broadcast daily from the station of the state university. He liked science. In his rural isolation he believed—then, early in the thirties, almost a full century after it began to dominate the life of the western world—that science was "the coming thing."

As he fell into the rhythm of it, he was enjoying his work as much as he ever had. The warming day, which would probably take the bottom out of the gravel roads between here and town before it was through, permitted him to take off his sheepskin coat. He was warm enough in a sweater as long as he kept busy, and for a good hour he worked without pause, bringing tin bushels full of corn from a pile in the slatted corncrib and feeding it into the machine.

While the ears ran down the trough to the hopper, Cory sometimes watched the throat of the outlet where the shelled grains poured into gunnysacks. Mostly the grains flowed out in a brisk, placid stream, but now and then above the main flow some single grains would leap like fast, yellow sparks from a grinding wheel. There was of course nothing extraordinary in the maverick behavior of these grains. They were the ones that had caught somehow between the cobs and the whirling spikes just long enough for elastic and centrifugal forces to build up, then hurl them like bullets ricocheting out the metal chute that filled the sacks. Still, their unpredictable flight suggested mysteries beyond the fringe of his experience. He had read in *Popular Science Monthly* where some Jap had invented a centrifugal machine gun. It pleased him mildly to think he was watching the principle of the gun being demonstrated by the apparatus he had put together. In another issue of the same magazine he had seen a photograph of electrons leaping through the dark of an experimental chamber, and though these pictures had showed no more than the scratch of a white line across a black rectangle, it pleased him to believe that electrons *really* looked like these hard-flung, zinging grains of corn.

Once that morning when Cory went out into the main storage bins of the crib to fill his bushels, he heard the electric motor change pitch. Its normal whine became a level, unpleasant hum. The slap and hiss of the driving belts had stopped. The motor was no longer turning over, and he had better shut down the current quickly before the armature burned out.

As he skipped for the door, the motor began to run again. A belt whistled on an immobilized pulley.

He saw his four-year-old son Bobbie standing beside the fly wheel with his gloved hand raised to the gear reduction. The boy's face was turned back over his sheepskin collar, and he was grinning the not quite honest grin he often showed when caught doing something destructive and forbidden—he grinned as if trying to minimize his offense.

Cory thought the boy had pushed a cob into the gears, experimentally, and thus had stopped the whole complex of machinery cold.

Then with a hawking scream that scalded his throat and the inside of his nose with bile, Cory called his wife's name. The boy's hand was in the gears. Down the fringed and starred cuff of his glove, blood was oozing briskly onto his sleeve and down the sleeve to the hem of his coat.

Cory had turned the power off and knelt with the boy in his arms by the time his wife ran from the car she had just parked.

As pain returned to the shocked nerves of the hand, the boy's grin merely enlarged until his mouth stood in a ridged O like the corolla of a white flower. He was now shrieking incessantly in fear and pain. He danced in his father's arms and jerked and jerked to free his hand. Urine bubbled through his overalls and mixed with the blood under his boots.

"Daddy'll get you out," Belle Johnson shouted in the boy's face.

"Daddy, Daddy, Daddy, Daddy," she moaned to Cory, depending like the child on his act to save them.

"Hold'm," Cory said. He vaulted the machine and knocked the belt from the drive shaft, vaulted back and set his shoulder to a spoke of the flywheel. When the gears moved, the boy shrieked louder and fainted.

"I'll take the sonofabitch apart," Cory said. He looked under the motor table for his toolbox. He remembered having put it in the trunk of the car. He was not sure whether he had left it there or had taken it out later in the barn.

"Daddy, he's swallowing his tongue," Belle said.

Cory put a finger and thumb in the boy's mouth. It was like putting them into an electric socket with the current on. The strength of the curling tongue seemed greater than any he could force into his own hand.

It took him five seconds to secure the tongue and press his wife's nails into it. He believed it had taken two or three minutes.

Sweat was blinding him. He thought the boy might die if he did not hurry, but he caught himself staring with revulsion at the machine, taking time to blame himself not only for the failure to enclose the gears in a safety box, but for making anything so ugly and rough—for presuming to do something that only factory technicians working for pay could do right.

He fished out his jackknife and cut away the blood-sopped glove from the jammed hand. He thought it possible that the jersey might have cushioned the bones at least. What he saw looked like boiled and shredded chicken in which a bad cook had left bits of gristle and bone.

"Daddy, his mouth is turning blue," Belle said.

"All right. Hold onto him. Hold him tight," Cory said.

He took a dark-bladed hatchet from its hanging place on the wall. There was not much room for it between the gears and the bottom of the hopper. With a three-inch blow he clipped the hand just above the wristbone.

"Get a tourniquet on him. I'll get the car," he told his wife.

The doctor in Boda, young Doctor Grant, said that Cory had done a pretty good job of amputation, all things considered.

"Bobbie probably never even felt what you did," Doctor Grant said, with his clean, pink-nailed fingers resting on Cory's sleeve. "There was quite a little shock. Naturally. But if his hand was so badly mangled you couldn't get it free, you can be sure that's where the shock came from. Say, it didn't take you long to get him in here to me," he said with an encouraging gleam of admiration in his eyes.

"No," Cory said. "I just didn't pay any attention to the mud-holes. I came through the bad stretch the other side of the bridge doing about sixty-five, I guess."

The doctor laughed quite loudly. "I'll bet you jumped that Model A right over the bad spots."

Now that he knew his boy was going to be all right—which at the moment meant that he was going to live—Cory felt an unaccountable but decent pride in his behavior after the accident. By God, he had held back nothing. He had ripped the guts out of his Model A, coming in from the farm in just seventeen minutes. By God, he had seen the mail carrier—the mail carrier, mind you—out beside his car studying the mire of gravel and standing water in the low spot beyond the creek and probably deciding it had thawed too bad for him to get the mail through. Now Cory could remind himself—what he wouldn't bend the doctor's ear with—that Belle had shouted from the back seat to go around the longer way by Hopewell Church when he took it on his own shoulders to give this way a try. He hated to think what might have happened if he had stuck the car in deep there, a mile and a quarter from town. And for a minute or two it had been touch-and-go with the mud geysering over his windshield and the car skidding always to the left against his pull on the steering wheel. He had seen the face of the mail carrier through a muddy window, puckered in disbelief, almost in awe, as he watched the Model A churn past him.

The car was still fishtailing uncontrollably when Cory took her up the bridge approach. The whipping rear end grazed half the girders of the span before he got her straightened. The rear bumper was gone and somewhere along the line he'd over-taxed the transmission so he couldn't get her shifted down from high when he had to wait for a truck to cross at the Boda stop sign. He killed the motor then and ran three blocks to the doctor's office with the boy in his arms and Belle unable to keep up with him. And made it in time.

In time. In time. In time. The thought quieted the thudding of his heart.

"I don't think there's enough loss of blood to worry us," Doctor Grant said. "The tourniquet worked very nicely." Doctor Grant was only concerned—just a little—about the effects of shock, he said. He wanted to drive the boy over to the hospital in the county seat as soon as he had seen two more patients. He wanted to make sure Bobbie had his strength built up "before I finish the job for you," as he put it to Cory, with a wink of complicity. The Johnsons could ride along in the doctor's car. Belle could hold the little fellow in her lap, and everything would be arranged so one of them could stay all night with him in the hospital.

In the meantime, while his parents waited, the boy was sleeping in one of the doctor's examination rooms. He had been given morphine. Everything seemed to be under control. The orderly flow of circumstance had resumed again.

Cory opened a magazine, there in the doctor's waiting room —not so much because he thought he could read anything just now as because he wanted some shield behind which to hide until he came to terms with himself. Most importantly, he had to choke down the boisterous, excessive pride that had come on the rebound of his relief. He kept wanting to grin when he thought of the mail carrier's face. But if he couldn't help grinning, no one ought to see him do it. Then, too, he might want to pray out some of his thanksgiving that the roads hadn't been too bad, that Doctor Grant knew his business, and so on. Cory was still religious in crisis, though in normal times he lived by the opinion that "a lot of people went too far" with the religious business.

"Cory?"

He heard Belle's whisper like something whispering to him out of the past—like his mother come to wake him for a fine day in summer after vacation from school had begun and he could enjoy himself helping *his* daddy around the farm.

He looked up from the magazine. Belle's face was so pale he was frightened for her. Her blue eyes looked black against her ghostly skin.

"Daddy," she said, "don't feel too bad. You had to do it."

Of course it would have occurred to him sooner or later, without any prompting from Belle, that he and he alone was guilty for the loss of Bobbie's hand.

Since Cory would rather—if wishes had anything to do with the matter—have given his own hand, the way the guilt came to present itself was especially hard for him to master.

The point wasn't his negligence. As his father-in-law said, "There's a great many dangerous things around a farm, Cory. There always will be for kids."

"I know it," Cory said. "There's got to be machinery and animals and the pony that Joe and Gordon ride. You take the windmill tower for an example. I've caught Joe and Gordon up there I don't know how many times. They might any time fall and break their necks. Or the fan's going and they stick their heads up through the platform. Pfffttt!"

The older man extended the rhythm of agreement. "That's a fact, and you know Belle, when she was little, one time I nearly toppled a horse tank I was loading right onto her." He shuddered even now.

"Ah, but Dad, you held it," Belle recalled.

"I did," her father said. "And I paddled you for it when I saw you were safe. And I always remembered what a scare I had. But the point is that accidents just happen, Cory. After all, that's what the word *accident* means."

"Yeah, it does," Cory said.

The conversation was one of a great many that took place in

the spring and summer after Bobbie lost his hand. They amounted to a kind of informal funeral, commemorating and at the same time draining away the immediate emotions of loss. It appeared, even to Cory, that it did him good to speak of the accident. He found no difficulty in saying man to man, man to wife, father to children—even to Bobbie—that an accident was something that just happened. Cory knew as well as any man that this was so.

Though he said many times that he could shoot himself for not having put a safety box around those gears on the sheller, this negligence was not the point that proved most crucial, either.

"You should have done that," his father-in-law said once when Cory lamented the absence of such a guard. "Well, we go on and try to make up for our past mistakes, and it does seem kind of sad to lock the door after the horse is gone, but that's what we do. I notice you took some rungs out of the ladder up the windmill."

"And Gordon climbed it the other night anyway," Belle said. "Shinnied right up the frame and had to yell for Cory to come and get him off."

They laughed and Cory laughed with them. Yes. Just to go on living he had to accept the likelihood of accidents, particularly where boys were involved, and he could do that.

But it wasn't the accidental part of Bobbie's misfortune that settled permanently into Cory's mind, freezing it to a pattern of distress. What he could never face—could never understand —was that he was guilty in taking that hatchet down from its hanging place on the wall and cutting off his son's hand.

"You had to do it," Belle said. She was willing to repeat this assurance whenever she thought it would help.

It never helped. Cory knew he'd had to do it. But necessity was no excuse at all for the guilt that rode him. The more he rehearsed his motives, the less important they seemed in comparison with the immortal act. If it was only bad luck that had put him in a situation where he had no choice, still, that luck was *his*. The guilt seemed to reside in that simple fact.

"It's like if I'd been someone else, not any part of this awful thing would have happened," he said to Belle.

Now that her emotions had resumed their normal level, she was almost as much amused as concerned at this odd way of putting it. She probably thought he was fishing for sympathy, and though she didn't mind sympathizing with him all he wanted, she didn't know how to offer the right response to his fancy. She said, "Sure. Sure. If you were someone else you wouldn't have this farm. You wouldn't have your nice kids. You wouldn't be stuck with me. Well, that's all a pipe dream, old man. You're stuck with all of us, and we'll get along. You know we will. Bobbie's a brave little guy. We might just thank God he was always left-handed."

"I know we'll get along," Cory said.

"You shouldn't punish yourself this way, because there's nothing to punish yourself for."

"I know that too."

"Then don't get depressed like this."

He had not spoken from depression, but from guilt. He knew well enough what depression was. He was depressed in those years of the thirties when the drought took most of his corn crop two years in succession; when he let himself be cheated in buying a secondhand car that turned out to have a cracked block; when he had trouble with his gallstones and had to cripple around all one winter; when his oldest boy, Joe, had trouble with his high-school studies and went off to join the Navy; when Belle's father, a man who'd been so good to Cory and his family and so dear to Bobbie, died of cancer; when the war came and Joe was out there at Pearl Harbor, where the Japs dropped on them with their newfangled weapons, and so many didn't have a chance on the anchored ships.

Year by year there were things to depress him. Big things

and little things. And through the same years there'd been good times and times of satisfaction when he *wasn't* depressed. Take the summer he'd put the family in the car and driven them out to Yellowstone Park. That trip was a pure satisfaction. He couldn't remember a thing wrong with it.

Easily he remembered the good winters when he and Gordon were teaching Bobbie to hunt with them. They would load the dogs in the back seat of the car and drive over to the creek bottom to look for rabbits, quail, or pheasants. Cory had his pump gun. Gordon and Bobbie "shared" the single-shot .410 that had been bought for Joe when he turned twelve. Off they'd mush through the snow and broken cornstalks, trying to keep up with the badly trained dogs, joking and trading insults like three men—or three boys, it didn't matter which. Once, Cory'd knocked down three cock pheasants from a rising covey. Bobbie clapped his mitten to the side of his head and howled in admiration and disbelief. "Purty good, for an old man," he yelled over the snow. "Purty good."

"Even if you did get more than the limit," Gordon put in. "You going to tell the game warden I shot one of them?"

What he'd seen in the boys' eyes that afternoon was unmistakable and worth treasuring—just standing there in the snow with the dead birds around them, the boys being proud of their old man. It was like the male satisfaction he'd felt the day he took Bobbie in through the mud to the doctor's. In time. Only now the boys were here to share and mirror back the lonely pride of his manhood.

There had also been the good times—not to mention *all* the blessings of the years—when Joe came home on boot leave; when prices picked up in thirty-nine and the same year Belle had another boy, Cory, Jr.; and when they got the first letter from Joe after Pearl Harbor saying he was all right.

The good things and the bad things of an ordinary farmer's life had happened to him. He had responded to them like an ordinary man, with satisfaction or depression.

But the guilt he endured was something else. It seemed to have a life of its own, to be almost a distinct life he lived when his ordinary life gave him the opportunity.

Weeks, months, years went by in which he forgot that he was guilty. During those periods he got quite used to Bobbie's disfigurement, as if it were a condition that had always existed, one intended by nature.

Fortunately, Bobbie wasn't the boy to feed on sympathy. He managed. As far as his parents could tell, he was a happier boy than Joe had been.

Cory watched without sentimentality as his maimed son grew up. But when the awareness of his guilt came back in one of its cyclic manifestations, he found that it had not diminished with time. After ten years it was as keen and lively as it had been that morning in Doctor Grant's office when Belle had unintentionally announced it to him.

An assortment of events served, through the years, to recall it, the way symptoms in the throat announce the approach of a general systemic infection.

For example, there was Bobbie's fight in the school yard when he was in the second grade.

Cory saw most of the mix-up. Driving homeward from an errand in Boda, he and Gordon stopped to pick up Bobbie from his play after school. From where the car was parked, they could see some boys darting back and forth beyond the schoolhouse, dodging, turning, skidding in the grass, swinging at each other in what seemed to be a game of tag. Then Glen Horstman chased Bobbie down into the corner by the well. Bobbie backed into the hedge separating the school yard from a cornfield. He sparred away the jabs and pokes the bigger boy aimed at him. It looked as if both boys were laughing breathlessly, having a lot of fun.

They saw Glen Horstman feint a kick and follow the feint with a blow of his fist that started Bobbie's nose bleeding. Bobbie signaled that he'd had enough: *Lay off. I surrender.*

Glen kept punching. He had knocked Bobbie to the ground and was sitting on him when Gordon leaped the ditch and went running to the rescue.

Laggardly, Cory followed. He was only a few steps from the car when he saw Gordon chase Glen into the schoolhouse.

"Gordon!" he commanded.

Gordon stopped on the wooden stairs by the door and turned. His face was quizzical and angry. "Why, I'll just knock *him* around a little bit," he said.

"No you won't," Cory told him. "You and Bobbie come on and get in the car now. Bobbie'd better wash his face at the pump."

"But he's bigger than Bobbie," Gordon said. He blushed because he did not want to mention that Bobbie lacked one hand to use in self-defense.

"Get in the car!" Cory shouted.

All the way home from the schoolhouse, Gordon sat in incredulous, wounded silence. Bobbie, though, was talkative enough. He wasn't in any pain from his beating. He wasn't really mad at Glen Horstman. Now that it was over, the fight seemed to him a pure entertainment.

But that, as Gordon's silence implied, was not all that must be taken into account. On almost any other day he would have been there at school to protect his brother. At least, without his father's inexplicable attitude to reckon with, he would have known what he ought to do tomorrow.

After supper, Gordon went to his mother about what had happened. She, in turn, spoke furiously to Cory as soon as the boys were in bed.

"I think I'd just better get on the telephone and find out from his teacher if this has ever happened before—the kids picking on Bobbie. I won't have it. Just because he's crippled—"

"Aw, Belle, that wasn't why Glen done it. They was playing and he got carried away."

"Playing? Gordon said he hit Bobbie with his fist. He was

sitting on him, pounding his head, and you didn't . . ." She
didn't say what Cory should have done that he had omitted,
but she shook her head bitterly. The more she thought, the
more worked up she got.

"Well, you go ahead and call the teacher if you want to put
your nose in it," Cory growled.

"I *will* put my nose in it," she said, "and you'd better go
over to the Horstmans' place and have a little talk with Glen's
dad, because I don't intend to have this kind of thing going on,
whatever you intend."

"But Bobbie wouldn't want—"

"You can drive me over and sit in the car while I go in and
have it out with them," she raged. "You can sit in the car if
you're scared to tell Ralph Horstman we want this stopped."

The Horstman farm was less than a two-mile drive.
Through the spring night and the murmur of a rainy wind,
Cory drove slowly, telling himself that of course Belle was
right. He sighed heavily and thought he'd want his friends
who lived around him to come and tell him about it if one of
his boys had done a wrong. But he seldom felt so uneasy about
anything as he did walking in under the elms of the Horstman
yard and knocking at the screen door of the back porch.

"He what? Glen done *what?*" Ralph Horstman bellowed.
He grabbed Cory's shoulder and dragged him in from the back
porch to the kitchen. "When'd he do that? This afternoon?"
Horstman's throat began to swell rhythmically. He seemed to
be growing taller and broader. "Mama, give Cory a cup of
coffee or—or some *beer!*" he shouted to his wife. Then he fled
the kitchen, pounding up the stairway from the living room
like a plow horse frenzied in a burning building.

Cory and Mrs. Horstman heard the thump of a body
dumped from its bed onto the floor and then a long, sleepy,
uninterrupted wail, accompanied irregularly by the sound of
slaps. In a minute Mrs. Horstman ran upstairs, too.

More slaps then. A more complicated sound of struggle began as the woman tried to mediate. Again and again, like the boom of outraged justice itself, Ralph Horstman's voice shouted, "He hit li'l Bobbie!"

After the condemnation, the smack of a hand on a rump, and then the woman's plea, seeming only to convince her husband that she had not understood the enormity of the offense. "But he hit li'l Bobbie!"

Downstairs Cory listened in what he could no longer doubt was envy. He knew well enough what he had no wish and no way of explaining to Gordon or Belle—that when he had seen Glen Horstman's fist bring blood from Bobbie's nose, he had felt a merciless identification with the agressor. He had been unmanned by the recognition.

He had not wanted Bobbie hurt. No! He had never wanted Bobbie hurt, but he had seen his own act reenacted and known himself as powerless to prevent the pain as before.

But Glen Horstman, because he was a little boy, could be punished for what was, after all, a small offense. Cory, for his immeasurably greater offense, could expect no such squaring of accounts.

Afterward, each time his guilt flared in his face, he had to endure it in the same way until, mysteriously, it faded in his mind again—not dead, not even eroded by the remorse he had paid for it, merely waiting to be wakened again and endured again like an operation submitted to without anesthetic because, though he was guilty, no one owed him punishment.

He was punished. In the last year of the war, Gordon had just been drafted and sent to Fort Bragg when Joe was killed near Okinawa. By that time Joe was a seaman first class serving on a destroyer escort. The DE was on picket duty about seventy miles east of Buckner Bay when it was attacked by a George fighter. The attack occurred near sundown. A broad highway of gold and choppy crimson opened away from the little ship toward the west. The fighter came down this road like an erratic spark of gallantry and panic, hurled without conscious aim. The big ring sights on Joe's 20-mm. cannon must have circumscribed the sun itself as he swung it over to defend the ship. The fighter struck just abaft and below the bridge. The ship lived for several hours more, time enough for the survivors to be transferred to a destroyer. None of Joe's shipmates saw him or his body after the attack.

When the news came to the Johnson farm, Cory wept like any father bereft. And his tears were partly tears of relief, for it seemed to him in the first debility of sorrow that this extravagant punishment might, at last, pay off his guilt. It was not even in his heart to protest that the payment was too great, though he saw no equivalence between the hand he had taken from one child and the life he must now yield helplessly back to darkness. If he was quits, he must be satisfied.

But when his grief diminished and his strength returned, Cory saw that whatever had happened to Joe had nothing to do with his old guilt, which was neither increased nor minimized by Joe's death. What little religion Cory had kept through the years melted with this discovery. Religion seemed foolish to him now, a windy pretense at linking things that had no real connection. The issue was between himself and a chaos to which only a fool would pray.

He had nothing with which to replace religion. His irregular and shallow enthusiasm for science had long since vanished of its own inanity. Besides, though science had once seemed to him "the coming thing," he had never been notified that science might pretend to explain what he thirsted terribly to know. It had been fun to read about the novelties science discovered. He had got bored. That was all.

In his whole life, as he could look back at it now, only one condition had given meaning to his work and the depressions or satisfactions that went with it. That condition was his fatherhood. Even if he had fathered his boys more or less accidentally, in lust, in lukewarm fondness for his wife, his fatherhood had come to be more than the sum of days and of forgotten wishes.

Before anything else, he was a father—and it was against this definition of himself that he had been forced to strike that day in the corncrib.

Belle died in 1950. Cory wept for her, too; envied her, too, for he suspected she must have carried through life some secret, like his, of undiminishable guilt for rebellion against the self that time and accident had given her. But now she was free of it.

They said Cory's mind began to fail him after Belle's death.

His mind was working better than ever—and he understood that was what his family and Doctor Grant *meant,* though they had to express themselves by an exact inversion of the truth.

If they had said he was troublesome and a bit frightening to live with, he could have agreed straightforwardly. But they needed more than that. Like most people, they needed a shallow burrow of "reasons" and "explanations" because they dared not deal with a sheer, objective fact. He could no longer live on their sort of explanations, but he sympathized with them. So he said, Yes, he reckoned his mind was going back on him. He didn't want to be a trouble to them, and if he couldn't straighten up by himself, he would certainly do what Doctor Grant recommended. He would go to the asylum "for a while." In the meantime, while they gave him a chance, he wanted to carry on his share of the work on the farm.

In this period there were five of the family living together there. Cory, Bobbie and his wife Lucy, and their little boy Ed (after Lucy's father), and Cory, Jr. Between them, Bobbie and Cory, Jr., could just about take care of the farm work. Bobbie had been to Ag school at the state university and he was a fine manager, very good with bookwork and planning ahead about the crops and machinery and soil, and figuring how they could afford the new things they needed. Farm work was more and more a matter of business brains these days, and he was sure that Bobbie was all right in that department.

Bobbie had got himself a new device to use for a right hand, too, now that they could afford it. There had been so much more money coming in during and after the war! Now you take Joe, Cory would tell himself, we just couldn't have afforded to send him to the university, Mother and I, back when he might have wanted to go. Then, quicker than anyone else could have reminded him that Joe was not a great one for study or using his brain, Cory would throw in that very qualification and go on: Yes, but things are getting so well-organized that they can take a boy who's not so bright to begin with and kind of guide him over the hurdles and give him remedial work and guide him into the right niche and he does all right! This was the way Cory's mind went on and on in an endless series of examinations and connections. His mind was far from failing. It dealt with more all the time, and, insofar as the mind alone was concerned, it was dealing more effectively. The sickness was elsewhere.

What Bobbie had was too grand and clever to be called a hook, though he good-humoredly called it that on weekdays. On Sunday, for fun, he called it a prosthesis. It was really three hooks and a bar, all with a bright chromium finish that twinkled wonderfully in the May morning sun when the young man swung himself up onto the tractor seat and headed out to the fields, while Lucy held little Ed and waved to him from the back door.

It was so strange, sometimes, to Cory to see that shiny batch of levered claws on the baby's back when Bobbie was holding him—as at the homecoming picnic in Boda when there was a crowd and the Johnsons drove in to see all their old friends come back to this hick town. Gordon was with them, too, on that occasion, visiting a week from his job in Seattle, where he'd remained with an opportunity after the service.

That *thing* on the baby's back would look just as firm and tender as a human hand. Odd how Bobbie could use it to caress with sometimes, as if it were alive, though of course it had no sense of touch. It could express feeling though it had none. The only time the baby minded being touched with it was in

cold weather. But Cory's thoughts were often busy on conjectures as to whether the baby *ought* to mind being touched
by the lifeless thing. No end to considerations involved there.

With his prosthesis Bobbie could manage nearly any chore
on the farm. No doubt if worst came to worst, everything
could be handled without hired help if Cory went away. But
Cory had made his place, now that the boys were taking over
so much, by doing the dirty and menial jobs that their machinery still left undone. True, they had a milker, and even Cory,
Jr., could handle the milking of their twelve cows without
complaining he had been put upon. Someone still had to shovel
up after the stock. The boys rented a corn picker from the elevator in Boda for the corn shucking. Someone had to drive the
tractor into town through a November rain to get the picker
and see that it got back on schedule. Cory always did jobs like
that.

Doctor Grant didn't like it much that Cory should make
himself into a nigger—that was his word—for the boys. As he
saw it, this was another symptom of Cory's mental deteriora-
tion. But the doctor's opinion on this account was only one
way of looking at it, and Cory was very well aware of this.

He realized that quite aside from any help he gave with the
work or any hardship he imposed on Lucy by giving her
another mouth to cook for, he *worried* his family.

He was sorry for this, but deliberately he went ahead with his
alarming and aberrant courses. In the winter of 1952 he spent
part of every day in the corncrib, where he was reconstructing
the corn sheller that used to stand in the corner room. He
scoured the neighborhood and the junk piles around Boda for
old parts. He rebuilt the wooden frame where the electric motor had sat. He drilled bolt holes in the concrete floor he and
Gordon had poured back in wartime when they junked the old
sheller. He begged some secondhand lumber from the people
who had moved onto the Horstman farm, not wanting to spend
any more good money than he had to on his "foolishness."

It took Bobbie less than a week to figure out what his father was doing—a little longer to decide to intervene. Then one morning he made a point of sauntering down to the crib and entering the room where his father was hammering and sweating.

"What you up to?" Bobbie said. "I thought since I didn't have much to do this morning, maybe I could . . ."

The brightness and pretense—from both sides—faded quickly enough. A reckless pity shone from Bobbie's face. He wet his lips.

"Dad, you're making that sheller again, isn't that it?"

"Well, Bobbie, yeah, I thought I'd run her up again and see if maybe I could improve the design. Like you say, there's not too awful much work to be done these days, though maybe I ought to be down at the barn having a look at that loader Cory broke last summer." He started to leave the room.

Bobbie stopped him. "I didn't mean that, Dad. You don't have to work every minute. But—but, it seems kind of useless for you to be making a sheller."

"Yeah, it does."

"Then—"

"It kind of—"

"Dad, Lucy and I've been talking and we want you to, well, go out to Seattle and see Gordon awhile. You keep saying it would cost too much, and Seattle's a big place if you don't want to stay with Gordon. Look, I'm going to come right out with it. Lucy and I don't feel right for having called Doctor Grant in on you. Doctors don't know everything. But a family is different, and I know that Gordon would want you to come."

"—kind of helps me think things out," Cory said mildly, touching the homely machine he was building. "I'm not a hand like you are to put things down on paper or in words, either, and if I can build something to see, that helps with my brain work."

Bobbie gritted his teeth. "But you're thinking about things you ought to leave alone," he said. He held up his claw, glittering and lightly sweating in the cold room. "You're brooding about *this* again. For my sake, leave it alone. You think all my life I've blamed you somehow and I haven't. Can't you believe me when I say it? You *saved* my life and everyone knows that."

"I don't know," Cory said. "Maybe there was some other way to do it."

"Was!" The horror of that exploded syllable stood with them like the angel of death. What had been in time was not, any longer, in time. The past was unalterable, and yet they could not shake from their minds the illusion of free choice.

"I've had a good life," Bobbie said—as if that bore on the enigma that Cory wrestled. He might have had *another* life if his father had been the man to find another means of saving him. "What more could I want? I've been happy," Bobbie said.

"I know, son," Cory answered. "What I'll do, I'll get the pickup this afternoon and carry this junk down in the east forty and dump it. Guess I'd better save the lumber and use it for kindling."

Bobbie snarled in his frustration. "You don't have to do *that,* Dad. You don't have to do anything I tell you or anything for my sake. That's the point. Don't you get it?"

"Sure I see what you mean," Cory said. "I wasn't thinking about how you—and Lucy, I suppose—would feel about this contraption. Now let's just walk up to the house for some coffee and I'll tell Lucy I'm sorry I started it."

Bobbie said, "Maybe you'd better not mention it to her."

"All right," Cory said. "Whatever you think is best."

The next morning he was working on the sheller again. He had got to the point of installing the gears and covering them with a steel safety box.

Probably his queer behavior and his family's concern with it had been going on longer than he realized. Because they cared for him they would have taken what pains they could not to let him notice their precautions. Noting their few failures to be discreet was like seeing an advance guard of rats begin to invade the farm. Experience had convinced him that if you saw only the signs of depredation, that meant there were ten rats around your buildings. If you saw one rat, that meant a hundred. If you saw two together, a thousand, probably.

Now, to all his other considerations, he added the task of measuring the impressions he made each day on Lucy, Bobbie, and Cory, Jr. Like a stock-market gambler he read the daily quotations of his stock with them. Better this afternoon. Low and worried this week. Cautious. Desperate. Better. Better. The same.

They could not bring themselves to wound him by flat and final decisions in his behalf. If Bobbie had really insisted, Cory would have packed and gone to Seattle. Probably he would never have come back from that city.

At the same time, he realized that he confused their impressions by the very act of measuring them. And if their sanity wavered to the magnetism of his craziness—as he saw it did— then how could he trust them for reliable guidance, even in what he ought to do?

He understood, sometime during 1953, that they had been cautioned by Doctor Grant—or another authority they might have consulted at Grant's recommendation—to be on the lookout for a suicide attempt. He knew this first by subtle signs, as he would have known about a family of rats in the corncrib before he saw the first darting black shape and prepared for a campaign of poison and traps. The subtle signs were followed by a blunder so loving and crude it made him weep.

One morning he found that his straight razor had disappeared from the cabinet in the bathroom and had been replaced with an electric shaver. The exchange had been made just one week before Christmas, and he knew the electric gadget had been bought as a present for him. In their anxiety they had been unable to wait.

He picked up the shaver without hesitation. He accepted whatever Lucy and Bobbie (or was it Lucy alone, weaker in her fear, who had made the switch?) thought had to be done. He put the plug into an outlet and set the humming head to his cheek. He saw his cowed eyes under the windburnt sag of lids. It seemed to him his courage was not adequate to his pity.

"Father," he said, as he used to pray in the time he had not taken religion seriously enough to reject it. "Father." He heard no distinct syllables, but a shapeless groan.

The futility of their gesture seemed unendurable. They had taken his razor—didn't these children know that, on a farm, as Belle's Dad had put it, the means to harm were never lacking? He supposed they had hidden away the shells for his pump gun, too, though he had not bothered to check for some time. Odds and ends of rope had probably been gathered from the barn and outbuildings (by Bobbie, careful not to let on to Cory, Jr., why he was being so neat these days). They probably timed his comings and goings, not to permit him to be too long alone. And what good would all that do if he could claim the right to kill himself?

To put their minds at ease he wanted to go to them now and tell them how he had once determined to do away with himself and why that was all past. The occasion had come soon after Joe's death. The absence of the coffin from the funeral services had served as a reminder of the absence of justice due from the empty heavens. That had been more than eight years ago. No one had worried then about gathering up ropes from the sheds, garage, or barn.

He had put a rope around his neck one morning before anyone else was out of bed, standing by the square opening in the floor of the haymow. There was enough light at that hour to show the churchlike vaulting of rafters in the empty mow. Nothing had ever tempted him more seductively than the black square in front of his toes.

But he had taken the rope off with the slow deliberation of a judge—not for a moment assuming that he was granting himself reprieve, but that in all solemnity he was refusing it. Self-execution was inappropriate to his guilt.

Well—of course he must not go to the children and tell them what he remembered of that morning. He was poor with words; he was more likely to scare them than to appease them.

They weren't prepared to understand that what he had sentenced himself to that morning in the barn was *to think*. Under that sentence, he was obliged to respect all the problems raised whenever he was rash enough to solve one of them.

He had to think, though it was not easy for him. It was not easy to rid the farm of a pestilence of rats, either, but, again and again through his years on this place, he had set himself the task of poisoning and trapping creatures who had over him the advantages of number, secrecy, and natures that recognized no obligation except to exist. He supposed there had never been a day when the farm was free of rats. Yet, by unwavering persistence he had thinned the rat population again and again to the point at which it was tolerable.

It wasn't easy for him to get ahead of the problem he now presented to his anxious children, but he set himself to find how to make it easier for them.

Through that spring and much of the following summer he appeared to be succeeding. The cycles of compulsive thought that had made him careless of his behavior since Belle's death sped faster—of necessity—as they seemed to settle down into the tranquillity of age. Once upon a time he would have refused to believe himself capable of the nimble calculations that now became a commonplace.

He gave up working on the sheller in the corncrib—because he had now got the whole material apparatus in his mind, from the grain of old wood to the bolts that fastened the electric motor to its bench, the pulleys and flywheel and their weight, strength, appearance, sound, and speed—all of this so completely transposed into an image that he could set the machine going in his imagination whenever he wanted. While he helped his youngest son with homework, or went over the accounts with Bobbie, or listened attentively to Lucy's frets about her new pregnancy, another part of his mind could repeat the crucial morning of his life.

So his family thought him better. They said he was "more himself" than he had been for years. They noticed how he gave up a share of the meanest work to each of his boys. Sometimes now he talked voluntarily of going to visit Gordon.

They were glad, again, to invert the truth. He saw that this second inversion did not cancel out the first—when they had believed him mad—but only made it incalculably more difficult to encompass, as if an already insoluble labyrinth should suddenly open out into its duplicate.

World without end, the world of thought that seemed bent on returning to some safe, lost starting point; but the prospect of its difficulty neither cheered nor daunted him. While he had strength of mind, he would go on as best he could, pretending that he was a juggler, an explorer, an acrobat, though he was only a big-footed farmer. At least he had learned to pace himself in his pursuit of multiplying complications. He had learned not to try too much at once. He was glad to think this adjusted pace—whether it meant success or failure to him—comforted his family.

One night in late summer he reached the end of thought. He had not foreseen (as a man with greater original gifts might have) that there could be an end of it. But there it was, confronting him. What had been a constantly accelerating series of wheels within wheels, wheels begetting wheels, a spinning and a spiraling that multiplied and exploded toward the ultimate horizons—all that was frozen in an instant into what seemed to him an immense sphere of light, motionless, achieved.

On the night it happened he was alone on the farm except for his grandson, who was sleeping upstairs. At suppertime Lucy had said with unusual petulance that she probably wouldn't get to go anywhere again for months or see any of their friends. The new baby was due soon. She would be tied down permanently after its arrival, so why didn't Bobbie take her anyplace any more?

Since he had been working hard in the hayfield all day, Bobbie might have snapped back at her. But Cory smoothed things over. He suggested that they drive through Boda to the county seat and find a place to dance or go to a movie. He was kind of tired himself, but would be glad to bathe Ed and read him a story and let him watch TV awhile before he went to bed.

Then Cory, Jr., had popped up and said he wanted to go along, too, and again there had been the threat of friction that Cory had to deflate judiciously. Why didn't young Cory ride just as far as Boda, he suggested, and drop off there to see some of his buddies? He could stay all night with Mickey Carnahan if he wanted, as a reward for working so well all day.

Cory had eased them away smoothly. The three young people left the farm after supper in a jolly mood. Young Ed had turned out to be no trouble at all. He nodded in front of the TV and went to bed early.

It was still not altogether dark when Cory took his cigar onto the screen porch to sit on the glider and do some thinking. On quiet evenings, left alone, he felt able to catch up on the arrears in his thought.

The night was faintly oppressive, though mild. He could hear the tree frogs dinning in the yard and the chug of the pump down by the barn. He heard the intermittent traffic of his neighbors going in late to Boda or the county seat, most of them traveling the new blacktop.

He thought about the highway and his neighbors and the way things had changed and the way things had been before. He thought, without emotion, of the difference between the blacktop and the muddy gravel he had charged through the day he cut off Bobbie's hand. Then he thought of the real sheller that had caused the accident and of the imaginary sheller that had duplicated it in his mind. And presently he was sure as could be that the sheller he imagined was run by the same principles that had run the sheller made of wood and steel. His creation and he were indistinguishable.

With that realization he reached the end of thought, knowing neither good nor evil but only guilt. The tree frogs, perhaps, continued their monotonous, hysterical song in the dark leaves around him. There may have been a continuing traffic on the roads and the sound of the pump's piston beating back and forth in its imprisoning cylinder. He did not hear them. Whatever existed was silent and motionless. Eternal. As it had been and as it would be when time ended.

In that silence he rose from the soft glider and let himself out the screen door onto the grass of the yard. He walked, without needing a light, to the shed by the back gate. The motion of his body was fluent and easy, but he felt nothing. It seemed to him that he was constituted of the same material as Bobbie's well-wrought hook and had been able, like it, to express love without the ability of knowing it. (The proposition was the same if exactly reversed: to know love without the ability to express it.) The only passion remaining was for a justice that would bring a man in phase with the total equilibrium of the night.

From the shed he took a short ax and went upstairs to his grandson's bedroom. He came down a little later without it.

He sat in the glider and relit his cigar. After a while he found himself straining to hear the tree frogs. To hear anything. Because he was not dead he had to break the motionless, soundless sphere of the thoughtless universe. He needed a noise to start him thinking again.

It was peaceful enough not to think—just to suck on the sweet cigar and let it all go up in a gentle exhalation. But he had to resume, if he could, the pain of thought so he could review what he had done in that silence when the sound of machinery stopped.

He had to plan the right way to present his act, or all those folks who relied on explanations would refuse to believe him sane. If they did not believe him sane, they would not punish him for this repetition of his guilt, and if he could not trick those who ought to love him into responsibility for a just punishment, then there was no hope for him in all this vast gleam of silence.